HAAKON
A LEADER TO FOLLOW.
A MAN TO LOVE.

"Hear me!" Haakon roared over the din. His face was dark with rage, and all his knuckles stood out white from his grip on the golden ax. "Hear me!" he roared again, and Rosamund wasn't sure if he was calling on his men or the gods themselves to listen.

"By this ax and by its giver and its makers, by my fitness to lead men and by my hope of a good death, I swear vengeance for those innocent dead. Two of Harud Olafsson's men will die for every murdered villager, and all of the abducted children will be safely returned! Now, who follows me?"

They crowded around him shouting, wave after wave of men, his new crew and his old together, swearing vengeance, swearing loyalty, swearing to follow anywhere Haakon Olesson took them.

Rosamund listened without taking her eyes off Haakon or wiping away the tears that streamed down her cheeks. She knew that either the children or Haakon's dead body would return at the end of this fateful journey. . . .

THE VIKING'S REVENGE

Eric Neilson

**Created by the producers of
Wagons West, White Indian,
Saga of the Southwest, and
The Kent Family Chronicles Series.**

Chairman of the Board: Lyle Kenyon Engel

BANTAM BOOKS
TORONTO · NEW YORK · LONDON · SYDNEY

HAAKON 2: THE VIKING'S REVENGE
*A Bantam Book / published by arrangement with
Book Creations, Inc.*
Bantam edition / March 1984

Produced by Book Creations, Inc.
Chairman of the Board: Lyle Kenyon Engel.

ISBN 0-553-23924-4

Published simultaneously in the United States and Canada

*Bantam Books are published by Bantam Books, Inc. Its trade-
mark, consisting of the words "Bantam Books" and the por-
trayal of a rooster, is Registered in U.S. Patent and Trademark
Office and in other countries. Marca Registrada. Bantam
Books, Inc., 666 Fifth Avenue, New York, New York 10103.*

PRINTED IN THE UNITED STATES OF AMERICA

H   0 9 8 7 6 5 4 3 2 1

THE VIKING'S REVENGE

N

NORTH SEA

NORWAY TRONDHEIMS-FJORD

SWEDEN

BIRKA

BALTIC SEA

BOOK CREATIONS INC. 198?   RON TOELKE '82

1

"Hear me!" The lawspeaker solemnly inspected the sheep's blood on the rune-stone and lifted his hand to make pronouncement. "I swear and bear witness before the gods that the omens are good, the marriage between Sigrid Briansdottír and Erik Allesson is lawful and binding, and no man may say otherwise."

The bride giggled, and the lawspeaker glared at her. Most of the morning had been spent in oath-taking between her son and the new men swearing to his service, and a good deal of beer had been drunk in celebration afterward, but a marriage between a landed widow and a new husband was an important matter. The lawspeaker haughtily knitted his eyebrows at her until Sigrid adopted a properly solemn expression. Almost everyone else was drunker than she was, and the lawspeaker was growing annoyed. He stepped back to let the other witnesses come forward and swear before they fell down.

Haakon Olesson came up, grinning broadly, kissed his mother, slapped his new stepfather on the back, nearly knocking him over, and planted himself beside the rune-stone. Haakon was not overly tall but solid, broad-shouldered as a bull, and his dark hair and beard made him stand out among the fair-haired Norse. "A fine day," he said approvingly. His old enemy Ivar Egbertsson was dead and buried with very few to mourn him; Ivar's men had just sworn themselves willingly into Haakon's service. His mother was finally married to Erik the Bald and in the future might be less

1

interested in running Haakon's household for him. And his stolen English woman was safe, standing on the edge of the crowd and smiling at him. All in all, a satisfactory conclusion to a dangerous year.

The lawspeaker irritably thumped his staff, and Haakon unslung his ax from the sheath on his back. Best to get on with the witnessing before the poor man lost his temper.

The axhead was strangely gilded, bright as the gold bands on Haakon's arms, and the crowd craned their heads forward to peer at it. Some had come more out of a desire to see the ax than to see his mother married, he thought. It was Haakon's war-luck and he had killed Ivar with it, and already the ax was beginning to take on a legend of its own. Gunnar Thorsten had made a poem about it, more fancy than fact, but Gunnar couldn't be faulted for that since Haakon never told anyone the truth about the ax. He was not wishful to have his people think he had gone mad. He put his hand on the axhead, feeling as always the sense of power, the *life* in the thing, that came from the god who had given it to him. It was Thor's ax, and a part of Thor lived in it.

"By the gods and by my hope of fair wind and a good end, and by the edge of my ax, I swear that the marriage between Sigrid Briansdottír and Erik Allesson is true and lawful, and that I am a witness to it. I, Haakon Olesson, son of Sigrid, swear to it."

Sigrid smiled at him, with her hand in Erik's, and Haakon kissed her again and stepped down to make room for the next witness.

One by one they stepped to the rune-stone to swear. The stone was carved with the runes of Frigg, who was queen in Asgard and blessed all lawful marriages, and the runes of Freya, goddess of love and fertility. Some put their hand on the stone to swear, some on whatever they held most sacred: Bjorn Karlsson, helmsman of Haakon's first ship, *Red Hawk,* and Haakon's comrade in battle and ale-drinking for over six years, with his pale, graying hair freshly washed and combed, and his hand on his sword; Gunnar Thorsten, the skald, who swore by Bragi Odin's-Poet and his own hope of future fame; Knut One-Eye, spear in hand, swearing on his ship, his honor, and his oath to Haakon Olesson; and finally Orm Persson, leader of Ivar Egbertsson's old crew, looking a little uncomfortable but plainly wishing to let his new loyalties show, swearing on the ship *Dragon Queen*.

The lawspeaker nodded gravely at each witness in turn and then thumped his staff on the grass for the next. At an important wedding there might be twenty or thirty who wished to make their assent to the match heard.

There was a quick murmur of surprise from the crowd and a collective indrawn breath as the next witness came forward. Rosamund Edmundsdottír moved with the grace of a stalk of grain swayed by a breeze and seemed not to notice the consternation she was causing. She smiled at Sigrid.

By law, Rosamund was not a wife but only a prisoner held for ransom, since Haakon had stolen her out of her father's English castle a year ago. But Haakon had never asked for the ransom, and if it had been paid, which would have been unlikely, he would have sent it back. Where Rosamund was concerned, he had very little interest in what the law might say.

By now most of the Trondelag folk knew that, and they had privately made up their minds that because Haakon's luck had held good since he had brought her home, she was probably *not* a witch, even if she was a Christian. Also it was hard to be in Rosamund's company for long and not learn to love her.

Nonetheless, she was not Haakon's wife by Norse rites or any other, and she was not Norse by blood or religion, and they looked warily at the lawspeaker as she stepped forward. If she swore on the rune-stone, it might be a sacrilege.

The lawspeaker stepped up to block her path, and she stopped abruptly, startled.

"No believer in the White Christ may bear witness," he hissed at her.

Rosamund turned toward Haakon, her purple-blue eyes wide with surprise. No one in the crowd moved, fearful that the slightest gesture or even an intake of breath could be construed as a taking of sides.

"You will let her come forward to the stone." Haakon didn't raise his voice, but there was an edge to it, and his meaning was plain in the look on his face.

The lawspeaker frowned momentarily but stepped out of Rosamund's path. Although his face was red with rage, he recognized the wisdom of remaining silent. Rosamund realized what she had done and opted for compromise. She had no wish to be the center of a dispute between her husband and the Thing and its lawmakers. She moved to the side, away from the rune-stone, to take Sigrid's hands in her own. Looking into the dark eyes that reminded her so much of Haakon's, Rosamund smiled fondly at Sigrid as she spoke.

"By the honor I bear Sigrid Briansdottír and Erik Allesson, by my love for her son, Haakon Olesson, and by the valor of the sons I shall bear him, I swear that this marriage is good and lawful. As witness of this, I bring a gift to Sigrid."

For the first time, Haakon noticed that the leather purse on Rosamund's belt was bulging. She opened it and pulled out a necklace that gleamed and flashed, catching the watery afternoon sunlight. Haakon recognized it at once. Rosamund had brought the necklace from England, a magnificent thing of silver links and pieces of fine amber set in gold wire. It had been her

mother's and was one of the few things her father had
let her inherit after her mother's death.

Lady Sigrid recognized the necklace, too, and looked
as if she might cry. After being publicly embarrassed by
the lawspeaker, the girl was giving her her treasure.

"Rosamund, this—" She stopped and lowered her
voice. "This is yours. I cannot take it." Her eyes dared
the lawspeaker to say one more word.

"You must take it," said Rosamund, with a catch in
her voice, half laughing, half crying. "I cannot wear it
now that I have a mother again." She unlooped the
catch of the necklace, raised it, and draped it around
Sigrid's neck. Before the older woman could move,
Erik stepped up behind her and fastened the catch.
Then he gathered Sigrid in his arms and kissed her
firmly to hide the fact that she was crying.

The crowd whooped at the ferocity of the kiss. The
cheers rolled and bounced over their heads, louder
than the cheers for the oath-taking of Ivar's men,
because now they too were shouting their approval of
Rosamund's gift. They had remained quiet during their
oath-taking. Swearing an oath to a new chief was something a wise man did cautiously, even if the oath was
lawful and the new chief had slain the old one in fair
combat. It was hard to know the will of the gods or the
Norns in such matters.

Everyone could cheer Rosamund's gift and its clear
message: *I make my home among you*. Haakon wanted
to sweep Rosamund into his arms, but suddenly there
were too many people crowding around her and the
wedding couple. For a moment she vanished in the
crowd, then her shimmering blond hair appeared again,
rippling as she tossed her head back. Haakon couldn't
hear her words, but he caught the tinkling sound of her
laughter, and he laughed, too, and shouldered his way
through the crowd to her. She had showed him so

plainly where her heart lay, and he thought she had
never looked so beautiful.

Rosamund beamed contentedly at the merrymakers
in the hall.

When Haakon had first brought her from England to
the Trondelag, the Norsemen's raucous feasts had seemed
appalling. Tonight she was drunk with happiness, like
the effects of strong mead. She felt as if she could fly up
to the rafters of Haakon's hall or lift a bench with one
hand or twist a sword into a knot.

Or maybe it *was* strong mead working on her. She
couldn't remember how many cups she'd emptied, but
the quantity was not much less than what Haakon had
drunk. And he was twice her size and hardheaded,
even for a Norseman.

Haakon was sitting next to her on a bench of honor,
absently running a hand down her back, while he
waved the other hand for another cup of mead. A
thrall-boy ran up and shouted in his ear that there was
no more mead. Haakon was not deterred.

"Wine, then," he shouted. "Bring out the wedding
wine!"

Rosamund carefully lifted Haakon's hand off her breast
and straightened up. She was pleasantly surprised to
find that she could stand and walk, and not float off the
floor. She wanted to make sure that the wine was
carried in by the soberest men in the hall, for it was the
finest sort of wine, brought all the way from the Rhine
Valley in Germany for the occasion. There was only one
barrel of it, and it was too costly to be spilled.

Rosamund steadied herself, then wove her way among
the revelers, treading on one or two along the way. By
the time she reached the wine stores, she was almost
too late. Four men were already lifting the barrel, and
from the way they lurched and staggered, Rosamund

knew none of them was sober. She stamped up to them and screamed above the din.

"Slow and easy, for the love of God! That's a wooden barrel, not an iron battle helm!"

One of the men was drunk enough to make a rude answer, grave disrespect to a lady, in particular the chieftain's woman. The man on the opposite side of the barrel let go of it, stepped around to his companion, and punched him hard in the stomach. The first man folded on himself like a comb into its case, then he sat down and gagged.

Fortunately, both men were Ivar's warriors. Even more fortunately, the remaining two men were able to lower the barrel gently to the floor instead of dropping it. Several men on nearby benches jumped up, eager at the prospect of a good fight, and one foolhardy soul had his knife out. Haakon took one look and stumbled after Rosamund.

He grabbed the man with the knife by the neck of his tunic and knocked his head against a pillar. When he let go, the man slithered down the pillar, coming to rest in a heap at its base. Haakon took the knife and stuck it in his own belt. Then he punched the next man who looked quarrelsome in the jaw, and the man flew backward onto the table with a crash and slid the length of it from the force of his chieftain's poke. He got up slowly, with roast goose in his hair. At Haakon's signal, a thrall-girl rushed over to sit on a third man's lap, nuzzling his neck and wriggling her hands inside his clothing. He promptly lost all interest in fighting.

By now everyone could see that there would be no fight, or at least not with anybody except their host. Meanwhile, Rosamund had found four men sober enough to be trusted with the wine barrel. Taking one cautious step at a time, they carried it to the bench where Erik and Sigrid sat. They occupied the other bench of honor, between the pillars on the opposite side of the hall from Haakon.

Under ordinary circumstances, Erik Allesson presented an imposing, dignified figure. He had pale blue eyes, high cheekbones, and a sturdy body with strong, thick arms and legs. His hair—what was left of it—was blond streaked with white. His appearance was strikingly similar to Haakon's father's. Just now, however, Erik was far from imposing. He was barely able to sit upright, let alone stand, and even Sigrid was a long way from sober. Her dark face was flushed, her eyes seemed to glow with a light from within, and some of her silver-tinged black hair had escaped from its braids. One of the brooches holding up her gown was unclasped, and she didn't seem to notice or care. Her hands were roaming over Erik, although more subtly than Haakon's had moved over Rosamund.

Rosamund watched them and thought with growing interest of bed and Haakon, while they were both sober enough to do anything. Her desire could so easily have been fear, she thought, when she remembered how she'd been at Haakon's mercy the first time he bedded her. She had offered Haakon her maidenhead as a means to escape her betrothal to Harud Olafsson, who had contracted with her father for a virgin. Having taken her father's hold, Haakon could have thrown Rosamund down on the floor and done as he pleased. Instead, he'd been as gentle with her maidenhood as if she'd been his lawful wife and had even been gentle afterward. That had been her first lesson in what love could be like, and it had left her wanting to learn more, and Haakon was her willing teacher. If only she could bear him a son!

She was certain that she had conceived, during an afternoon of lovemaking by the little pond in the woods. But she'd been taken captive right after that by her less-than-loving brother and Ivar Egbertsson, and her brother had had an herb-woman try to abort the child. Rosamund had missed only one moon-time, so it was still possible she could lose the child.

Rosamund's reverie was interrupted by shouts and cheers. Erik was on his feet, apparently standing through sheer strength of will and Sigrid's grip on his belt. He held high a drinking horn, with the fine Rhine wine sloshing over the edge. Then he threw his head back, raised the horn first to his guests, then to his lips, and started drinking. He was obviously planning to empty the horn without taking it from his lips, a favorite Norse drinking challenge. Rosamund had seen it done many times with ale and a few times with mead, but never with wine, and she watched him nervously.

Erik's throat pulsed with his frantic swallowing, and wine dripped into his beard. His head went back farther and farther, and the tip of the drinking horn rose steadily toward the ceiling. For a moment it wavered, and Rosamund thought with some relief that Erik was giving up. Then he straightened, turned the drinking horn mouth-down to show everyone that it was empty, and tossed it across the hall.

Everyone in the hall cheered and stamped their feet. Erik raised his hands high over his head, reveling in the loud appreciation, a wide and sloppy grin gracing his face. Suddenly his expression changed, as if he realized he had forgotten something important. Then his face went blank, and he fell over backward, stiffly, like a fir tree brought down in the forest. This was also heartily cheered by the guests. Sigrid shrieked, and Rosamund picked up her skirts and stumbled through the chaos, hoping her mother-in-law wasn't going to find herself a widow again.

Fortunately Erik had landed in a pile of boots and cloaks, which cushioned his fall. He was senseless, but his breathing was deep and steady. Rosamund suspected that he was suffering more from the effects of the wine than from the impact.

Sigrid sighed, then bent over her fallen husband, kissing his eyes and running her fingers through his wine-soaked beard. From the look on her face, it was obvious that Sigrid's plans for the night had been frustrated by Erik's losing bout with the wine.

Rosamund didn't remember much of what had happened at the feast after she had found two men who were sober enough to carry Erik to the nuptial bedchamber, and she had sat back down beside Haakon. She vaguely recalled that he fondled her breasts again, but she didn't mind enough to move away from his explorations. She vaguely heard various drunken bets on the outcome of the athletic games planned for tomorrow, commemorating both the wedding and the oath-taking, and wondered if anyone would remember making them in the morning.

She remembered for certain only that by the end of the feast, she had retired with Haakon to their bedchamber, with half her clothes unfastened before they were through the door.

Haakon was drunker than she was, dancing her about the room like a playful bear, pulling her against him, kissing her, fondling every part of her body he could reach, and singing bawdy songs at a bellow. Rosamund collapsed giggling, and finally he let her take the rest of her clothes off, while he swept all the fur coverings off the bed and onto the floor.

By the time Rosamund had stripped, Haakon was on the furs, lying on his belly, humming cheerfully. Rosamund grinned and prodded him in the ribs with her right foot, exactly where she knew he was most ticklish. He let out a yelp and turned over. Before he could sit up, she jumped on him, pressing her body down on his and biting his neck.

He happily bounced her up and down on him and proceeded to prove that he was soberer than she had thought. She gasped and straddled him, and his hands rose to cup her breasts and play with her nipples.

They made love drunkenly, giggling, and tried once to get up on the bed and fell off. Afterward, Haakon burrowed his face into the furs and fell asleep immediately, snoring. Rosamund curled up alongside him and pulled the rest of the furs over them both. She went to sleep with her head on Haakon's chest and the fingers of one hand twined in his hair.

II

When Knut One-Eye waked at dawn the day after the wedding feast, he found himself in an outbuilding, in the arms of a thrall-woman he didn't remember seeing before. She looked pleasant enough, though— asleep as she was—and Knut was sorely tempted to wake her up, make brief introductions, and tumble her again. But Haakon had scheduled the athletic contests to start at dawn. Knut thought he might be still drunk, but he didn't want to disappoint Haakon or miss the fun, so he gave the thrall-woman a farewell pinch and heaved himself up and went outside.

There was no movement on the steading. In fact, it seemed that he was the only person awake, free man or thrall. When he walked to the field where the games were to take place, no one was there, and he sat down with a lurch on a rock and contemplated the wisdom of putting off the starting time until noon.

"I think it would be better if the prizes went to the best athletes, not the best drinkers," he told Haakon when his chief finally crawled out of the furs. He had to repeat the message three times before he was sure Haakon was listening to him and not to his headache.

Haakon really wanted to crawl back under the furs, make love to Rosamund again, and go back to sleep. Instead he dragged himself out of the hall, stumbled down the hill to the fjord, and plunged into the water. The icy fjord cleared his head and started the blood flowing reluctantly through his limbs.

The field for the games was marked at the west end by the two gigantic pines that Haakon's grandfather had left standing when he had cleared the rest of the land. Haakon watched as the men lined up on both sides of the trees, and he grew uneasy as Ivar's former followers clustered together to the south of the pines, while his men from last year gathered to the north. A few of Ivar's men at first stood on the north side but moved south when they saw how the teams were forming. Only two bold spirits held out. Otherwise, the two pine trees stood between the men who'd served Haakon before his duel with Ivar and those who'd joined him afterward, almost as if the two bands were lined up on a battlefield, behind their shields, ready to fight.

Although no one seemed ready to go that far, Haakon saw a number of looks he didn't like. He turned to Bjorn Karlsson and said in a low voice, "I think I should hold a sacrifice and declare that the omens are bad for the games today. This dividing into two bands is not good."

Bjorn looked steadily at Haakon. "What will the gods say if you lie about a sacrifice?"

Haakon didn't much care what the gods might say about a lie that might keep the peace. "I'm not looking for blood-feuds today."

Bjorn shrugged. "I can't say I like it myself. But these men have got some old scars to make them touchy. Your men beat them in battle, and they'll be remembering it. Not everyone is as ready to forgive as you." Bjorn was being polite. He usually thought Haakon's willingness to forgive enemies was foolhardy. "Also they haven't fought together under you yet. *Wave Walker's* men helped you storm Earl Edmund's hold ten days after swearing their oaths to you. When we've gone after Olaf Haraldsson, I don't think you'll find Ivar's men standing apart."

That seemed like wisdom to Haakon. With a hundred and fifty fighting men sworn to him, he could take a fine red vengeance against Olaf Haraldsson, the man who had defeated and disgraced his father. They would sail in no more than a few days, probably not enough time for real trouble to blaze up between his men and Ivar's former warriors. And before summer's end, Olaf would be dead and his lands in Ireland a waste. And the two bands one. "All right, I won't interfere. But I think I should stay out of the *stangstortning*."

Bjorn grunted disapprovingly. "I was looking forward to watching you. Some of the men were laying wagers."

"Tell them to keep their money."

"Orm will be in the *stangstortning*."

"All the more reason for me not to." Haakon knew he could beat Orm, and that would be too much provocation.

In the *stangstortning* a man balanced on the palm of his hand a wooden pole as thick as his arm and as tall as three men and heaved it as far as he could. It demanded the sheer strength of an ox and the delicate touch of a juggler, and few men had both. Haakon was one, Orm Persson was another, and everyone in the Trondelag knew this. Haakon decided he would rather bury his pride and give Orm an easy victory than rub Orm's nose in a second defeat.

"Oh, very well," Bjorn grumbled. He knew that Haakon usually thought things out before he did them, even if it didn't always look like it. "But *I'm* going to be in the *stangstortning*, and I won't hold back for Orm or anyone else."

"Nobody's asking you to," Haakon said. He punched Bjorn in the shoulder. Bjorn couldn't beat Orm.

By the time the games began, all but a handful of Haakon's fighting men were out on the field, and there was a straggling, unruly crowd of spectators ready to enjoy the games. Most of the free men and women from Haakon's and Ivar's steadings were there, everyone who had come for the marriage and the oath-taking and to take advantage of Haakon's reputation for open hospitality, as was every thrall who could find an excuse for shirking work.

Haakon lifted a hand to Rosamund, who stood in the crowd with Sigrid. Her Irish wolfhound, Wulf, was beside her and looked ready to enjoy the games as well, tail fanning in the grass and ears pricked up and interested. Erik stood behind them, but he looked as if he should have stayed in bed. His eyes were red pits, and every time someone near him shouted, he winced and swayed and put a steadying hand to his head.

Watching the crowd grow, Haakon was uneasily aware of how many people would witness anything that went wrong today. He rested his hand on the head of the golden ax and asked Thor to remember that even gods' work could be undone by brawls or blood-feuds; then Haakon walked to the center of the field.

"Hear me!" he bellowed across the field, and Gunnar Thorsten beat his spear against the pine trees. The clatter silenced the spectators, and Haakon cupped his hands and shouted, "We are gathered today to celebrate! This is a friendly showing for enjoyment! I call on the gods to bless these games and the men who play in them, and I will break the head of any man who breaks the peace!"

Haakon fixed his eyes on the men who looked less

than friendly, one by one, and they looked down or away, somewhat shamefaced. He nodded, satisfied, and called out six men, three from each team, to help him judge the ground, the sun, and the wind.

They inspected it like priests looking for omens, but in the end conceded that the ground gave no one an advantage. It was as level and free of rocks as could be found in the Trondelag, although at one end it dropped sharply into the fjord. The sun was only a faint glow through low, gray clouds. No one would have it in his eyes. The wind was light and seemed to come from a different direction each time Haakon raised a wetted finger to test it. It might affect the archery contest, but it was impossible to predict how.

Haakon announced himself satisfied, and the other six nodded agreement. Someone started beating a drum, and the rest began to stamp their feet and shout as the pole for the *stangstortning* was brought forward.

Orm Persson was the first, and to no one's surprise he made a fine throw. Orm was tall and muscular, and no one had beaten him yet. The pole sailed cleanly, like a spear, and landed just ten feet short of the marker stone. Orm looked pleased with himself, and there were cheers and shouts of "Well thrown!" from both sides of the pine trees. The point of impact was marked, the pole was brought back for the next contestant, and Orm swaggered back to his team, where he was greeted with slaps on the back.

The next up was a Trondelag boy, no more than eighteen, who'd be making his first viking voyage this summer with Haakon. No one had ever seen him throw, and he was sweating, his face twisted in concentration, and painfully aware of four hundred pairs of eyes on him. The pole swayed on his hand like a tree in a gale. He gulped, took a deep breath, and threw, and the pole landed an arm's length farther than Orm's.

This time the cheers from the north side of the pine trees rattled the branches. Those from the south were ominously low. Haakon didn't like that much, but Orm was past thirty, while the boy was in the first flush of his strength. Maybe Orm's men would see it that way, even if Orm didn't.

Unfortunately, that explanation didn't hold for long. Man after man stepped up and threw, and time after time Haakon's men threw farther. The newly sworn men were doing their best, and getting red faced over it, but they were clearly outclassed by their opponents.

The last man to throw was Bjorn Karlsson. He lifted the pole as if it were a stalk of grain and balanced it with the ease of a man picking up a drinking cup. Every muscle in his body seemed to tighten and release as he heaved the pole. Bjorn swung full around from the momentum of his throw and landed facedown on the field, facing the other way. When he looked up, he saw the faces and pointing fingers of the crowd, and he heaved himself out of the grass and spun around to see the pole disappearing over the slope to the fjord.

It had sailed clear over the marker stone and kept going for half a ship's length before it struck. Then it had bounced end over end, come down again, and started rolling. At the edge of the slope it vanished, and the splash as it hit the fjord was drowned out by the cheers for Bjorn. No one had ever seen anything like it, and likely Gunnar Thorsten would make a poem of it.

Wulf's ears pricked up as the pole disappeared over the slope. Then, barking furiously, he raced after it, ears and tail streaming out behind him. Haakon ran after him in time to see Wulf plunge into the fjord after the pole. After several tries he finally got his jaws around one end of it and started paddling. By the time he had nearly reached the beach, Rosamund was standing behind Haakon, laughing so hard that she had to press her hands to her stomach.

"At least his wound must be healed," she said, when she'd caught her breath.

"Good as new," Haakon chuckled, as Wulf worried the pole uphill. Rosamund loved the Irish wolfhound dearly. She had had him since he had been a pup, and when he had helped to rescue her from Ivar, he had taken a deep wound in the fight. Rosamund had nursed him with as much care as she had given the human wounded, but for a while no one had been sure he would live. Haakon was nearly as fond of the dog as Rosamund, and just now he was grateful for his antics, but even the laughter of the crowd as Wulf finally heaved the pole over the crest of the hill didn't hide the fact that Bjorn's throw had made Ivar's men look foolish. He scratched Wulf's chin absently as Wulf stuck a wet snout in his hand.

There were more contests to come, and other opportunities for Ivar's warriors to salvage their pride. Haakon hoped they'd win *something*. The next contest was the throwing of ten-pound stones at a stake a ship's length away. Each competitor was given three chances to throw the stone as close to the stake as possible.

Haakon was mildly surprised to see Hagar the Simple step up. "I thought you'd be saving yourself for the archery." Haakon wished he had.

"I feel lucky today," Hagar said. That was about as long an answer as he ever gave anyone. Haakon hoped he wasn't, but he didn't say anything. Arguing with Hagar when he'd made up his mind was like arguing with a stone wall. Hagar stripped to the waist and picked up the first stone. Hagar was not overly talkative, but he was a gifted athlete. It was as if some magic connection existed between his hands and his eyes, sending his aim true to any target he chose.

Hagar's first throw landed almost at the foot of a marker stake, and everyone cheered. The second throw landed on top of the first and cracked both stones. This time the newly sworn men didn't cheer quite as loudly. And they didn't cheer at all the third time, when the stone hit the stake at the base and snapped it off clean. Haakon heard a shout from one of his older men: "Why don't you admit you're beaten now? Or are you waiting for the knitting contest?" He also saw Knut moving in to have a word with the heckler. After all, there was only one Hagar the Simple. The new men had no real reason to give up now.

Unfortunately, it wasn't long before the newly sworn men realized the stone throwing was going to be worse than the *stangstortning*. Haakon's men consistently outthrew Ivar's, and the climax came when one of Ivar's men twisted his right arm out of its socket, trying for extra distance. He howled like a wolf as he lay on his back while his comrades stepped on his shoulder and yanked the arm out and then back into the socket. With all his parts back where they belonged, he staggered off the field. He wouldn't be crippled, but Haakon knew he was going to be in pain for several days.

The archery came next, and Hagar stayed out of it to keep the peace, but it didn't help. Black Ayolf did what Bjorn had done in the *stangstortning* and Hagar in the stone throwing. He put his first arrow right through the target, then split its still quivering shaft with his second. The cheers of last year's men were frightening. So was the silence of Ivar's.

And to make matters worse, the first of Ivar's men to come after Black Ayolf was obviously nervous. His first arrow went wide of the target and skittered along the ground in a spray of earth. "Are you plowing, then?" someone taunted from the north side of the pine tree. "I'd heard Ivar was no good chief, but I never heard that he was served by farm boys!"

This time Bjorn had to wave his sword in the man's face to make him apologize and shut his mouth, but the gesture didn't mollify Ivar's men. They looked sullen, and some of their sullenness was now aimed at Haakon.

At least their anger inspired some of Ivar's men. They lost the archery contest, but not by so disgraceful a margin as in the first two contests. Unfortunately, whatever goodwill this produced promptly vanished in the wrestling. The only good thing that could be said about the wrestling was that by the time it was over, Haakon had figured out why Ivar's men were losing so badly.

It was not for lack of spirit or desire or fortitude. And in spite of the taunts, Ivar's men were not weaklings. They were as tough and as strong as most Norsemen, who knew that their strength and weaponscraft could make the difference between life and death. But the men of Ivar's *Dragon Queen* were not the men of the *Wave Walker* and *Red Hawk*. Haakon's men had exercised, trained, and practiced until they might have been made of leather and iron. And they had done it on Haakon's order, to fight the very men who were now their sworn comrades. It was why they had won the battle, and why they were now winning the games.

Thor's hammer, this is my doing, Haakon thought gloomily. If today's games caused bad feelings, he would sail to Ireland with a war-band divided against itself. And that was as dangerous as going into battle with a spear loose on its shaft. But, by Thor, he was not going to postpone his sailing, not give up the vengeance that had been too long coming. Not for his men and their jealousies or anything else.

Something had to be done to cool the hot tempers. Haakon waved Gunnar Thorsten over. "Gunnar, I want a verse on the fickleness of luck. Something to take the sting out of this and put some sense in their heads."

Gunnar looked dubiously at his prospective audience. No poet likes to recite to men who look ready to stick spears into each other or into him if they don't like what he has to say. But he owed his freedom and honor to

Haakon, and he was reasonably proud of his skill as a poet. Gunnar nodded and stepped up to the pine trees. He thumped on both trunks with his spear and began to recite, keeping the spear in hand.

Only Haakon heard the first few lines because everyone else was too busy glowering at each other. They bristled and snarled like two packs of dogs, Haakon thought, disgusted. If he wasn't careful, they would fight like hounds, and he wouldn't be able to knock all their heads together before someone got killed. He bellowed at them for silence, and after they had noticed Gunnar, most had enough respect for the poet's art to listen. Gunnar continued, looking wary, and Haakon realized that it wasn't one of his best efforts. He was repeating himself more than he usually did, and he kept a good grip on his spear.

> . . . Warriors' lesson, battle-learned,
> That the Norns determine Fate.
> Only gods may judge man's fitness,
> Game or battle, lost or won.
> All are victors, all are vanquished,
> As the gods send, so we take.

It wasn't brilliant, but it bought time, and that was enough. While Haakon stood glaring at them from the field, Bjorn, Knut, and, finally, Orm moved among their comrades with whispered advice, warnings, and, when that failed, threats. They persuaded the cooler heads on both sides to see that a day's athletic competition wasn't worth losing their chance at Irish loot, let alone worth a possible blood-feud. The more recalcitrant merely had a fist shoved in their faces. By the time Gunnar had finished, there were still a few black looks but no shouted taunts or insults.

Erik the Bald lent a hand by having his men bring up

a barrel of ale. Gunnar drank first, and then the athletes,
and by the time they'd finished, the low, gray clouds
had fulfilled their promise, and it was starting to rain.
Before the barrel was empty, the rain was coming down
in sheets, and the ground was rapidly turning to mud.

Haakon eyed the miserable weather with relief. The
last event of the day was a footrace, with thirty men to a
side, and he knew his own men were certain to make
Ivar's look like cripples. But no one could be expected
to run a footrace in mud up to his ankles, and he said a
silent prayer of thanks and thought that it was the first
time he had ever counted rain as weather-luck.

Haakon raised his voice to be heard above the rain
and the noise around the ale barrel, and declared the
games over. No one took the time to cheer. The men
wrapped themselves in their cloaks and hurried toward
the nearest shelter. Haakon and Gunnar were the last
to leave. By then the rain was coming down so hard
that Haakon could no longer see the tops of the pine
trees, and a rising wind kicked up foam on the
Trondheimsfjord.

III

There were fewer guests in Haakon's hall that night.
Some of the men who lived nearby had left and were on
their way home. At another time, he would have been
insulted at their refusal of hospitality. Tonight he wasn't
sure they hadn't been wise. To get through the evening
without bloodshed or oath-breakings would need luck.

Rosamund breathed a sigh of relief at the absented
men. "You must think we have bottomless barrels, like

the bottomless drinking horn the giants gave Thor. I don't know if there's enough ale on the whole steading to let everyone wash down his food."

Haakon looked weary, but he smiled. "Good. If they stay sober tonight, they may behave themselves and forget what happened today."

She kissed him on the cheek. "I think so. I've seen a war-band that was broken open because of a feud once, and these men don't look the same. They're already making some amends. I heard Knut tell Orm he'd judge Ivar's men after the first fight."

"Well, let's hope everyone has that much sense. I'm going to Ireland to bring back Olaf Haraldsson's head, and I don't want feuds on the way—we can't afford them."

Haakon put his arm around Rosamund's shoulders, and they went into the great hall to greet their guests and hope for peace.

The pork and fish, bread and onions and peas were passed around and disappeared rapidly, although there was plenty, even for men who'd worked hard all day. To Haakon's relief, the men were mingling with each other, laughing and telling stories of old fights, much embroidered. The atmosphere had improved noticeably in the warmth inside the hall, with the sound of the rain on the walls and roof, the crackling and the smoky fragrance of the fires, and the old ritual of breaking bread with comrades. Also, Bjorn and Knut and Orm had their eye on them.

Haakon took a deep swallow from his beer horn and wiped his mouth on his hand, looking thoughtful. Maybe it would help unite Ivar's men—no, *his* men; he must start thinking of them as one group—if they heard the story of Olaf Haraldsson and why this sailing for Ireland was so long overdue. He squeezed Rosamund's hand and made his way into the center of the hall.

Rosamund nodded at the thralls to fill the men's beer
horns with what little was left and hoped they'd be
content with that. They looked up, interested, as Haakon
planted his feet in the straw on the floor. He raised his
horn to the men in the hall, drained it, and tossed it to
a thrall. The thrall dived and caught it; thralls were
used to that.

"You did well today. *All* of you. The man who says
otherwise is no friend to me or the rest of his band." He
let that sink in for a moment. "But we sail in three
days, and you will have the chance to test yourselves in
real battle, and I am thinking that you have the right to
know why. You are free men, and free men, even
oath-bound, should not follow blindly."

Knut and one or two others looked uncomfortable at
that. They had blindly followed a treacherous leader
once and attacked under a peace shield in sheer
desperation; Haakon had forgiven it and taken them,
hungry and half-starved, into his own service. It was
not a thing they were likely to forget, but Knut, looking
at Haakon, decided that the jarl was not rubbing their
noses in that. He merely spoke the truth as he saw it.

"It is no secret to anyone that I have a blood-
vengeance due me against Olaf Haraldsson." Haakon's
voice was low now—perhaps he felt the ghosts crowding
in—and the warriors put their beer horns down to hear
him. Two hounds under a table began to quarrel over a
bone, and someone kicked them into silence.

"Olaf Haraldsson has thief's eyes and little honor,
but he calls himself a jarl, and now he sits fatly on my
father's lands in Ireland! My father was a good man
with only one fault—trusting the honor of a man who
had so little."

Rosamund sent a thrall up with Haakon's horn, filled
with the last of the beer. She could see Sigrid, crying,
at the other end of the table, and Rosamund knew that
this was no easy story for Haakon to tell. He took the

horn from the thrall and drank from it absently. And the
story began to take shape, calling up its ghosts in the fire-
light.

Ole Ketilsson had been in his first youth when he
had come from the Trondelag to take his holding in
Ireland, and there was no one who would not say he
had been a fine man—spearman, father, husband; wise
in judgments and openhanded in hospitality. He had
married a girl of the Irish, and even though she had
abandoned her birth name and her religion for him,
Ole somehow had stayed a friend to most of her kin.
That was the mark of his nature and the trust that most
men placed in him. Ole Ketilsson and Sigrid Briansdottír
had had seven children in Ireland, four who lived past
infancy: Thorgrim, then Haakon, then two girls, Gwyntie
and small Asa. Haakon had been fifteen when Olaf
Haraldsson had asked for Ole Ketilsson's alliance in a
war to make Olaf overlord of the Norse in Ireland.

"My father refused in mild words, to give no offense,
but he thought that Olaf Haraldsson was no lord for a
free Norseman to follow and no good ruler for Ireland.
He was right in that. His only fault was in not seeing
that for men like Olaf Haraldsson there are only allies
and enemies and nothing between. And he didn't mend
his walls."

The rain was still falling, and a rising wind was
blowing it against the hall with a steady *tak-tak-tak* like
tiny arrows. It was a night for the Wild Hunt, when
Odin rode out on his eight-legged horse, Sleipnir, with
the souls of the dead behind him. A night of evil
memory and pale, sad ghosts. Haakon stood looking
into his beer horn for a long moment before he went
on.

"It was on a night like this one, with the wind and
the rain to hide his coming, that Olaf Haraldsson rode
to my father's steading. . . ."

Only the rain and Haakon's voice broke the silence in

the hall. He spoke and the scene formed, lit by blood and torchlight in their minds. . . .

It was the thralls' shouting that woke him. At fifteen, a boy sleeps deeply and wakes slowly, and the sound of splintering wood from the hall came vaguely under the frightened screams of the thralls.

Haakon shook the sleep from his eyes and felt on the bed for his shirt. There was more shouting now, deep voices, harsh as hawks—the war cries of fighting men—and a cry of pain and fury that Haakon recognized was his brother, Thorgrim's, voice. Haakon dragged the shirt over his head, snatched up his sword, and ran.

"Stay out of the way!" Haakon bellowed.

In the hall he fell over the thralls cowering against the doorway. He pushed them back, toward the bedchambers, and ran for the chaos in the hall. In three steps he was in the middle of his first battle.

They were Olaf Haraldsson's men, and they were already in the hall, outnumbering Ole Ketilsson's by nearly two to one. Haakon saw Thorgrim fighting desperately, with an arrow in his left shoulder and the blood coming out around the shaft each time he raised his shield. At last he couldn't raise it fast enough, and a spear drove into his neck. He coughed blood and would have fallen if the press of men around him hadn't been so dense. Haakon watched his brother dying, head lolling sideways, his body caught between two others in the swaying mass of men. Something snapped in Haakon.

Sword raised, he hurled himself through the defenders in his father's hall and caught Olaf Haraldsson's spearman as he drew his spear back for another thrust. Haakon was shorter than the spearman, and his charge was unexpected. He dove under the other man's guard, his sword slicing through the spearman's leather jerkin. When the press of bodies shifted, the spearman fell with Thorgrim on top of him. There was no time even to take his brother's hand. Haakon snatched up the dead spearman's shield, tugging its strap free of his gloved hand, and flung it up in time to stop a battle ax from coming down on him. He swung and missed, and the sword caught only the axman's ear before a spear thrust from one of his father's men knocked the man back.

Nearly half of Olaf's men in the hall were dead, but the sounds of battle came wildly through the open hall door from the yard outside, and Haakon knew that there were more warriors to be reckoned with. His father would be out there somewhere in that desperate stand. Haakon shouted at the defenders to move back and hold the doorway that led to the sleeping chambers at the rear. If they could hold them there . . .

The hall doors slammed back, crashing against the timber walls on either side, and a confused mass of men from both bands staggered in. The uproar of war cries, the clash of weapons, and the shouts of rage and pain doubled and redoubled. They pounded in his ears. Haakon could see his father swinging an ax in the press of men around the door.

Behind him a woman screamed. He spun and saw his mother in her night shift, her face taut with horror, reaching out her hands for Haakon's five-year-old sister, Asa. Awakened by the noise, the child had crept from her bed into the hall, and now she stood, transfixed with terror, one hand to her mouth and the other clutching a rag doll.

Haakon ran for Asa as his mother struggled forward, but one of Olaf Haraldsson's men was before him, sword in hand, not caring what he killed, striking blindly. He swung his sword, and blood sprang from Asa's face and head. She gave a high-pitched scream and fell. With Haakon at his back, the swordsman swung wildly at Sigrid as she closed with him, her eyes blazing like a she-wolf's, but he only slashed the linen of her shift. Her long fingernails raked across his face, turning his eyes to bloody pools, and Haakon's sword cut into his back. The swordsman fell, and Sigrid, sobbing, pulled her dead baby clear. Haakon stood above the swordsman, hacking at him until long after he was dead, not really caring if Olaf's men killed him or not. . . .

"But we drove them off," he said wearily. "They left thirty dead behind them, and half of the ones who escaped were wounded. We were tougher meat than a wolf like Olaf Haraldsson could stomach.

"But he won in the end. Thorgrim was dead, and my father couldn't walk, for a wound in his thigh. Another battle would have been the end of us, and my father wouldn't ask anyone to fight a fight that he could only lead from a litter. We knew Olaf would be back before my father could ask for help from his kin in Norway, or even his wife's kin in Ireland."

Haakon took a long drink and avoided his mother's eyes. She was weeping silently, and Erik had his arm around her and Rosamund was holding her hand.

"We buried Thorgrim and Asa in Ireland, rigged and stocked two ships, and sacrificed the last of our horses for weather-luck."

But weather-luck hadn't come. The desperate voyage to Norway was cold and storm filled, and off the Orkney Islands Haakon's other sister, Gwyntie, died of the illness that comes from a broken heart. The baby, Asa, had followed Gwyntie like a puppy since she had been old enough to walk, and without her Gwyntie didn't care enough to eat or stay dry in the storm that followed them like a pursuing wolf. They found an island on which to bury her. The island had a Norse settlement, and even though there was a chance that the inhabitants might be Olaf Haraldsson's allies, Ole Ketilsson insisted on the burial; he wouldn't bury his daughter on an empty rock where her ghost might roam alone and frightened.

Haakon stared at the wall, and the picture came up sharp and clear—the shabby village on the shore of the windswept island, the gray ocean all around it, and the dull boom of the surf on the rocks. And at the hilltop a small and lonely grave with a kneeling dark-haired boy piling stones on Gwyntie's mound while his mother stood sobbing by her husband's litter.

"Then we limped home to the Trondelag, and my father's wound never healed rightly, and in the end he died, too." Haakon's face was bleak, grim as the island where he'd buried his sister. "For this I will have vengeance," he said finally.

There was silence, taut, sharp as a sword edge. *They are caught in it*, Gunnar Thorsten thought. *I am not such a skald that I can do that to men*. But stories such as Haakon had told came out of a sadness and a wild rage in the heart, wrenched from inside a man, and it was a gift that Gunnar thought he could do without.

Suddenly the hall exploded. Orm Persson started it, but in an instant every man was on his feet. *"Haakon! Haakon! Haakon!"* They shouted and pounded their beer horns on the tabletops, and their noise drowned out the wind and rain and washed over the old, dull ache that the storytelling had left in him. They would fight for him now, as one man, with one sword. Someone pushed a beer horn into his hand, and then another. The second had wine in it.

But after he had drunk it, he didn't feel like drinking any more, and he took Rosamund by the hand and led her off to their bedchamber and left them behind him, cheering him.

When he got into bed, he didn't want to make love, but only to have Rosamund hold him, under the furs. It was cold, nearly as cold as it had been on the island by Gwyntie's grave.

IV

The battle raged outside the house, and the thralls were screaming. Olaf Haraldsson's men had come! Haakon knew he had to get up, get his weapons, and fight his way to his father and brother in the hall. There was blood on the floor. He reached for the edge of the bed and found bare skin between it and it. He groped in the darkness, and his hand slid along the shape of a woman's breast.

That was wrong. There hadn't been a woman in his bed when Olaf Haraldsson's men had come. Something was *definitely* very wrong. The battle had faded to a hammering on the door, and he dragged himself up out of sleep as Rosamund swung her bare feet over the edge of the bed. Haakon closed his eyes momentarily, then propped himself up on one elbow, opened one eye, and saw Rosamund standing by the door, with a fur-trimmed robe wrapped loosely around her slender frame and her long, blond hair tangled. She was talking to someone outside the bedchamber.

And who was the fool of a thrall to wake him at this hour? Rosamund turned toward him, and he saw tears in her violet eyes.

"Haakon," she said softly. "Oh, Haakon!"

Beyond the door he could see Knut, his lined face somber, and Guthrun, Rosamund's maid, wiping her eyes on her apron.

"What is it?" he snapped, still half asleep and in no good temper.

Rosamund swallowed. "Bjorn Karlsson is dead,

Haakon—*dead*. He drowned last night—" she choked,
"—in an *ale vat*."

"He couldn't have. There's not enough ale left on the
steading—" The full impact of it hit him. "Bjorn?
Dead?"

"Yes."

"He can't be!"

Bjorn *was* dead. Kare Ingstad and Thorfinn Solvisson
had laid him out decently on a clean, dry sheepskin by
the door. As Haakon came in with Rosamund they
stepped back. Rosamund knelt, and her lips moved in a
silent prayer. Probably a prayer to the White Christ,
Haakon thought, but the prayers of a good woman to
any god never did a man harm. He put his hand lightly
on her head and stood looking down at Bjorn.

Good-bye, old friend. Was Bjorn's ghost close enough
to hear him? *Good-bye, and thank you for what you've
done for me and for others.* Haakon and many other
men he knew owed their lives to Bjorn's skill in battle.
And Bjorn's counsel was wise and reasoned and always
worth following. But most of all, Bjorn was a friend, and
his willingness six years ago to swear his allegiance to a
young and unproven chief had gone a long way to
starting Haakon's reputation as a war leader. Without
Bjorn he would never have come so far or as fast as he
had. And always, for six years, Haakon had known that
he had a comrade at his back.

*Sleep in peace, Bjorn. It was not a death to win you
Valhalla, but it's no straw death, either. You always did
love good drink, so maybe it was not so ill chosen.*

Haakon knelt beside Rosamund, not to pray but to
look at the body. It looked no different from other
drowned men Haakon had seen, but there were bruises
on his left temple and the knuckles of his right hand.
They could mean much or nothing at all. Certainly
Bjorn might have bumped his head against a doorpost
and skinned his knuckles when he fell into the vat. The

ale was low in the vat. He might have overbalanced when he tried to drink from it, fallen in headfirst, and breathed in ale—

Someone coughed behind Haakon. He rose and found Magnus Styrkasson, Bjorn's nephew, in the doorway. Magnus was twenty-two, married, a father, and a successful trader who had sailed as far as the Slavic lands along the Baltic coast. Right now he looked about fourteen, and he miserably twisted the hem of his tunic between his fingers as he looked at his uncle's body.

"I just came back from Hedeby," he said, answering Haakon's unspoken question. "I was told he was here." Magnus choked. "I had come to say good-bye to him before he sailed to Ireland. . . . Haakon, that man was father and brother to me. I want to go to Ireland in his place. My sword is not as good as my uncle's, and my advice is worthless, but I won't disgrace my blood."

"Your youngest child is only two seasons old," Haakon said. "Do you have kin to guard your wife and family while you're gone?"

Magnus thought and nodded. "If I didn't, I still owe Bjorn that much. I would leave my wife and children under the hand of any man you name, as surely as kin."

That was such high praise that Haakon wondered if Magnus was trying to sway him with flattery. But it made no difference. Magnus was more a trader than a warrior, but he'd fought off pirates often enough to be no stranger to battle. As he'd said, he would not disgrace his blood. And Haakon thought maybe *he* owed Bjorn that much, too.

"Get your weapons and armor ready, Magnus. You have a place on my ship." He listened politely to Magnus's thanks, with half his mind, and then walked sadly back out into the morning, with Rosamund beside him. It would be a long time before he grew used to not having Bjorn on his other side.

* * *

Everyone had his own notion of what happened to Bjorn, and some didn't have the sense to keep their theories to themselves. It wasn't long before Haakon knew his own doubts were echoed in the minds of other men. Was Bjorn's death an accident or murder, or was it some unlucky mixture of the two that could only be guessed at?

"And if all you can do is guess, why are you doing it out loud, trumpeting like a bull seal in the mating season?" Haakon growled at Hjalmar Sitricsson two days later.

Hjalmar planted his feet stubbornly. "It is simple enough, jarl, if you would think it through for yourself."

Haakon frowned, but he listened. The right of a fighting man to speak freely to his chief was sacred among the Norse.

"Very well. Tell me this simple reason."

"We are wondering, jarl, if Bjorn's fate is an omen for our sailing to Ireland? Your oldest man struck down? What can the ones who haven't followed you so long expect?"

Haakon looked exasperated. "Do you expect me to know the will of the Norns, Hjalmar, or only to promise you a whole hide in a battle?"

"No. Not that." Hjalmar dug in his heels. "Only— take some time to be thinking if Bjorn's death's a sign, jarl. If you do that, I'll be following you with an easier heart."

Haakon only grunted and made no promise, but he had to admit that Hjalmar had some justice on his side. It could be that Bjorn's death was an omen for the voyage to Ireland and his hope of vengeance on Olaf Haraldsson. But *what* omen?

The irony of his dilemma was that Haakon wanted to talk it over with Bjorn, as he always had. Rosamund was not the one to go to for counsel here. She would only try to persuade him to stay in Norway. But Haakon had to face the fact that a bad omen could be a death-omen, and he was acutely aware that his death in Ireland would leave no man of Ole Ketilsson's blood alive, unless the child that Rosamund was carrying survived. Erik would do his best for Rosamund, but she wouldn't be in a good position if Haakon died.

Unfortunately, the best evidence that Bjorn's death was no ill omen was something Haakon couldn't tell to Hjalmar. He had put his hand on the ax already and asked Thor for the meaning of Bjorn's death, and he had received no sign that it meant anything, for good or ill.

But maybe he was asking Thor for more than he was prepared to give. And maybe he was letting his desire not to have his long-deferred vengeance on Olaf Haraldsson snatched out of his hands at the last moment get hold of his wits. Still, it seemed unlikely to Haakon that after going to the trouble of making him his servant, Thor would now start speaking to him in riddles. The golden ax and its stipulations had been plainly and truthfully spoken by Thor Odinsson. Haakon remembered the clarity with which it had told him that he must do the god's bidding on earth, righting wrongs among mortals. Haakon had never encountered two people as thoroughly evil as Harud and Olaf. Surely Thor would have no objection if Haakon rid the world of son and father both.

The more Haakon thought it over, the more the matter seemed settled in his mind. Thor had spoken to him before, and there was no reason for him to keep secrets now. If the death were an ill omen, Haakon would have been told. So Bjorn's loss gave no reason not to sail to Ireland. Now for a tale that could make Haakon's men think the same. He had until Bjorn's funeral to think of one.

V

Haakon knew that Bjorn's kin could not provide the sort of funeral he deserved without beggaring themselves, so Haakon stepped in with silver and gifts to make sure that Bjorn's ghost slept well. Bjorn's funeral was scheduled for ten days hence, to give his kin and friends time to reach his nephew Magnus's steading. Magnus went home immediately with his uncle's body, preserved in a barrel of ale, and a rich load of gifts from Haakon: enameled brooches, fine blue cloth, red bronze arm rings, shoes of tooled red leather, Frankish knives with amber set in the hilts, a bag of silver for Magnus, and a small herd of livestock—two bullocks and a good many pigs, sheep, and goats.

Rosamund understood the Norse custom of gift-giving well enough to anticipate most of this. Bjorn had been a valued helmsman, and English customs and Norse in this matter were not so far apart. One of the complaints most commonly voiced against her father, Earl Edmund, had been his stinginess with gifts and hospitality. The gift of the livestock, however, confused her.

"Magnus's herds are small," Haakon explained. "The feasting could leave him without breeding stock. This will let him feed his guests and not strip his herds bare."

Rosamund looked blank. There had been no feasting when her mother had died. "The feasting?"

"Yes. There will be feasting at Magnus's steading on most evenings from now until the funeral. I'd have sent him ale and mead if we'd had any to spare."

"But—his uncle is *dead*."

"Of course. All the more important, then, to be generous with the mead and ale."

Rosamund looked at the ground, the sky, the trees, anywhere but at her husband's face. There was so much that she thought she would *never* understand. Deeply as she loved Haakon, she had yet to feel entirely comfortable among his people, largely because the teachings of the English Christians were so contrary to those of the Norse. Sometimes, when she thought she was doing her husband a favor, it ended up as an insult or disservice. Then they would suffer, sometimes for hours or even days, until the hurt feelings had been soothed and the trespass shown as unintentional. Rosamund had the feeling that she and her "husband" were about to fall into another one of those times. Even now, as she forced herself to look at Haakon, he was frowning down at her.

"Rosamund, do you still bear Bjorn ill will for the time when he thought you were not a good influence on me?"

She looked so shocked and surprised that he knew she was telling the truth. "Oh, no! Nothing like that. He only spoke his mind, as he always did. And he helped make me friends with your mother. No, Haakon, I wouldn't say a word against Bjorn, or hear one said."

She walked off briskly after that, saying that she had to see to the stocking of some meal barrels. She was desperate to escape before she made more trouble by letting him see that she found feasting at a funeral hideous, a lack of respect for the dead and a mockery of the funeral ceremony.

Wulf trotted at her heels with Gerd, the wolfhound bitch that was now his constant companion. She was a gift from Ragnar the Noseless, who'd sold cargo for Haakon in Hedeby and made a fair profit on it. Haakon doubtfully watched them go, one eye on Rosamund,

but was momentarily distracted by the bitch. If she
mated with Wulf—well, she was big and strong, intelli-
gent and quick. She was also the ugliest dog of the
breed Haakon had ever seen in his life. This didn't
appear to bother Wulf, but it made Haakon wonder
what the puppies would look like. He hoped Wulf's
canine beauty would carry down into the litter.

He stood for a minute looking after the three of
them, and then shook his head over Rosamund and the
dogs. Women had their fancies, particularly when they
were breeding, as Rosamund still seemed to be. He
doubted that whatever troubled her was so serious that
it could not wait until she found words to tell him
herself.

Haakon needed a man to act as steward, to run the
steading and, if need be, defend it after he had sailed
for Ireland. He finally settled on Gunnar Thorsten.

"Guthrun isn't threatening to have your manhood if
you don't go this time, is she?" Haakon asked with a
grin. It was no secret that Gunnar was in love with
Guthrun, Rosamund's maid, and that she was leading
him in a merry dance. Also, she had definite opinions
about what a warrior should do.

"No," said Gunnar. "And I *am* going." He grinned
back. "But this time she has said she'll miss me."

"Good. You can continue your courting while I'm in
Ireland."

"You're *not* going to leave me here when you go to
Ireland! Haakon, I have—"

"Gunnar, listen to me. I have many good strong arms
and not so many wise heads among these men. Yours is
one of the wisest, and you'll do more to keep your oath
to me by keeping them in hand while I'm gone."

"Erik can—"

"They wouldn't follow Erik the way they would you.
He hasn't fought beside them. Besides, he's a newly

married man. You'll be learning that that can take a man's wits from his work."

Gunnar glowered. Haakon's confidence in his leadership was all well and good, but it still added up to sitting at home like a housewife while other men took vengeance and loot and, more important, fame in Ireland. And when Haakon had sent Olaf Haraldsson down Hel-Road, there would be no skald with him to make a poem by which men could remember his vengeance and his victory.

Haakon took Gunnar's elbow and pushed him to a more secluded corner of the hall. "There is something else I want you to do for me. I have another reason for leaving you behind." Haakon leaned closer, and Gunnar looked suspicious. "I want—"

"Haakon! Harroo, Haakon!" Black Ayolf came into the hall. "Snorri wants you to see the ships."

Haakon looked at Gunnar and shrugged. "We'll finish this later," he said, and slapped Gunnar lightly on the shoulder. Then he left with Black Ayolf, leaving the poet to cast dark looks at his back.

Over the winter Snorri Longfoot had given Haakon's old ship, *Red Hawk*, two extra strakes of planking on either side. This raised her freeboard by nearly two feet. When Haakon saw how good *Red Hawk* looked, he told Snorri to go ahead and do the same to Ivar's captured ship, *Dragon Queen*. Snorri was now rushing to finish the work in time for the sailing, driving his shipwrights with threats and insults and was seemingly in six places at once. The third ship, *Wave Walker*, was so large she needed no extra freeboard.

All three would now be fit to carry heavier loads than Haakon had ever before put in a longship, and it gave him an idea. He bought a shipload of hides from a Trondelag merchant who was about to take the cargo on to Hedeby and had Rosamund gather every woman on

the steading who knew one end of a needle from
another. He had the women cut and sew the leather
into tents, which could be set up ashore or even aboard
when the ships were at anchor. His men would sleep
drier and warmer in Ireland's mist and rain, he thought,
and there would be less sickness.

The sentries would have to keep alert, since attackers
shooting fire arrows or cutting the tent ropes could trap
the men inside, but a chief who didn't have trustworthy
men on sentry duty had no business as a war leader in
the first place. (Haakon felt a twinge of pain, like the
old ache of a tooth, when he remembered that it was
Bjorn who had first given him that piece of advice.)
Also, it occurred to Haakon that if Rosamund kept busy
with the tents, there would be less time for fretting
over whatever troubled her. Or at least so he thought.
By the morning of Bjorn's funeral, she still looked
tense and as if she were beginning to be ill.

Rosamund remembered the sunrise of the day they
buried her mother. It had thrown a deep red with
streaks of purple up into the sky before it rose over the
mountain at Ram's Head. The colors were beautiful
but strong and violent, as if the dawn were bruised and
bleeding. The wind blew across the land, and the trees
shook their limbs like ghosts over the little grave in the
hard ground—so small a grave to hold her mother's
body and Rosamund's despair.

Bjorn's funeral was marked by paler colors and a
calmer day, as if nature were more accepting of his
death. Haakon's party left the steading with the gentlest
yellow dawn's light in the gray sky, with the sun still
below the hilltops to the east. Rosamund rode a shaggy
pony and wrapped her cloak tightly about her against
the morning chill. Sigrid and some of the older men
were also mounted, but everyone else, including Haakon,
was on foot.

The fighting men carried their weapons, and most had their shields, as well. Haakon and the few who owned it were wearing mail. Without the women in it, the column marching beside the fjord would have looked more a war-band than a funeral cortege. No one spoke. There was no restriction against it, but the men and women were lost in their own thoughts of Bjorn, who had been loved. He had never married and had been instead a member of everyone's family. The silence was a simple indication that Bjorn's memorial service had already begun, privately, in each mourner's thoughts. When they reached Magnus's steading shortly before noon, Rosamund rode her pony to the head of the column and kept it beside Haakon as they switchbacked down the last, long hill.

A narrow, open boat rested on the shore twenty paces from the water's edge. A miniature hut of planks stood amidships, with Bjorn's shield hung on the end and, inside, Bjorn's bier. The boat rested on rollers, and half a dozen men, stripped to the waist, were piling smaller logs and branches and resin-soaked straw around them. By the time Haakon's party reached them, the kindling rose halfway up the boat's hull.

"Look at the size of that boat!" Haakon hissed suddenly. "Bjorn deserves better! If they'd told me this was the best they had, I'd have given them our *knarr*, at the least."

He'd spoken loudly enough for Magnus's men to hear, and Rosamund leaned down from her pony and put a hand on Haakon's shoulder. "He's their kin, Haakon. They know you've done him much honor and would gladly do more. But they can't let you do everything they're supposed to do themselves. They must do the best they can and feel proud of it. You embarrass them."

Haakon looked at her, his head cocked to one side and his free hand tugging at his beard, thoughtful.

Then he smiled. "You're right. I'll have other chances to honor Bjorn's memory. They won't."

Rosamund sighed with relief. She'd spoken purely on impulse, knowing nothing of Norse funeral customs. And she had felt muzzy-headed and slow-witted since she woke up this morning, not giving thought to the words that spilled out of her mouth. Now she felt sick to her stomach, too, as if she'd eaten too much breakfast instead of hardly any at all. It was a wonder, she thought, that she hadn't said the wrong thing and made trouble.

Haakon helped Rosamund dismount, and she followed him over to the boat. Magnus was piling wood at the stern. "Thank you for all you've done, Haakon. I hope I can repay you for it in Ireland."

"You'll be worth your food and booty," Haakon said. "If I didn't think so, I wouldn't be letting you set foot aboard any ship of mine. Your uncle's ghost would haunt us both."

"Yes," Magnus said solemnly. "He had war-wisdom."

"He had no patience with fools in a fight." Haakon looked around him. "Are those the beasts for the offering? No thralls?"

Magnus shook his head. "Bjorn told me once not to ask anyone to join him when he died, and no one came forward, but I wasn't surprised. Since the last Angel of Death is dead, we could not be sure their spirits would follow Bjorn."

Haakon nodded and walked over to inspect the sacrificial animals before Rosamund could ask him what an Angel of Death was. Obviously it was something to do with a Norse funeral, but she had no idea what.

Haakon and Magnus inspected the ship and the tethered beasts and pronounced everything in order. Then Haakon, Knut, and Orm joined the five men of Bjorn's family around the boat, and Rosamund stepped back among the witnesses. Each of the five male relatives carried either a soapstone bowl or a brass jar of corn or beer. They put them in the boat and stepped back to let the women of the family come forward. The women had lengths of cloth, shoes, and a belt for Bjorn's use in the hereafter, and they laid them inside the hut beside the bier.

When the women had stepped back, Haakon came forward, with a taut look on his face, and a sword, wrapped in silk, under one arm. He lifted it in both hands.

"Be witness," he shouted. "To arm Bjorn's ghost, I give the sword that I myself have carried in battle, a blade that has shed blood of Bjorn's enemies, and mine. I do this so that Bjorn's ghost may walk armed, and his own sword may fight on in the hands of his nephew Magnus."

Haakon hid the sword in the boat and then untied the scabbard at his belt and put Bjorn's sword in it. He laid the scabbard and sword across Magnus's hands, which shook as Magnus tied the weapon to his own belt, but he kept from dropping it, which would have been an evil omen. The look on Magnus's face said plainly that Haakon had gained his gratitude for life. Rosamund smiled in spite of her queasy stomach. There was great kindness in Haakon.

Nevertheless, she turned her head away as well as she could without making a scandal while the sacrifices were made: a ram, a goat, a boar, a goose, and a cock, throats cut and then piled in the boat on top of the rest.

When that had been done, Magnus's son brought several torches and a soapstone pot of coals. Magnus stripped his clothes off—Rosamund tried not to watch that, either—and stuck one torch in the pot. The fire blazed up red, and Magnus waved the torch above his head like a banner.

Haakon and the others stepped back and took the torches that Magnus's son handed to them, while Magnus began to run around the boat with the red fire streaming behind him. He looked only at the gathering, never at the ship. When he had made the circuit nine times, he stopped and caught a deep breath, his bare back straight and tense, and then whirled the flaming torch into the ship. It caught the kindling with a roar, and Haakon and the rest stuck their torches in the pot and threw them after Magnus's. They picked up their weapons and slammed them hard against their shields, shouting over the roar of the flames, sending Bjorn to his gods.

The black smoke poured up from the boat, billowing in the windless air, and the whole gathering began to shout. Their voices, strident as the hungry roar of the flames, and the clash and clang of sword and spear on shields made a din that grew until Rosamund wanted to clap her hands over her ears to shut it out. But still, these people *cared* so greatly. The burning of a body was anathema to Christians, but as the flames rose up, Rosamund began to think that maybe the shouting and the din and the love that prompted it were a better way to send a man to the next world than the stony, bitter silence that had marked her mother's funeral. The only sounds then had been the priest's monotonic chanting of the funeral mass, the rattle of pebbles and stones sliding into the grave, and her own stifled sobs. There had been tears other than hers that day, most of them from the servants, who knew the difference it would make with Lady Jeannot no longer there to stand between them and her husband's temper. Earl Edmund had kept his eyes on the ground all through the funeral, with Rosamund's three stony-faced brothers beside him. Afterward she had heard people say how deeply Earl Edmund grieved. Rosamund thought he must have looked down to hide a smile at being free of his wife's restraint. And her brothers had cared very little more. They had lost any love for their mother on the day they

were weaned, and the earl had then taken them to train
and cast in his image.

*At least Bjorn has more people who mourn him from
their hearts.*

She thought of Bjorn, lying alone in the flames on the
boat, burning into ashes until there were only bones.
Burning— Suddenly, unwillingly, she could see in her
mind his body burning, and the wind came up and the
black smoke rolled her way.

Whether or not she actually smelled burning flesh—
and if she did, whether it was Bjorn's or the animals'
—suddenly she knew she was going to be sick. With
one hand over her mouth and the other frantically
clearing a path ahead of her, Rosamund pushed her way
through the crowd and down to the shallow water at the
shore. At the water's edge she dropped to her knees
and threw up everything in her stomach. With her
arms wrapped around herself she retched again and
again.

Vaguely she was aware that a boat had grounded on
the beach and two men were climbing out of it. Then a
fresh spasm of nausea hit her, and she clamped her
hands over her aching stomach and forgot them. Eventually her heaves subsided, and she sank onto the sand,
drained and crying. Her gown was wet with sweat.

*Jesus, Lord, help me accept the ways of my husband's
people.* Then suddenly she was frightened—terribly,
terribly frightened that her illness would return because she had come here to worship Norse gods. *She*
had not prayed to them, but she had been here, and
that was as bad, the priests had always said. She knew
she was being punished already. No one else at the
ceremony was vomiting, and she knew it was her
penance for abandoning her faith for the rituals of pagan
gods.

"Here, dear, drink this." It was Sigrid with a wet

cloth in one hand and a cup in the other. "Drink. You will feel better."

There was cool ale in the cup. Rosamund swallowed just enough to wet her mouth and then waited until she was sure it would stay down. When it did, she drank enough more to get rid of the sour taste of bile, and felt her stomach begin to unknot. Sigrid wiped Rosamund's face and began to comb her hair for her. Rosamund put an arm around her, grateful, and tried to think what to say. She was terrified—of God, and of what Sigrid and Haakon would say if she admitted her fear.

Sigrid smiled. "I saw you go. I *thought* I knew what was wrong. Is it better now?"

"It's still—" Rosamund felt her stomach heave again and clenched her teeth. After a moment it subsided. She sipped at the ale again.

Sigrid cocked her head to one side, at an angle so like her son's that Rosamund now knew where the pose came from. "Rosamund, are you pregnant?"

Rosamund forced her mind away from her stomach. "I *believe* I am. I've passed through one moon-time without bleeding. It is about time for the next, and I don't feel like I usually do."

"But you *do* feel sick to your stomach?" Sigrid chuckled. "Then you're breeding, definitely. Two moon-times without blood and then a queasy stomach make it almost certain."

Rosamund sat back down. It hadn't occurred to her that that might be what was making her sick. But Sigrid had borne seven children and helped at least twenty other women through their pregnancies, so she ought to know.

"There is nothing wrong with you that doesn't come to most women when they're breeding," Sigrid said briskly. She looked at Rosamund thoughtfully. "So you needn't frighten yourself by thinking your god is punishing you for coming to a Norse rite."

Rosamund jerked her head up. Was she that transparent? "I was afraid," she said miserably.

"I know," Sigrid said. "Remember, I had to walk the same road when I married Haakon's father. It was harder for me than it will be for you. My father was a great patron of the Church, and one of my brothers is a priest. He hasn't spoken to me since I turned to the gods of Asgard."

Rosamund looked unhappy. "If Haakon's people know the trouble I have accepting their gods, they— I don't want to make trouble for Haakon."

"No one will learn it from me. And I don't think anyone will care when they find out you're carrying Haakon's child." Sigrid put an arm around her and helped her to her feet. "I wouldn't have said anything, child, but I do remember how all this troubled me. It will get easier."

Rosamund rested her head against the older woman's for a moment. "I don't know if I can *ever* accept these gods as you have. And if I don't, what will Haakon say?"

Sigrid replied slowly, "He may say a few harsh words. Our gods are close to his heart. But he will also regret them, and he will *understand*, whatever he says. Only" —Sigrid's voice became brisk again—"try to tell him so that he thinks he has learned it for himself. It is much easier to deal with a man who *thinks* he has found out something for himself. And his temper will be greatly eased if you *first* tell him you're breeding."

Rosamund managed a weak chuckle and started to speak, but Sigrid wasn't listening. She was looking toward the crowd. Suddenly she stiffened and said sharply, "Something's happened. And I don't like the way it looks."

Rosamund turned and saw everyone gathered in a half circle beyond the blazing ship. Haakon was in the middle with the two men from the boat. Even at this distance, she could see their fists shaking and hear the anger in their shouts.

Sigrid picked up her skirts and ran, with Rosamund stumbling after her.

VI

". . . from Rogaland," one of the men was saying. "We tracked you here, jarl, because we don't have enough men left for vengeance." There was old blood on his clothes and a bandage around one arm, with fresh blood seeping redly through it. He staggered, and someone gave his shoulder to lean on while he spoke. "All dead—" he choked on the words "—and the children—"

Harud Olafsson took a swallow of the ale, then spat it on the ground. It was no better than he'd expected from this pigsty of a Rogaland village. But his two ships needed water, and his men needed a chance to stretch their legs ashore if they were to be fit for the work coming up. This village was a good place for his purposes, in spite of its sour ale and unwilling women. It was far enough from the Trondelag that word of this visit would not reach Haakon Olesson in time for him to put his sword into Harud's plans.

Harud was rinsing his mouth out with water when he saw one of his men running up to the guards on the hilltop above the ships. The man was clutching a bloodied hand and arm. Harud swore and buckled on his sword and went to meet him.

It was Thjodhulf, half out of his mind with anger and pain. He collapsed at Harud's feet, rocking back and forth, cradling his wounded arm.

"What happened?" Harud snapped.

Thjodhulf gave no response beyond hysterical wailing. Harud reached down and grabbed his axman by the tunic, ignoring his wounds, and hauled him back onto his feet. He held Thjodhulf within inches of his own face and spoke to him from between clenched teeth. "I asked what happened. Tell me now, or I'll take that arm right off your body."

Thjodhulf struggled for control, but the pain was excruciating. "They killed Svein Ulfsson," he sobbed. "She wouldn't go with him. She wouldn't. So they killed him. They killed Svein." This said, Thjodhulf dissolved into muttering and weeping.

Harud threw Thjodhulf from him in disgust. He could guess what must have happened. Svein had a name for liking women too well and too often, without regard for what they or their kin would say. He'd finally paid the price everyone had always expected he would. But that didn't make any difference to Harud. Svein had been one of his best axmen, and the village was going to pay for his murder. If they paid willingly, he might ask a reasonable price. If not . . .

"Send someone into the village to get our men out of it," he shouted to the shipguard. "Go armed."

At least twenty more of his men were still in the village, seeking fresh meat and playful women. If word of the violence got around, the villagers could trap the men and use them as hostages for Harud's good behavior.

Harud's war-luck got the messenger there before enough of the villagers knew what had happened to make trouble. Harud's crew got out of the village and back to the ships with no more bloodshed, but not long after, two men came from the village as emissaries to Harud. Neither was armed with anything but a knife, and one of them looked close to sixty. He stooped from the pain in his joints. Harud kept his men armed, and he laughed. The villagers could hardly be sending men like these to do anything but submit to whatever terms he set.

"So the fathers come to demand a higher price for their whoring daughters?" He grinned at the men standing before him.

The younger one bristled, but the older only shrugged. "You may shape your tongue to whatever vile names you wish, Harud Olafsson. They will make the injury to us no greater and no less."

"What injury to *you?*" Harud took a step forward. "It seems to me that *I* have a claim against *you* and your village. One of my men is dead, and another may never fight again."

"And both in a brawl caused by the dead man," the emissary said. "He was trying to force a free woman of the village, Harud Olafsson. Did anyone tell you that the woman's jaw and arm are broken, and her skull may be?"

"If she resisted Svein that long, she's a fool and deserves it," Harud said. "Isn't that right, men?" He looked to his warriors for verification, and they laughed and cheered.

The younger man spat on the ground. "Karl, I told you this was a fool's errand. Nothing less than a king's fleet will make this—"

Harud turned again toward his men and nodded his head almost imperceptibly. The name the younger man was going to call him changed into a grunt of surprise as two of Harud's men put their spears through his chest. The older man, Karl, stood unbelieving until Harud's sword bit into his neck a moment later.

Harud looked around at his men and laughed again. "These village folk are fools! Did they think I would let them go when they threaten me with King Harald's fleet?" King Harald Fairhair was ruler of the Vestfold, where Rogaland was located. He grinned ironically. "Are we pirates such as Harald fought at the Hafrsfjord?

What sort of jarl would I be if I let pass that sort of an insult against my men?"

That brought a cheer and loud laughter. Harud raised his sword and pointed it toward the village. "Now—let us take the blood-price for Svein. Make certain they won't forget Harud Olafsson's men in the Rogaland for a long time."

Harud's men grabbed their shields and weapons and descended on the village like wolves on terrified sheep. They poured into the town, bent upon destroying the village and any living thing in it. Karl and his companion were the first from the village to die, but far from the last. There were perhaps fifty men of fighting age in the village, but they were outnumbered and ill prepared.

In the time it would have taken a man to walk from the ships to the village and back again, the serious fighting was over. Some of the villagers escaped to the hills, but the only refuge for most was death—a hard death for the women.

There were also some two-score prisoners: children too young to fight or to be used as vassals by Harud's crew, and men too old or sick to fight. Harud sat on an upturned watering trough in the village square and looked them over. From the huts around him came smoke, the crackling of flames, and sometimes the raw screams of women who hadn't yet lost their voices.

There were twenty children among the prisoners, ranging from a girl of two to a boy almost old enough to have fought if he had had the chance. Harud got up and walked through the huddled villagers. The children cringed away from him, and many of the youngest were crying for their mothers. An old man reached down to pick up one baby. Harud, who had worked up a rage as senseless as it was uncontrollable, shouted at his men to drag the old and sick away. Grinning like wolves, his men herded them behind a hut and slaughtered them.

Harud turned his attention back to the children, and

it was only his greed and dawning fear of retribution
that saved them. They were too young to fetch a good
price as slaves, but Harud thought of a better use than
that—he would sell them back to their own kin. And if
he was outlawed, the children would die slowly and be
returned in pieces, if at all.

The children would be well worth the trouble of
sending them back to Ireland. The plan he had in mind
for Haakon Olesson and his English bitch could be
easily accomplished with one ship. And meanwhile, the
children were his surety that he would face no new
enemies until he'd settled with Haakon. Harud laughed,
and one of the girls began to scream. She went on
screaming until a warrior struck her in the head with a
spear butt. . . .

When the Rogaland messenger had finished his horrify-
ing tale of Harud's atrocities, there was a terrible
silence, with only the crackle of the burning ship to fill
it. And then suddenly the air was full of a wild howling
that sounded to Rosamund more animal than human.

"Vengeaaaaance!"

Haakon lifted his ax, and it whirled around his head,
burning brighter than Bjorn's fire.

"Hear me!" Haakon roared over the din. His face was
dark with rage, and all his knuckles stood out white
from his grip on the ax. "Hear me!" he roared again,
and Rosamund wasn't sure if he was calling on men or
the gods themselves to listen.

"By this ax and by its giver and its makers, by my
fitness to lead men and by my hope of a good death, I
swear vengeance for those innocent dead. Two of Harud
Olafsson's men will die for every villager, and the
children will come home! Now, who follows me?"

They crowded around him shouting, wave after wave
of men, his new crew and his old together, swearing

vengeance, swearing loyalty, swearing to follow anywhere Haakon Olesson took them.

Rosamund listened without taking her eyes off Haakon
or wiping away the tears that streamed down her cheeks.
She knew that either the children or Haakon's dead
body would return from Ireland, and that these men
would follow him down Hel-Road itself.

With such a man it did not matter that he swore on
his ax instead of on a cross or that he got drunk at every
feast. Nothing mattered except what she saw so clearly—
virtue was in each man as his own will put it there. God
or gods did not matter, at least not much. A small voice
in the back of her mind whispered "*Heresy!*" but she
knew it wasn't so, would never *be* so, not to the kin of
those stolen children.

She wanted to run to Haakon and throw her arms
around him, and took a step forward before she felt a
hand on her shoulder. Sigrid whispered in her ear,
"Stay back. Find another time to tell him what's in your
heart. Now he is a man among men, with no time for
anything a woman has to tell him."

"That's not fair."

"No, it isn't. But that's the way the world is, fair or
not." Rosamund wriggled indignantly, but Sigrid's grip
was too strong to break easily. Then Sigrid said, "You
were betrothed to Harud Olafsson by your father, and
you probably know his mind better than any of us
here. Why do *you* think he took the children?"

Rosamund turned to Sigrid. That was an important
question, and it might be that she was the only one who
could answer it. She had studied Harud Olafsson like a
bird studies snakes.

"The kindest thing I can suppose is that the man has
gone mad," she said slowly. "But that is not very
likely, although not impossible. I think that the fight in
the village came about because his temper got the

better of him after one of his men was hurt. He does try
to do a chief's duty to them, you know."

"I have heard as much. But—why the children?"

Rosamund pressed her hands to her eyes. The noise
of the clamoring about Haakon roared almost too loud
for her to think. "He knew there would be a strong case
against him under the laws of any Norse land. He took
the children to bargain with, I think—their lives against
weregild or any other judgments."

Sigrid caught her breath. "And he may threaten to
kill them if Haakon's voyage to Ireland becomes known
to him?"

"Yes."

"I think Haakon should know this."

"I will tell him when the time comes to speak to him
about everything else," Rosamund said. That would
come soon enough. She loved Sigrid like a second
mother, but she would not hop every time the woman
said "Frog."

Rosamund had her chance that night. She was already in bed and Haakon undressing when he stopped
with one leg still in his trousers and his tunic dangling
in his hand. "I'm thinking of leaving one ship and her
men behind to protect our steading. You know Harud
Olafsson. Is he likely to strike here?"

Rosamund sat up and crossed her arms on her knees.
"I don't know. But if his *father* is so strong that he
doesn't miss Harud's hundred men—"

"Olaf *wasn't* that strong, the last time I heard. Harud's
hundred must have been a good half of his father's
strength."

"Then I think Harud will be sailing home, not here.
He'll want enough men in Ireland to enforce any ransom he demands for the children. He may have hoped
to strike here in the Trondelag before the fight at the

village, but I don't see how he can do it now. No one in Norway would help him now, would they?"

"There are always men with the honor of mad dogs, but this time I think you're right. Harud has made himself a pariah, and I think he'll be sailing home, whatever he planned to do before. Even if he does come here while I'm gone, he'll have a good many enemies he didn't have before. Enough to put the fear of Odin in him. So, I should be safe taking all three ships to Ireland, but I'll leave Gunnar here with some men, just in case. I was planning to do that anyway. And I'll either bring back the children or I'll die in Ireland." He looked grim now. "I swear it."

"That's an ill omen. Don't swear anything like that, Haakon. I want you back here in the winter to see your child."

The words caught Haakon in the act of pulling his trousers off the other leg. He started, lost his balance, and sat down hard on the bed. He disentangled himself from the furs with some care for his dignity, finished pulling off his trousers, and looked cautiously at Rosamund, almost afraid he had heard wrong.

"My—child? You aren't going to lose the—"

"Your mother says not." Rosamund smiled, content with Sigrid's judgment. "I've missed two moon-times and I was sick this morning. Sigrid says that makes it certain."

Haakon let out a roar of delight, Ireland forgotten. He scrambled over the bed coverings, hugged her soundly, then kissed her. After a moment she pushed him away gently and sat so that she could look squarely into his face. "I wanted to say this earlier, but it wasn't the time. I want this child to know the kind of man his father is. I want him to know his father is the best, noblest, wisest—" Her voice broke, and she blinked in a fruitless effort to force back the tears. They wouldn't stop, and her throat was so constricted with emotion, she couldn't speak. Instead, she put her arms around him and her head against his chest.

"Haakon, I love you, all that you are or ever can be. I wish I could say more. I want to say more. I can't think of the words." She cried because she couldn't and because she was happy. He put his arms around her and ran his hands down her back. He patted her buttocks gently, then held her close to him until the tears stopped.

Slowly the tears faded, and she wriggled under his hands on her bare skin. She ran her hands across his chest and let her fingers drift down the hard muscles of his belly. He was already stirring, but he looked at her dubiously.

"Rosamund, if you're not well—"

"I said I was with child, not sick. I'm not made of glass." She broke off in a sigh as he pressed her to him happily and raised one hand to her breast. It would be a long summer with Haakon gone in Ireland. . . .

She pulled him down into the furs with her and wriggled her legs apart for him. A few more days to put a whole summer's lovemaking in. . . . Haakon had never had to be coaxed to bed. Assured that she was not fragile, he threw himself on top of her hungrily and pushed in deep, tangling his hands in her long hair as they rolled together in the furs. It was nearly dawn before they slept.

VII

Even with the unsettling prospect of Haakon's sailing and her sheer fury at Harud Olafsson over the stolen children, Rosamund felt like singing. Sometimes, when she thought no one could hear her, she did sing. It wasn't long before everyone on the steading knew that Lady Rosamund was wonderfully happy, and from there it wasn't much of a step for those who knew how desperately she had prayed to keep this child to figure out why. The women smiled and giggled and kept bringing her things to eat.

Haakon wasn't so lighthearted. More and more of his fighting men were muttering over Bjorn's death and evil omens, and Knut One-Eye finally came and told Haakon he had best do something about it.

"There haven't been any accusations between our men and Ivar's, have there?" Haakon asked when Knut was finished.

Knut shook his head. "No. But the mystery makes them uneasy. There's a smell of murder in it, and they don't like it any more than any man would, leaving Bjorn unavenged, and maybe sailing with a murderer. If we could settle the thing before we sailed, it might save trouble later."

"Thor's hammer, they're as suspicious as old women. Bjorn could have fallen into that vat with no help from anything but his thirst! Turning the whole band inside out looking for a murderer who may not exist will split them in half if we don't find one."

"You seem too easy in your mind about not avenging Bjorn. He was your oldest comrade," Knut said bluntly. He took two steps backward as a precaution. The jarl's temper was not at its mildest these days.

"You're an odd one to speak against me for not taking blood-vengeance when it's due," Haakon said grimly. "Where would you be now if I'd done that last year?"

Knut shut his mouth tight and bit his lip. That was unanswerable. If Haakon had taken blood-vengeance last year when he had the right, neither Knut nor anyone else who had sailed on *Wave Walker* would be alive. They had attacked under a shield of peace, and they owed their lives and their honor, which was the more important of the two, to Haakon. Knut looked ashamed, and Haakon's expression grew milder. Still, Knut thought he was keeping his temper on a tight rein.

"If Bjorn was murdered, something will happen to show it," Haakon said. "And believe me, there will be a vengeance." Knut looked at Haakon and thought that he would not care to be the man who had killed Bjorn, if anyone had.

"You're right in one thing though," Haakon said. "Something has got to stop the talk, and I spoke with Gunnar about it this morning. With Harud raiding in Rogaland, we need a stronger guard here. Anyone who fears the omens can stay behind under Gunnar's command and keep his oath to me by spending the summer here, weapons in hand. Will that content you?"

"That will save their oaths," Knut said, practical. "What about their share of the booty?"

That was important. "I'll make that up out of my own share if I have to," Haakon said. "I'll have no man in my ships who's not easy in his mind about this. A man seeing ghosts and omens under every tree is a danger to himself and to the rest of the men. I won't make any man who honestly thinks the gods have an ill hand in the matter sail just to save my pride."

Knut went away satisfied, and the next day, Haakon led the hundred and fifty men who would be sailing with him to Ireland up-country to the field where they held their weapons practice. They watched curiously as he strode out to the center of the field.

"I will ask no man to go or stay, fight or drink, tumble a woman or even steal a chicken—" Laughter drowned him out. "I will ask no one to do *anything* if he feels the omens are bad." They listened, quiet now. "So. We need a guard here, at our backs. Any man who stays here at the steading over the summer will have kept his oath to me. He will answer to Gunnar. Each man's honor will be safe, and his purse no lighter for not sailing." He looked around at the men, meeting each one's eyes. "Now. Who will stay?"

It was a Norseman's privilege to argue with his chieftain, but now, actually given the choice, only eight men came forward. The first two were jeered, and Haakon roared for silence. "If *I* say nothing against them, who else dares say anything? *Their* honor is safe, but I don't know about the honor of anyone who mocks them." He pounded one fist into the other, and the men closed their mouths. He was not making the threat idly. He had no use for louts willing to insult men who had a reasonable fear of evil omens.

In the silence that followed, the other six men came up quickly. Knut was not among them, Haakon saw. And neither was Hjalmar Sitricsson, who stood at the back of the crowd, looking stubborn. He still didn't like it, his expression said, but he wasn't going to miss a fight. The last man was Kare Ingstad, one of Ivar's best spearmen, a tall, handsome man with pale green eyes and ruddy cheeks. He had long, bushy eyebrows and a drooping mustache that gave his face the look of a wild man.

"I ask to stay behind, jarl, less out of fear for myself than for fear for you," he said dubiously. "*I* may be a bad omen. All three chiefs I've served in the last six years have died. If you count Bjorn, four. I've no wish to leave your service, but I will ask to stay behind. I was thinking to ask, anyway. That should take away any ill luck I might bring you in Ireland."

Haakon considered that. Kare had been one of Ivar's most trusted men, but also one of the first to swear to Haakon. He was a strong fighter and a loss to be regretted, but his doubts did not sound like those of a coward, a liar, or a fool.

"Very well, Kare. You will swear to answer to Gunnar as to me, and swear to sleep sword in hand."

Kare swore, and the other seven men who would stay behind repeated his oath. Satisfied, Haakon faced the whole band again. "You will have one more chance to be sure that neither god nor man stands against my vengeance. We will go to the June *Eyrathing* to get the law's sentence passed on Harud Olafsson. If anyone feels an evil omen there in the sight of the gods and the lawspeaker, he may come to me then and ask to stay behind. After that, we sail to put an end to Olaf Haraldsson and his bloody-handed son!"

Two days later, Haakon led his fighting men and much of his household aboard his three longships and the *knarr*. By either rowing or sailing, the sacred grove of the *Eyrathing* was easier to reach by water than by land. With no need to load food and gear for a long voyage in the open ocean, there was plenty of room for the women and children. Haakon loaded only the leather tents for everyone's comfort at the law courts, which sometimes went on for several days.

The men who stayed behind at the steading had their weapons ready at hand, and their orders. With Harud Olafsson perhaps loose in Norway, Haakon had no mind to let his guard down. Haakon didn't think Harud would attack during the *Eyrathing*, not with hundreds of the fighting men of the Trondelag gathered for it. It would be too easy to come after him. No sensible man would risk it. But, as Rosamund had said, it *was* possible that Harud was mad.

It was a bright, sunny day, with a breeze promising good sailing. Oars clattered, sails rustled as they filled with wind, and the children giggled and had to be held lest they fall overboard looking. From the *knarr* came the neighing of the stallion Haakon would offer in sacrifice for a good judgment and good vengeance.

In the bow of *Dragon Queen*, Kare Ingstad stood a little apart from everyone else. He had done his share of the work in setting sail, and he didn't want to talk to anyone. Let them take it for worry over himself as an ill-luck bringer. And in truth he was so close to grasping fortune that he feared anything that had the smallest chance of changing his luck. He had already tried to sweeten the odds somewhat and had come close to losing everything.

Until then, the gods had sent him good fortune, and if nothing of his careful planning came unbalanced now, they would send him good fortune still. Kare grinned into his mustache. The men who had started it all hadn't fared so well—they were dead.

It had all begun the night that Lady Rosamund's brother Mark had come from England and from Harud Olafsson, who was in a rage over losing his bride, to make a bargain with Ivar Egbertsson. And Kare, who had an ear for what might mean profit, had listened at the door. What he heard had been dangerous enough to keep quiet about, but he listened anyway and went on listening all through that winter and into spring. By the time Mark and Ivar stole the lady Rosamund out of Haakon Olesson's steading and got killed for it, Kare knew more about the chief's dealings than anyone suspected. He even knew which man a suspicious Harud had placed in the Trondelag to watch Mark and Ivar. So Kare went to him and promised to do what Mark and Ivar had failed at—for a sufficient price in gold.

Harud's agent agreed. The man hadn't been able to salvage the first plot, and Harud Olafsson was not a notably patient man to serve. If Harud's agent couldn't retrieve the situation, he would soon be as dead as Mark and Ivar. He grasped at the first offer of salvation that came his way and struck a bargain with Kare.

With Harud's gold, paid by Harud's agent, in his

pocket, Kare began to enjoy himself. For the first time
in his life, he could feel himself a leader with men of his
own under his command. He hired a group of knifemen
in one of the coastal towns and settled down to wait
until Haakon had sailed for Ireland. And that was when
he had made his mistake. He had tried to hire Bjorn
Karlsson, too.

It had seemed a good enough idea to begin with.
When Jarl Haakon had first brought Lady Rosamund
from England, Bjorn Karlsson had said she was a witch.
And she had taken some of Bjorn's place in Jarl Haakon's
life, too. Likely Bjorn was afraid of her, and most
certainly he was jealous of her. Men had committed
murder for less cause.

So the night after Lady Sigrid had married Erik
Allesson, when Bjorn was still a little drunk from two
nights' feasting and probably in a receptive frame of
mind, Kare took him aside into the brew house to talk,
and found out how wrong he had been. His only piece
of luck had been that Bjorn was older and drunker.
Bjorn was so outraged that he forgot his sword and tried
to punch Kare in the face instead. He might have had
some idea of dragging Kare bodily into the hall to give
to Jarl Haakon. Kare ducked, and Bjorn's fist smashed
into the wall. Frantic, Kare kicked him, and Bjorn went
over backward and hit his head hard on an ale vat.

Kare had his sword out before he realized, through
his own drunken panic, that if he put a sword in Bjorn,
the hunt would be on for the murderer. And if he
didn't, he wouldn't live longer than it would take Bjorn
to get to Jarl Haakon. He stuck the sword back in its
sheath and quickly dragged the half-conscious Bjorn to
the ale vat. The ale was low, and he tipped him into it
headfirst and held him under. Bjorn struggled, but
Kare's grip on his hair and the back of his neck was too
strong, and after a few minutes he grew still.

In the morning, Kare had waited fearfully for someone to find the body, his nerves so tightly strung that he had had to fight to keep himself from going to the brew house to make the "discovery" himself. Finally, Thorfinn Solvisson had come out of the brew house shouting, and Kare had gone to "help." Even then, his stomach had been knotted into a hard ball until the jarl had decided it was an accident. He had been lucky there, too, Kare thought. The jarl might have his doubts, but he wouldn't do anything about them until he came back from Ireland. And after that, Kare Ingstad wouldn't care because he would be elsewhere, with a purse full of Harud Olafsson's gold—enough to be a jarl himself, in Ireland, maybe, or the Orkneys.

Kare leaned on the shields hung along *Dragon Queen's* side and tried to think about that, and not the little twist of doubt that had begun to run through his mind. He stared into the wind-ruffled blue waters of the fjord and then up at the green pastures that ran down to it on either side, looking for something, anything—a sign that his luck was still with him. It should be. He was free and unsuspected, his men ready for his word, and his own excuse for not sailing with Jarl Haakon easily accepted. Also there was no Bjorn Karlsson now to grow suspicious. It was as well that he had killed him, Kare told himself. He should be confident now, sure of success, with his gold and his land and his place in the world just waiting to be taken. Instead he found himself starting at too many noises, and the breeze that blew on the Trondheimsfjord felt cold to him, even through his cloak. He had made one mistake. There could be no more. Harud Olafsson was not forgiving with men who made mistakes.

VIII

Red Hawk slid easily onto the gravel beach with a grinding of stones and a groaning of timber. Haakon was the first man to leap over the side into the shallows. Then he held his arms to Rosamund, and she eased herself down into them. As he carried her ashore she felt his concerned eyes searching her face, then running down her body. When she and Haakon were ashore and he'd set her on her feet, he looked at her suspiciously. "You are pale. Is it the child, or are you getting ill?"

Rosamund sighed. It was going to have to come out now. She had put it off for as long as she could, and she *would* make herself ill if she went on gnawing at the question like a bone, and being afraid to ask Haakon. "Haakon, there will be a sacrifice at the *Eyrathing*, won't there? An important one?"

"Yes."

"Does that mean there will be . . . men?"

Haakon shook his head and led her to a large boulder, where they could sit and talk. He spread his cloak out for her to sit on and held her hands in his own. "No men will be sacrificed. Not this time, not here. . . . This has been bothering you for a long time, hasn't it?"

Rosamund's eyes filled with tears. She sat looking miserably down at their interlocking hands and nodded her head.

"You've heard too many Christian priests' tales," Haakon said. "I don't understand why they make such a noise. I *have* heard it said that the followers of your Christ *ate* his flesh and *drank* his blood—"

"No!" Rosamund said, horrified. "That is—is a symbol."

"Well, our sacrifices are symbols too, in a way," Haakon said. "We give a beast—or a man—to the gods for their own use, or to follow his master in the next world. I can tell you what is approved by most lawful men among the Norse. No men or women are sacrificed against their will unless they are criminals or captives in war. And even then they are given the choice—to offer themselves to the gods and be honored after their deaths, or be executed and die in shame. Most *choose* to go to the gods, for their own honor and their kin's.

"Otherwise, those who are sacrificed go of their own will. For some it is a desire for a better life in another world. For some, the fear of being sold after a master's death. And some go out of love for someone they have served for many years.

"No man has offered himself for this sacrifice, so no man will die. And even if someone *had*, it might not be lawful. We have no Angel of Death here now, and it is never a good omen to ask an Angel to come from somewhere else."

He said it as if he assumed Rosamund knew what an Angel of Death was, like a longship or a watering trough. This was the second time she'd heard those ominous words "Angel of Death," but she decided not to ask Haakon. She'd look too much a fool. And she was so relieved that she was not going to witness a human sacrifice that the question seemed unimportant. Besides, there was a whole host of men coming toward them, shouting greetings and questions at Haakon and all no doubt curious to see the English captive he'd taken to his bed. She forgot the Angel of Death and set her face into an expression of appropriate friendliness, the jarl's lady greeting the jarl's comrades. They would be quick enough to criticize if they found her haughty.

*　　*　　*

The grove of *Eyrathing* was ringed with ancient oaks, gnarled and old as time. They formed a rough triangle, with the apex pointing toward the fjord and the base to the hills. On either side of the apex were altars and rune-carved memorial stones, and behind them, wooden images of the gods. Rosamund recognized some of them: Odin, the gallows lord, rune lord, god of wisdom and poetry and all knowledge; Thor, the thunderer, protector of man; Frey and Freya, the twin gods even older than the lords of Asgard, givers of fertility and harvest and the cycle of the seasons; and Tyr, the war god. There were others that she didn't recognize.

Before the lawspeakers of the *Eyrathing* heard the cases and made their judgments, there must be sacrifice, to ask wisdom and truth-speaking of the gods. In the shadows of the grove stood a stone hut that had been there longer than any man present could remember. It was densely covered with moss and vines, almost a part of the grove itself. A tall man with a white beard and an arm that dangled uselessly stood before it, apparently giving orders to the men who scurried in and out with stone and bronze vessels and old bronze knives that they laid before the altars. He saw Haakon and raised a hand in greeting to him.

Haakon whispered to Rosamund that that was Egil Kjotvisson, who was chief priest in the Trondelag this year. "He lost that arm last season, raiding in Frisia. Prideful old man, too stubborn to admit he should bide by the fire now. He had to go raiding with men no older than his grandson, and cripple his arm to prove it." Haakon chuckled. "I still wouldn't want to fight him though."

Egil Kjotvisson stepped up with the lawspeaker, whom Rosamund recognized from Sigrid's wedding, and shouted for silence. Rosamund looked down at her toes while Haakon and two other men dragged up to the altar the stallion that he had brought, and the other sacrifices were made. On either side of the grove rose the grave mounds of long-dead jarls, like great ships rising through the grass, some crowned with rune-stones to mark the deeds of the men who slept in them. Rosamund felt almost as if those men watched her, waiting to see what the Christian Englishwoman would do. She gritted her teeth. A bull bellowed at the blood smell on the altar and backed away, fighting the men at his head. The whole grove seemed to Rosamund to smell of blood. Haakon came back to stand beside her, and she could see from his face that the sacrifice was no light matter to him. As Sigrid had said, the Norse gods were close to his heart, and this was the way he gave his worship.

Mother Mary, Sweet Jesus, this is the man I consider as my husband, and I love him. I am carrying his child. These are his people, and this is the way he worships his gods. But I cannot do this. Must I stand apart from my husband's people all my life because of it?

No answer came, only the chanting of the priest and the lawspeaker. Would her God even speak to her in a pagan grove? Would He abandon her altogether and leave her with nothing to hold to at all? Wulf came up from the ships, where he had been napping in *Red Hawk*'s hold, and stuck his nose in her hand, and she scratched his head gratefully, glad of any companionship here among her husband's dark and alien gods.

When the sacrifice was over, the lawspeaker stepped up and cleared his throat, and Rosamund breathed more easily. This was safe, familiar, nothing more sinister than an old man hearing cases, not so far different from her father's yearly courts—although the lawspeaker and the others who came forward with him to sit in judgment seemed a good deal more honest than Earl Edmund had been with his slaves and sworn men in England. Haakon had said it was a disgrace to offer a bribe at a Thing and that it would not be taken.

There were a number of cases to be heard, major quarrels that could not be settled at home—killings and the resulting blood-feuds mostly—brought when someone felt that the feuding had gone too far and that the Thing had best step in and set weregild and force an agreement before the feuding spread to all the combatants' neighbors and kin. There were also a few land disputes and some grievances over trade, and one broken betrothal involving a dowry that both sides now claimed they didn't have. That *someone* had it was obvious. It would be up to the Thing to decide who, and order restitution.

Haakon was called to judge some of the cases involving matters that neither he nor his kin were concerned with, and it was evident that his opinion was highly valued. When it came time to consider the matter of Harud Olafsson, there was little argument. Haakon had already sworn to go after the children, and the Thing merely gave him its official sanction. And after they had heard the two men who had escaped from the slaughter Harud had left behind him in Rogaland, they named Harud Olafsson outlaw. Strictly speaking, Rogaland was not their jurisdiction, but Harud Olafsson was a wolf that no one wanted roaming in his pastures.

When the last case of the day ended, the *Eyrathing* became almost a fair, a meeting place for old friends and gossip, with ale and games on the shore. A multitude of people Rosamund didn't know came to greet Haakon and wish him fair wind and to drink and talk while the evening meal cooked on spits among the beached ships by the fjord. Rosamund sat down gratefully beside Haakon to listen and to drink the ale that Guthrun brought her. Her mouth was dry, and as usual now, she was ravenous. It would be at least an hour until the meat was cooked. She gulped the ale gratefully and then wondered if she should have. With no food in her stomach, she felt a little giddy.

A jarl from upfjord, who had been talking about the spring sowing with Haakon, heaved himself to his feet and went off to see about his dinner, and Haakon tapped her on the shoulder as another man took his place.

"Rosamund, this is Egil Kjotvisson," Haakon said. "He is the keeper of the altars and the sacred grove, but not quite like a priest of your Christ. Our priest is chosen by lot every three years from among all the lawful men of the Trondelag."

Egil raised one eyebrow. "I think in my case the lot was not wholly the master of the affair. I *heard* it said that Jarl Haakon wanted me chosen so I shouldn't go hungry after I had lost the use of one arm."

Haakon tried to look indignant. "Who told you that?"

"*That* is a secret of the sacred grove," Egil said piously. "But I didn't come to talk of that. And Jarl Haakon knows I'm grateful. Lady Rosamund, for a year past now, the Trondelag has had no Angel of Death."

"I have heard as much," Rosamund said and wondered what was coming. Now she definitely wished she'd drunk a little less ale.

"Those who wish to go to the gods with their dead masters have not been able to do so. And the *Eyrathing* can send no captives or criminals, either. There is no way to be sure they will go lawfully."

"No one should be asked to face an unlawful death or make an unlawful sacrifice," Rosamund said. An Angel of Death must be some sort of attendant to the priest. She meant it as a polite formality, proudly exhibiting the knowledge learned that morning from Haakon. Haakon and Egil looked delighted.

"Very true!" said Egil expansively, his face brightening. "So you *do* understand the importance of what you would be doing for our gods and the Trondelag if you become our Angel of Death. Of course *my* voice is not the only one that must be heard in this matter, but—"

"Oh, trolls carry off your modesty," Haakon said.
"You know perfectly well that if Rosamund has your
voice, no one else in the Trondelag would dare to raise
his above a whisper." He beamed at her proudly, and
she thought that he looked slightly relieved. She began
to be uneasy.

"That *may* be so," said Egil. "What *is* so is that Lady
Rosamund is very worthy of the office. Her strength,
courage, wisdom, and honor are known to all."

Rosamund nearly said that it was equally well known
she was a Christian, and some people had suspected
her of being a witch. A look at Haakon made her keep
her silence. This was not the time or place for her to
decline. She gulped and smiled. "I had not expected
this. I am honored, but in truth I am also too surprised
to accept just now. May I have time to think about this,
maybe until Haakon returns from Ireland? I need to
consider whether I am fit for the office." *Please God
that that would content them.*

"*I* think you're fit," Haakon said. "But of course you
can have that much time, or more if you need it."
Rosamund wanted to kiss him, and Egil Kjotvisson
nodded solemnly.

"Very proper. Very proper."

Haakon poured more ale in her cup, only a single
swallow. There was no telling what might happen next,
and he wanted her sober to deal with any eventuality.
Egil Kjotvisson took his leave, but Rosamund could see
another horde of men and women coming toward them.
They would have to be greeted properly, and then
there would be tonight's feast to get through, and still
more greetings. *But no more mysterious honors,* she
prayed. She slipped one arm through Haakon's and
turned to face the newcomers. As soon as she could be
alone with someone who knew, someone who was *not*

Haakon, she would ask what an Angel of Death was.
And what one did.

IX

Before the *Eyrathing* ended, Rosamund could have
asked Sigrid, who was there with Erik the Bald, what
an Angel of Death was, but she found she didn't want
to. If she didn't like the answer, it might be awkward.

She finally decided to ask Guthrun, who would be
less inclined to give unwanted advice on top of
explanations. Rosamund's maid had been born and
raised a Christian, but she had Norse blood in her from
both parents. More important, when Gunnar Thorsten
had come to Earl Edmund's hold as a thrall, Guthrun
had fallen in love, and she'd slipped off her Christianity
as easily as she changed her shift. Rosamund marveled
at her maid's adaptability and felt Guthrun would undoubtedly know everything about Angels of Death. But
if she didn't, she could find out without making Rosamund
look foolish.

The day before Haakon sailed, Rosamund picked up
her sewing and dragged Guthrun to a quiet corner of
the hall. They had made shirts and new breeches for
the men and had patched the old ones, but there was
still a tear in *Dragon Queen's* sail that had to be
mended. Rosamund looked at her needle wearily. She
was tired of mending, and the sail wouldn't last more
than one more trip, she thought. It would be a fine
thing to make a new one and have it waiting for Haakon
when he came home. He was vainer of his ships than
he was of himself. She spread the sail out across both

their laps and whispered, "Guthrun, what is an Angel of Death?"

Guthrun looked startled. "Well, it's no great secret. Although they don't have one here now, and I've heard that's ill luck. But it always takes a great deal of time to choose a new one. The Angel of Death is important, and someone is always insulted if *everyone* doesn't have a chance to approve the choice. She's a priestess, in a way. Not always highborn, but of an old family. Maybe a farmer's wife or widow, or a jarl's lady even. Always someone who is married, or has been." She looked at Rosamund's dubious face. "Oh, Freya, have they offered to make you Angel of Death?"

"Yes."

Guthrun swallowed. "Well, it's an honor. Especially for someone who wasn't born here. I—to be truthful, I think the honor may be mostly for Jarl Haakon. He is a powerful man now, and it may be someone wants his friendship."

Or thinks Haakon is owed a debt, Rosamund thought dismally, thinking of Egil Kjotvisson. "I'll decide if it's an honor when I know what one *does*."

Guthrun looked nervous. "I don't think you can refuse."

Rosamund found her patience beginning to slip. "I can't even accept until you tell me what this honor *is*! Guthrun, you are hiding something."

Guthrun wished fervently that the priests had had more sense. And how could Jarl Haakon have let them? They must have been mad to pick Lady Rosamund, and now if she refused, they would be offended and it would make bad blood, and likely they would start saying she was a witch again. The trolls take all slow-witted men! "When a man or woman consents to go to the gods," she said slowly, "it is the Angel of Death who sends them."

"Who—sends them?" Rosamund's blue-purple eyes snapped open wide. *Oh, dear God.*

"Yes." Guthrun made her voice matter-of-fact, giving a lesson. "She dresses them in fine clothes and gives them ale to drink, and then leads them to the place of sacrifice. Then she puts a cord around their neck, and while two men pull on the cord she takes the sacred knife and—"

Rosamund put one hand out and the other over her stomach.

"My lady, you do not look well."

"I am *not* well," Rosamund said. "Guthrun, what have I done? When Egil Kjotvisson asked me, I didn't want him to know I was so ignorant, or Haakon, so I—I pretended I knew all about it and only said I needed time to think it over. Haakon looked so relieved. Dear God, he must have been afraid I wouldn't do it, and when I—when I didn't say no, he looked so *proud* of me. He *knows* that the idea of the sacrifices troubles me. He must have thought I was doing it for him."

"Well, I don't see how you *could* have said no," Guthrun said practically. "Not with the priest standing right there and the whole *Eyrathing* to gossip over it."

"And now I can't say no to Haakon, either," Rosamund said. "After he looked so happy over it."

"How long did you say you wanted to think about it?"

"Until Haakon gets home from Ireland."

"Well, something may happen between now and then," Guthrun said. "Although I don't know what," she added.

"And pigs may fly," Rosamund said. "Oh, I *don't* feel well." She bent over with her arms around her stomach.

"That's the baby," Guthrun said. "It's bad for you to fret yourself like this. I'll talk to Gunnar. Maybe he can think of something."

"No! Gunnar is too much Haakon's friend. I won't

have Haakon made to look foolish. This is my fault."
She stood up. "I am going to lie down. Maybe I will
think of something," she said drearily.

Haakon wasn't in their bedchamber, and she crawled
into the bed and pulled the furs up over her head. One
thing was clear. She could *not* be an Angel of Death.
She would respect the Norse gods for Haakon's sake,
and the Norse way of worship, even the sacrifice—
human sacrifices—if she had to. But she could *not* lead
another person to his death, much less kill him on an
altar with a knife while two men strangled him into
helplessness. Her stomach turned over. She thought
God might understand if she gave the pagan gods
respect for Haakon's sake. But this was a sin black
enough to burn her in hell forever. Even without the
sin she couldn't have done it, she thought. If she tried,
she would only give herself away and make a scandal.

She knew that Haakon was going to pay a price for
her refusal. She suspected that what penalty *she'd* pay
would depend very much on what happened to him.
Suppose the men who'd offered to make her Angel of
Death turned against Haakon and supported one of his
enemies? Haakon was no saint. He would not easily
forgive his wife for that.

*Must all we've built break apart now because in this
one thing his ways can't be mine?*

She put her face into the furs and cried, desolately,
yet quietly so that no one would hear her and come to
see what the matter was. After a long time she raised
her head, spent, and tried to think again.

At least she had until Haakon came home from
Ireland, which wouldn't be until the end of summer.
Surely she could find a way out by then—some way to
evade this appalling "honor" and still not destroy Haakon's
standing. If she couldn't, she thought miserably, maybe
she didn't deserve him.

* * *

Four days later Haakon and his men sailed for Ireland.

Even some of the women whose men were aboard the longships said it was none too soon. Most of the fighters had been around the steading long enough to eat and drink nearly everything in sight. They hadn't reached the stage of quarreling yet, but some of them were beginning to bother the women, not much caring whether they pestered an honest wife or a light-skirted thrall-girl.

"If they leave now, we *may* be able to put things right before they come home," Guthrun said briskly.

The day of the sailing was gray, and windy enough to raise whitecaps out on the fjord and make watchers draw their cloaks tight. Rosamund, Guthrun, and Gunnar stood side by side, with Wulf at their feet, as the men scrambled aboard the ships. Rosamund wavered between loneliness at Haakon's going and relief that now she wouldn't have to talk about Egil Kjotvisson's offer. She reached down and scratched Wulf behind the ears.

The warriors took their places at the oars, and the men who were staying behind waded into the water to help push the ships off. Haakon stood up and waved to Rosamund, then started the heaving chant. The men in the water put their shoulders to the hulls, and the oars dug into the water. From the shore there rose the familiar thud and crash of iron weapons on leather-covered shields. The men on shore cheered, and someone shouted, "Fair wind!"

Suddenly Wulf leaped to his feet and gave a great bark of protest. Before Rosamund could grab his collar, he was hurling himself down the slope to the shore, scattering unwary onlookers as he went.

As the ships floated clear, Wulf hit the water and threw up a sheet of spray. The men laughed and started cheering, and Rosamund saw Magnus Styrkasson stand up and throw off his cloak. A moment later he dove over the side of the *Red Hawk* and swam for Wulf.

Rosamund couldn't help laughing. Magnus was getting wet for no reason. Wulf could swim like a fish. Once he had grappled with a half-grown stag a hundred yards out in a lake and nearly dragged it to shore before Earl Edmund's hunters could wade out to help him.

Wulf swam straight past Magnus to the *Red Hawk*, and a dozen pairs of hands reached down. Someone tossed Magnus's cloak down into the water. Magnus wrapped it around the hound in a sling, and they started hauling. Haakon was standing on deck bellowing with laughter. "Have you sent your dog to protect me in Ireland, Rosamund?" he shouted. A moment later he was yelling and trying to get as far away from Wulf as possible as the hound shook himself furiously. They lowered the sling for Magnus, and Haakon reached over and hauled him up. He turned and waved to her again.

Rosamund pulled her cloak tighter as the masts of each ship rose into place. As the sails swelled to the wind, her eyes started to sting, and she couldn't stop the silent prayer, to whichever god gave good luck and safe homecoming to honest men: *Bring him home*.

X

In all his years of sailing, Haakon never had weather-luck to match that vengeance voyage to Ireland. All his past had been marked by the evils of Olaf Haraldsson and his twisted son. Taking both the price they owed him for his father, his brother, and his sisters and the price they owed the Rogaland would change the course of his own life, Haakon thought, and give a new beginning for the future. And Thor had sent him a wind out of Asgard to sail on.

They sailed north around Scotland and the Orkney Islands—a longer and stormier way, but also less used by Norse ships, except those from the Orkneys themselves, and Haakon knew that the jarl of the Orkneys was no friend to Olaf Haraldsson: Because the Orkney jarl thought *he* should be chief over the Norse in Ireland, he would have no mind to warn Olaf of Haakon's coming. The Orkney route gave more chance of surprise, and so an easier fight and a better hope for the children seemed likely.

The sea stayed empty and the wind fair all the way to the Orkneys, and they made such good speed that Haakon turned aside to find the small, sad island where his sister Gwyntie lay buried and make sacrifice to her memory. It took two days beating about the Orkneys to find it, but no man aboard grudged Haakon the time. When they found it, he climbed the hill to the grave and stood over it a long time. There was nothing to sacrifice, and he cut his own thumb with a knife and rubbed the blood on the old stones, so that there should be some part of him to stay with his sister in this lonely place.

From the Orkneys south to Ireland, the oars stayed inboard most of the time. The ships rode easily in spite of their heavy loads, moving with the waves as if they were living things. Maybe they were, Knut thought, hand on the tiller—Snorri Longfoot always said a ship was more likely to have a soul than most women he knew.

When they raised the north coast of Ireland, they put in to shore by night for the final council of war. Haakon gave his orders, ax in hand, and one other stipulation that came as a surprise to the men who hadn't sailed with him before.

"No woman is to be harmed unless she has a weapon in her hand."

"Does this mean the Irish thralls, too?" Orm asked, perplexed.

"It does," Haakon said. He wasn't sure why he made that rule, but when he felt the golden ax quiver lightly in his hand, he thought he knew the answer. And the men grumbled, but they did it.

The mist hung low on the river. Haakon thought that the masts of his ships probably rose above it. He thought about taking the time to unstep the masts and decided it wasn't worth it. A man on a hilltop might see them, but no watcher down on the riverbank would, and time was important. The odds for surprise increased with each mile up the river and each hour of darkness gained.

Wave Walker's bow was so close to *Red Hawk*'s stern that Knut One-Eye, in the *Wave Walker,* could lean out past the stem piece and speak to Haakon, in the other boat, without raising his voice. "I hope your memory of the river's shoals is as good as you think it is."

"Some of the men I've talked to are sailors who travel this river every season. Unless the river's thrown up whole new sandbars since spring, we're safe. You worry overmuch, Knut."

"I sound too much like Bjorn, you mean, and you're not ready to hear from another man what you heard from him," Knut said. Haakon couldn't see Knut's face in the mist, but he could hear the kindness in his gruff voice. It took away much of his annoyance.

"True enough."

Someone gave a sharp order to *Wave Walker*'s rowers, and the ship's prow faded back into the mist. Haakon walked forward and sat down near a bundle of torches wrapped in oiled leather.

I'm sorry, old friend. You were never so thin-skinned as to be jealous if another man tried to give me advice. But while I think your ghost is watching, I can't bear hearing from another man's lips the things you always said—not until I know how you died. And that was another debt waiting when he got home to Norway.

The three ships had entered the river mouth just after dark, sailing straight in from the sea. By midnight, shrouded by the darkness and the mist, they were halfway to Olaf's steading—Ole Ketilsson's steading. It was better land than Olaf's, and when Ole left, Olaf moved in, like a rat into another animal's nest. The oars thumped steadily, the water chuckled at the prow, and metal scraped on stone as men not needed at the oars sharpened their weapons. Haakon saw Hagar the Simple testing each of his bowstrings in turn, then greasing them against the damp air.

Occasionally they could make out a hill looming in from the bank, but they saw only one light. When it appeared, the oarsmen slowed their stroke until the ships were barely moving upstream. No one spoke, and few breathed deeply until the light faded away astern.

Not long after, Haakon felt a puff of wind on his face, and before long, a steady breeze was blowing. Grateful now that they hadn't unstepped the masts, he ordered the sails raised. They would make the ships more visible, even in the darkness, but it would speed their passage as long as the breeze held. It was a contrary breeze, blowing the wrong way for this part of the coast; the weather-luck—and whoever had sent it—was with him still.

The breeze held. There was still only a faint hint of gray to the east when they reached the point where Haakon planned for them to leave the ships. The lay of the land would hide the ships from the steading and also make it easier for only a handful of men to defend them. A shipguard of thirty would be more than enough.

Haakon was the first man ashore as *Red Hawk* grounded, wading through the shallows and then snaking his way cautiously up the hill that masked them

from the steading. On the banks on the far side of the
river were two longships, a small *knarr,* and several
boats. From beyond the shoulder of another hill, inland, he saw the faint glow of fires and lanterns at
the steading.

Fifteen years of waiting were ended. Haakon unslung
the golden ax and charged the longships with all the
fury of those fifteen years. Behind him he could hear
his men shouting and running.

He had always thought that the ax increased his
strength, and now he was sure of it. He reached the
first longship too far ahead of his men, and a guard in
the prow peered down at him, spear in hand.

The golden ax whirled. The first blow cut through
the spear and sank deep into the hull. Splinters flew as
Haakon wrenched it free, and the man in the prow
jumped to his feet to run. The ax snaked out and laid
his leg open, knee and thigh. He toppled out of the
ship to lie writhing on the ground, screaming for the
rest of the guard.

Haakon raised his ax to finish him. *Don't waste your
time on a dead man when your back isn't safe.* Bjorn
had said that. Haakon ducked and started running as an
arrow sang past his ear. By the time the archer shot
again, Haakon was a moving target. The arrow slammed
into his shoulder and slid off his mail. There was a thud
and a yowl, and he turned to see the archer sprawled
on the gravel. There was blood on his head and a
fist-sized stone by his ear. Hagar the Simple trotted up,
bow still slung and another stone in his hand.

"I thought I could throw quicker than I could shoot,"
he said. Haakon reminded himself to see that Hagar got
a helmsman's portion of the booty, even if he did
nothing else before they sailed home.

Hooves clattered on the gravel, and a horse and rider
came out from behind the *knarr,* riding hard for the
steading. Hagar shot, and the arrow took the rider in

the neck. He crashed to the ground, and his horse bolted squarely into the tents that were pitched on the hill above the beach. The tents collapsed, and by the time the people inside struggled out, Haakon's men had caught up to them.

They were Olaf's thralls, for the most part unarmed, half-naked, and babbling in Gaelic. Haakon thought they probably had had no mind to come out of the tents at all when they had heard the fighting and would be there still if the horse hadn't charged through their midst.

"Don't be afraid," he said gently in Gaelic and found that the old tongue came back to him easily. "I am an enemy of Olaf Haraldsson but not of his thralls. You are all free if you wish it." He had to repeat it twice, chafing at the time lost but knowing that honor demanded at least getting these poor wretches clear of the fighting.

At last they understood and snatched up their scanty possessions and ran as if dragons were chasing them. By now Haakon's straggling men had caught up, dragging the ladders and the battering ram. Most of the men assigned to the shipguard were among them, as well as Wulf, and Haakon cursed them roundly, but they looked so eager for the fight that he hadn't the heart to send them back. But it was asking too much of the gods, though, to guard his ships for him.

"Very well," he growled. "If you're feeling so strong, use some of that strength on Olaf's ships. Shove them into the river."

Thirty sets of muscular Norse shoulders promptly threw themselves against the ships' prows. Knut called out the heaving chant in a low voice, and they pushed with a will. Soon every ship and boat bobbed in the current in midriver. Whatever else Olaf might bring to his defense, he would have no ships to aid him.

Haakon knew that the alarm must have been sounded by now. He leaped on top of a boulder, with the ax in his hands. To his men he looked the same color as the gray dawn's light, something not quite human. He raised the ax over his head.

"Tell Olaf who is coming for the children! Tell him!"

"Haakon!"

"And tell Olaf who is coming for his blood!"

"Haakon! Haakon! Haakon!"

XI

Five days after Haakon sailed, Kare Ingstad came to Rosamund, saying he felt sick. He had pains in his joints and could not keep his food down.

Rosamund had doctored her father's thralls and household for years, and she was not overly worried. Pains in the joints were common enough, although mostly in men older than Kare. She was less certain about the rebellious stomach. That sort of problem usually came with a fever, but Kare was not complaining of one and, in fact, did not feel hot to her touch.

With only the aching joints, Rosamund would have given Kare a bed in the main house; but with the sickness in his stomach, she had to be more cautious. Because the malady might spread to other people on the steading, she had the thralls clean one of the guest huts and put Kare to bed there. Two thrall-women gave him fresh drinking water and hot bricks to ease the pain in his joints. Rosamund herself visited him every morning and night, conscientious of her duty to her husband's household.

Gunnar was unhappy about these visits and said so. "And I don't like your going about alone after dark, even on the steading. If you must go, let—"

"Gunnar Thorsten, this is Haakon's steading, and I am his wife whether any priests have made it legal or no, and I have a duty to his people!"

"Kare was Ivar's man," Gunnar said.

"And how many times have you and Haakon both said they are not 'Ivar's men' but only 'Haakon's men.' Kare stayed behind to keep from bringing bad luck to a chief who has so far given him little. That is loyalty, and we owe Kare something for it."

"How deep a loyalty?" Gunnar said. "He swore mighty readily for a man who was Ivar's right hand."

Rosamund lost her temper. "I am the jarl's lady, this is my responsibility, and I won't have *anyone* say I didn't live up to it. Or tell Haakon his wife cares so little for the man who has sworn to him. Kare is *sick*, too sick to do me an injury. And *I* am sick to death of the subject." She glared at him. "Do you wish to explain to Haakon why you were willing to let one of his men die for lack of care?"

"No."

"Good. I did not think you were such a fool as that," she said briskly. "Now do not speak to me of this again, or I shall be angry."

She gathered up her medicines and swept out of the hall, and Gunnar resisted the temptation to ask what she'd been for the past few minutes. He decided to let the matter rest. He and Rosamund had to be on good terms for the sake of the steading, and she did have a point about her own responsibilities. Ivar's other men wouldn't like it if it was said that Rosamund didn't trust Kare. *Gunnar* didn't trust Kare, but he supposed that she was going to have her own way in this. When Gunnar had been a thrall in Earl Edmund's hold, he had learned that it was only Lady Rosamund's kind heart that made life there endurable. The same kind heart that led her to defend her father's thralls was now leading her to doctor Kare Ingstad. It might lead her

into trouble someday, but until then, kindness would
continue to outweigh caution. And no man, except
possibly Haakon, could tell her anything.

So for three days matters rested as Rosamund wanted
them. On the evening of the fourth day Gunnar made
his usual rounds of the steading, set the night guard,
and went to report to Rosamund that all was well. That
done, he could go to sleep and spend another night
wishing he had Guthrun instead of an empty bed, he
thought irritably. He had sworn to sleep alone as long
as the responsibility for the steading was his. He still
thought it was a good idea, but that didn't make it any
more enjoyable, especially since Guthrun, who thought
it was a silly idea, made it plain that she would be
happy to move over in the bed for him, vow or no.

Gloomily resigned to more weeks of celibacy, Gunnar
knocked on Rosamund's door. She always checked on
Kare before retiring, but she was usually back from
tending him by this time. Tonight, however, there was
only silence from beyond the door. Gunnar knocked
again, trying to make enough noise to rouse Rosamund
without waking the rest of the house. Still silence. He
knocked twice more, and the last time he didn't worry
about other sleepers. Finally he pushed hard on the
door, and it swung open easily.

Inside, the bedchamber was so dark that Gunnar had
to go back for a lamp. Its fitful light showed the bed
empty, the furs and woolen coverlets smooth and tidy.
Unless Rosamund had made it up herself, she hadn't
been to bed yet. Gunnar went out, closed the door, and
leaned against the doorpost to think.

Should he sound the alarm? Shout for a couple of
men to go with him and look for her? He was younger
and less experienced in war than some of the men
under his orders, and he had not been sworn to Haakon's
service as long as some. Likely he would have trouble

with them if they thought he had the habit of sounding the alarm for trifles.

As for taking men with him—well, it was unlikely that Rosamund was doing anything that should not be seen by any eyes but his. He tried to imagine her in bed with Kare Ingstad and succeeded only in making himself laugh. But if he took men with him, Rosamund would be in a fury, and assuming she was all right, she would have a right to be. Gunnar was in no mood to have a crowd of laughing men witness him being tongue-lashed by the jarl's lady.

Still—it was unwise to rule out danger merely because they were on their own steading. They should have warning of Harud Olafsson's coming, but a handful of outlaws was another matter. Gunnar made up his mind, got a spear and a long knife, and put his helmet on over his woolen cap; then he headed for Kare's hut.

The night was overcast and windy, and several of the torches set up to light the grounds had blown out. The guards' watch fire was burning briskly, but it was at the other end of the steading yard. By the time Gunnar was a dozen steps from the hall door, it was as dark as the belly of a whale.

Except for the wind and his own footsteps, there was silence all around as Gunnar made his way to Kare's hut. He tried to walk softly but didn't waste time looking for footprints in the small areas illuminated by the torches. The ground between the hall and the outbuildings was packed so hard by generations of feet, human and animal, that a small army could have crossed it without leaving any traces a man could see on a night like this.

No light showed from the hut when Gunnar reached it. And no doubt Rosamund was already on her way back to the hall, and he was stumbling in the dark for nothing—except that she would have had a lantern. If she'd passed him on the way, he would have seen her. The lantern could have gone out, he thought dubiously.

"Rosamund," he called softly. "Rosamund? My lady? Are you there?"

No answer.

Gunnar stepped back from the doorway and thrust his spear cautiously into it. On the left, the spear point met solid wood. On the right, nothing. The door was partly open.

"Rosamund? Kare?" Gunnar shouted loudly enough that anyone inside should have heard him. When silence still answered, he pushed the door open hard. Silence, darkness, and an open door did not add up to things as they ought to be.

Inside the hut, a lamp was burning low, and there was no one there. Not Rosamund, not Kare.

Gunnar turned and ran for the door. Fool not to have called out the men! He shouted, but they were at the other end of the steading, and the wind carried away the words.

Something heard him. There was a sound from a stand of young pines ten paces from the hut. Gunnar ran for it, spear out, and a man leaped out in front of him. Gunnar thrust with his spear in the darkness, and its point drove through the man's belly. His breath hissed out of him, and Gunnar withdrew his spear and looked frantically into the dark for whoever might be with him.

Another form slipped from the trees and hooked an arm around the first man's throat, cutting off what was left of his breath. Before the wounded men could make a sound, the other had drawn a knife across his throat. Gunnar hesitated—a man from the steading who'd also stumbled on these raiders? Or another of their band?

"Who are you?" He hesitated too long. There were running footsteps behind him, and something crashed down on the top of his helmet, making his head ring like a gong. Gunnar jerked his spear around, but his head was pounding, and he was off balance when the second blow struck at the base of the skull, below his helmet. He fell, and someone kicked him hard in the stomach, and the world vanished in black agony. Just before his sight faded, Gunnar saw, bending over him, the man who had cut the other's throat. It was Kare Ingstad, with a smile on his face.

Gunnar awoke with pains in his head and stomach and a furious ache in his back from lying on a damp wooden deck. As he came to, the deck tilted, and he rolled over and banged his head against an oar bench.

He was aboard a ship, apparently a fair-sized *knarr*. And the pains in his head and stomach weren't bad compared to the pain in his heart. He had been too concerned with his own precious honor and not making a fool of himself, he realized, sickened. If he had had enough armed men with him, he could have saved himself and Rosamund both, and Kare would have been a corpse in a tree at the bounds of the steading.

Instead, Kare was standing at the steering oar of the *knarr*, his hair blowing freely in the wind. He was smiling broadly down at Gunnar. The grin cut through Gunnar's misery, infuriating, taunting. Gunnar would cheerfully have traded all his skill as a poet for the privilege of smashing that grin and shoving the pieces down Kare's throat.

The *knarr* was larger than Haakon's and not crowded. There was no one else in the hold amidships and no gear or ballast, except a few barrels and a pile of furs in one corner. Gunnar counted six men sitting or standing on the decks fore and aft and heard voices hinting at a few more.

The men he could see all wore ragged clothes but had new cloaks of heavy wadmal and good boots. They also had new weapons—short spears, long knives, and a couple of axes. None had bows, and Kare was the only man with a sword. Outlaws, most likely, or men with no masters or poor ones, but certainly too many for him to entertain any notion of escaping. He saw no sign of Rosamund and felt sicker. Had they killed her in cold blood? Or had she been too badly hurt fighting them to be worth carrying off?

Gunnar was about to swallow his pride and plead with Kare to tell him where Rosamund was when he saw that the pile of furs in one corner of the hold was crowned by a pale face framed in long, golden hair. After a moment, unmistakable violet eyes opened in the face and turned toward Gunnar.

"Are you all right?" he said in a low voice, which croaked like an old raven's, and he coughed.

Rosamund nodded, stiffly, as if all her muscles and joints hurt. They probably did, after spending a chilly night bound and perhaps senseless. She nodded once more, then somehow managed to smile. "You were right," she whispered.

Some of Gunnar's pain faded as he returned the smile. Rosamund was alive and well, more than he would have wagered on before. Men like Harud Olafsson had been known to order women they hated as much cut open and left for others to find, with the unborn child cut in pieces and scattered around the mother's body.

Harud Olafsson. He had to be the master in this business, with Kare only his chief servant. Even if he'd thought of the scheme, Kare couldn't have hired, clothed, and armed half a score of men and bought a *knarr.* Gunnar and Rosamund were surely on their way to Harud Olafsson, wherever he might be.

Gunnar gritted his teeth and tried to call back the habits of mind that had kept him from going mad as a slave in Earl Edmund's castle. *Don't worry about what can't be helped; it wastes strength. Don't sacrifice your honor, but don't waste your life in foolish defiance. A live slave can become free. A dead man cannot become anything, not in this world.*

Rosamund would suffer for anything Gunnar attempted. They would count on his knowledge of that to keep him docile. No doubt he would also be punished if she disobeyed, but it was unlikely that she would; she was carrying Haakon's child. Rosamund would eat Harud's offal and smile as she did so if that would save the child.

Gunnar knew he could do no less. Were he by himself, he might have thought it better to die and take Kare Ingstad with him if he could. But he was now the only friend and helping hand Rosamund had, or might ever have, and he was miserably aware that that was his fault. It was all very well to say that Rosamund should have listened to him. But Gunnar Thorsten should not have listened to her or his pride. Gunnar Thorsten should have done what Haakon had left him to do and guarded Haakon's wife. And he hadn't. So now he would swallow his accursed pride and stay by her, whatever it cost. Maybe Haakon would forgive him eventually.

Kare Ingstad didn't call for any of his men to relieve him at the steering oar until he saw that Gunnar and Rosamund were asleep again. The fools had proved reluctant to pass too closely to the captives while they were awake, and Kare was in no mood for more trouble with them. The men he'd hired with Harud's money were not the best, but certainly they should prove good enough to guard a bound man and woman for two days.

Most unsettling to his knifemen were Rosamund's violet eyes. Those pools of purple fire might hide anything. They even made Kare nervous, but he told himself that it didn't really matter what Rosamund was thinking. She might be dreaming of slitting his belly open and packing it full of red-hot coals, but she couldn't do it.

And in two days, Rosamund and Gunnar wouldn't be his worry. They would be aboard Harud's longship, bound for the slave markets at Birka and a journey down the rivers to the East, from which they would never return. And Kare would be free to go wherever he wished, with enough silver to make himself a jarl in a fine house, with better men than these. He would have to walk carefully, with steel ready to hand, until Haakon Olesson was dead, but with the jarl's berserker's lust for battle, that shouldn't take long.

It would have been easier if Harud hadn't wanted Rosamund alive and refused to pay if she wasn't. It was always easier to deliver a person's head than his or her living body. But now that Harud wouldn't have her to wife, his lust for vengeance wouldn't be satisfied with only a quick death. Harud wanted to be able to think of her dying a little at a time through long years of slavery, far from any land she knew. There was a black twist in Harud somewhere, Kare thought, to take so much pleasure in that idea and spend so much money achieving it. But Kare was a practical man, and for the price Harud was paying, Kare was willing to let him take his pleasure as he chose.

Kare found that he needed a second cloak, even though the sun was still high. The warmth of the second cloak made him feel better. And so did the coming of darkness, when he could no longer see the two sleeping shapes in the hold of the *knarr*.

XII

Haakon's men marched in battle order through the fields that had once been Haakon's father's. They went behind their shields, arms at ready, and in the dawn's light the thralls in the fields saw them coming and ran. Olaf Haraldsson no doubt awaited them.

Haakon put Knut One-Eye in the lead on the right and Orm on the left, with himself at the center. They marched straight for the steading, veering only to keep clear of thickets and possible ambush. Most of the hilltops were so bare, they would see any archer who could see them, and Hagar the Simple could hit any man he could see.

As the dawn light grew they tramped steadily inland, weighed only by the siege equipment. If Olaf Haraldsson would not come out and fight, Haakon would break his walls open for him. The ladders were built by Snorri Longfoot, with pine uprights and rungs of stout, plaited leather as thick as a man's wrist. It made them easier to stow aboard ship and easier to carry, but it didn't make them much lighter, particularly with the leather wet from the night mist.

The battering ram was a hefty, long log with iron bands around the head to keep it from splitting and leather handles to provide grips for twenty or thirty men. Snorri had also carved solid wooden wheels for it, but on the muddy, hilly trail, they were almost useless. In desperation Orm finally kicked the wheels out from under the ram and ordered his men to take turns carrying it, fifteen at a time. The muscles popped out in their necks and the sweat poured down their foreheads, but the ram moved faster.

They saw no signs of the enemy except six horsemen along the crest of a hill, too far off to be identified. Haakon wondered if they were running away or going for help. He almost hoped it was the latter. Finding allies for Olaf would not be an easy task; Olaf was not a well-loved chief. And if help did come, it wouldn't come in time. But Haakon liked less the thought of Olaf fleeing, perhaps to die a straw death elsewhere. If he ran, he would wear the name "coward" as long as he lived, but that would not give Haakon or Ole Ketilsson's ghost the satisfaction he wanted.

The fields around the steading were dreary. Olaf's negligence had made a sad, ruined land of a once prosperous farm. And the Irish tenants and thralls in their huts were afraid of their shadows and pathetically ragged. They ran away so fast that Haakon had no chance to tell them they were free.

They crossed the last little stream, where Ole Ketilsson's children had played. Beyond it a short slope, cleared of trees, ran down to the wooden walls.

The steading itself was reasonably well kept up. The log wall enclosed several longhouses, with barns, granaries, sheds, and more thralls' huts scattered out-side it. These thralls, too, were running from the huts, clutching geese, chickens, piglets, and their household goods. Haakon laughed.

"Even if Olaf lives through this day, he'll have to chase his thralls halfway to the Hill of Tara to get them back." They weren't even pretending to fight for him. Ole Ketilsson's thralls would gladly have done so if they'd had the chance.

Certainly the steading was expecting unwelcome visitors. The gate was shut, and two carts were overturned in front of it. A shed close by the gate, which might have given cover to Haakon's archers, had been demolished and was now just a pile of planks. Helmeted heads and spear points lined the walls. From their positions, Haakon knew that Olaf had built a walkway around the inside, where his men could stand above their attackers to fight them off. Ole Ketilsson could have built a walkway, but Ole had been too long at peace with his neighbors.

I am sorry, Father, Haakon thought, in case Ole's spirit was listening. *But you taught me to see the truth and speak it plain.*

"Olaf Haraldsson's men! Hear me!" The helmeted heads on the wall looked down at him impassively. "Olaf's whelp, Harud, stole children in the Rogaland! If they are here, they are not to be harmed! When I am done here, there will be two men dead—slowly—for every child harmed! Do you hear me, Olaf Haraldsson's men?"

For answer an archer drew his bow and shot, then flattened himself behind the wall before Haakon's archers could take aim. The arrow whirred past his ear, and Haakon lifted his ax.

Three-fourths of the men behind him hurled themselves at the walls like a wolf pack, with the rest out of arrow range in reserve, in case anyone was so foolish as to come to Olaf's aid. Haakon doubted it. Most men would help an unpopular jarl only if there was a promise of rich booty after the battle. There was no chance of that here, only the certainty of a hard fight against a war-seasoned chief who was about the lawful business of avenging his father.

Orm's band took the ladders and attacked the wall, while Knut's men dragged the carts away from the gate and began to hammer against it with the ram. Their archers tried to pick Olaf's bowmen off the wall, and Haakon moved between them, shifting men, shouting orders, keeping the balance of the battle right. A Norseman in a berserker's rage saw only the man or the

wall in front of him, and Haakon had learned long ago
that the men with a chief who could hold them steady
were the men who won, unless the odds were greatly
unequal.

Hagar the Simple worked alone. He stood on the roof
of a shed, out of arrow range for any bow but his, with
his store of arrows spread out around his feet, and
picked off Olaf's archers carefully.

The defenders were throwing stones from the wall, as
well. These crashed down on the besiegers, crushing
shields and knocking a few of them senseless. Haakon
shouted at the men at the rear of the press, and they
began to roll the fallen stones away where they wouldn't
be under the attackers' feet. The gate groaned and
began to splinter, and on the wall Olaf's men frantically
redoubled their efforts. Haakon threw his shield up as a
hail of arrows rained down.

"It's going!" he shouted. "Keep at it!" There was a
ragged cheer, and Knut's men lumbered forward again
with the ram. Haakon shifted a few men off the ladders
to help the ram crew. He saw with satisfaction that the
two bands fought tenaciously side by side with old
rivalries long gone in the wind of the battle and the rain
of arrows that poured down on them. One of Orm's
men fell, and Black Ayolf stood over him with a shield
until someone from the rear could drag him clear. The
archer shifted his aim to Ayolf, but Hagar had seen him
by now. He fell writhing and twisting with his arrow
half-nocked and one of Hagar's shafts in his belly, and
his comrades pulled him back out of sight. But the gate
was still holding.

There were gaps in the men on the wall now, and the
shouting from behind the gate indicated that the defenders
were trying to pile more weight against it. Orm's men
had most of the ladders up and had made some inroads
on the defenders at the top. Magnus Styrkasson even
pulled a man bodily over the wall. The ladder toppled

and went down, but Magnus proudly dragged his prisoner to Haakon.

Haakon hauled him out of arrow range, and Magnus stood over him with a knife until he was willing to talk. It didn't take long. Olaf Haraldsson appeared to command no great loyalty.

"Where are the children?" Magnus wiggled the point of the knife against his throat.

"Inside," the man gasped. His eyes swiveled between Haakon and the knife.

"And where is Olaf's pup, Harud?" Haakon said.

"At sea, lord. I don't know where. That is truth!" he wailed as Magnus took a good grip on the knife.

Haakon looked at him thoughtfully. "Take him to the rear. I don't think he's lying. He hasn't the stomach for it." He looked a little disgusted. His own men would have given their lives for him. Still, it might be that Olaf Haraldsson wasn't worth it. And the information about Harud was welcome enough—it meant Olaf had a disadvantage in numbers. If only they could get in. . . . So far Olaf's men were holding, and Haakon had lost more men than he liked.

"Pull back!" he shouted.

Wearily they fell away from the wall, dragging the ladders after them so that Olaf's men couldn't pull them inside. The gate was splintered but showed no signs of giving way, with what must have been every heavy object in Olaf's steading piled behind it. Haakon sent Black Ayolf running for Hagar's shed with a pot of coals from one of the abandoned huts.

In a few minutes Hagar was leisurely shooting fire arrows over the walls, and the curses from behind them said that they were having some effect. Haakon's men righted the carts that Olaf had used to block the gates and piled the carts full of straw. With a guard to make a shield wall over their heads, they shoved them back against the gates and set fire to the straw. With luck the cart fires would either burn through the wall or force Olaf's men to push them away. Hagar stood on his shed and picked off any man who tried to pour water down on them.

The smoke rose straight and slowly in the windless air, and Haakon swore as he realized that the straw was damp. He said a prayer to Thor for a good wind and, being practical, used the time he waited to drag up the roof of the dismantled shed and lash it to spears to make a shield for the ram. If they could char enough of the gate, the ram would go through it, but every man in Olaf's steading would be shooting down at them, and Hagar couldn't hit them all.

They lifted the roof over the ram; Haakon felt a faint breeze against his cheek, and then the smoke began to fan out. Wind! It would seem that the gods liked a man who did his own work.

There were still no flames, but as the wind rose, the thick gray smoke began to pour along the wall like a fog, blotting out defenders and attackers alike.

Black Ayolf and Hjalmar looked at each other and grabbed a ladder, and Haakon shouted, *"Now!"*

They swung the ladder, and Haakon was on it before they were. "You'll both have a share for first man over," he shouted down at them, "but this is *my* vengeance!" He unslung his ax and climbed, swinging the blade at a spear that came out of the smoke at the top. The ax was light in his hand, *alive*, and it cut through the spear shaft and bit into the spearman's arm. Haakon swung the ax again, under the spearman's chin. Bone crunched, and the man staggered backward off the walkway and fell howling into the yard below. Haakon scrambled over the sharpened points of the palisade and onto the walkway with Hjalmar and Black Ayolf behind him. All down the wall other ladders were going up. An arrow cut through Haakon's shirt just below the sleeve of his mail, and caught, hanging by its feathers. He broke off the shaft and pulled it free, and held his ax out against the men who were coming along the walkway at him. Black Ayolf and Hjalmar were back to back with him. The next axman who came at Haakon thought, just before he died, that there was an odd light in the smoke and that it came from the head of the golden ax and the grim dark-bearded man who swung it.

Behind the axman were two spearmen, but they had no swords. Haakon ducked under the spear points and rose up between them. He lashed out at one man and toppled him from the wall, and before the other could shorten his grip on his spear, Haakon pinned him against the wall and split his head open. A grim satisfaction was pounding in his blood now, but these were only carls, and it was Olaf Haraldsson that he wanted. The walls were swarming now with Haakon's men. He grabbed a ladder that had been thrown up against the wall and hauled it over, wondering as he did it where the strength came from. He dropped it into the yard, and his men swarmed down on it after him. Behind them the gate was still holding, and tables, barrels, and meal sacks were piled against it. Those would have to be cleared away so the gate could be opened, letting his other warriors inside.

An arrow bit into Haakon's thigh, and he yelped and went on running. It wasn't deep, but it hurt enough to let his temper off its tether entirely. He whirled the ax around his head and charged for the defenders at the gate. With Ayolf and Hjalmar and twenty others behind him, the men at the gate began to scatter, and Haakon could see others running along the walkway, looking frantically for a place to jump down outside. As he watched, they poured down one of Haakon's ladders, and the shouting told him that they met the besiegers at the bottom.

"They are running!" he roared. "We have the bastards now! Olaf Haraldsson, come out and fight!"

"Haakon! Haakon! Haakon!" The wolf pack behind him acknowledged its leader.

Then there were no more words, only curses and howls of rage, wails of pain, and the hammer and clash of weapons. Some of Olaf's buildings were burning now from Hagar's fire arrows. Through the smoke and din Haakon saw a man with one ear fighting among the defenders at the gate. The man's eyes widened in recognition. Fifteen years had not dimmed his memory.

"You have my mark on you," Haakon growled at him. "Look to your sword, because I have come for the other ear! Where is your thief of a master?"

The man didn't answer. He came at Haakon, and the golden ax leaped and twisted, and sparks flew as it smashed the man's sword from his hand. He had courage; he drew his dagger and tried to get under the ax's murderous arc. That would have taken luck, and this was not a day for ordinary men to be lucky against Haakon Olesson. The ax handle slammed into the man's throat and knocked him backward, and the blade came down like a fire to split his skull.

At the gate the smoke was thickening, and Haakon's men and Olaf's moved through it like phantoms, choking and gasping. But Olaf was a lax chief in every way, it seemed. His men were not as strong as Haakon's. They had spent the winter growing fat, and now they paid for it. For every man of Haakon's who doubled up in the smoke, three of Olaf's gasped and strangled on it. A few fought their way clear, but most died in the smoke on a spearhead, and in a few minutes Haakon's men were hauling the debris away from the gate while the men outside dragged the smoldering carts clear.

A small band of Olaf's household warriors, more loyal than the rest, gathered themselves for one last desperate rush. At their head was a lean, gray-haired man, more bent with age than the last time Haakon had seen him. A pair of green eyes were painted on his black shield. It was Olaf Haraldsson.

There was no spear in reach, and Haakon didn't want to throw the golden ax, even with victory a certainty. He grabbed a long balk of timber from the pile, lifted it with both hands, and whirled it around his head. Men scattered as the timber hissed, and Olaf and his men turned and ran. Haakon let go, and it flew end over end and caught Olaf Haraldsson across the back of the legs. His men tried to get him to his feet, and two of them crumpled, one after the other, with arrows in their throats. Haakon saw Hagar the Simple on the wall, smiling grimly, nocking a third arrow.

Haakon's men swarmed forward from behind him. They knew that green-eyed black shield from Haakon's description. Eight of Olaf's men met an honorable end, refusing to leave their chief and dying beside him. By the time the last of them was dead, Haakon was standing over the still supine Olaf, and now he was not sure what to say, with the death of his old enemy and a fifteen-year vengeance only a single swing of the golden ax away.

So it was Olaf who spoke first. "Welcome to *my* steading, Haakon Olesson. I am sorry that our hospitality isn't more worthy of you, but that is as Fate sends. I am an old man, and my heart is failing. It seems I have no more strength left for such work." He looked up at Haakon with a dark smile.

"As for my son, other business has kept him away. No doubt you and he will have occasion to exchange greetings another time."

"Enough!" Haakon snapped. "Where are the children?"

"Here. Safe." Olaf's face twisted. "None of my men would lay a finger on them after your noble ultimatum." His voice was heavy with sarcasm.

"That was wise of them. And your son?"

"I do not know exactly where Harud is, but I think I know what he is probably doing about now. He should be receiving some stolen goods from your house. The lady Rosamund, to speak plainly."

For a moment the world spun slowly around Haakon. He wished he could be sure the man was lying, but a voice in his mind said that he was not. He made an animal noise in his throat and raised the ax. And stopped. There would be no vengeance now, not the way he had wanted it. If Olaf died, the knowledge he had would die with him.

Haakon put the golden ax down carefully. He wanted no messages from the gods just now.

"Take this thief away. Take him away, and make him talk about his theft and his son's. Do not be gentle."

Knut and Orm took Olaf by the arms and dragged him into the hall.

Haakon was sitting on a bench in Olaf's hall, cleaning the golden ax, when the first screams began. He looked down at the ax, but it didn't move or glow. Whether or not the gods approved, it seemed they knew their servant well enough to know when he would not have listened.

XIII

Haakon had a kind of vengeance before nightfall. Olaf Haraldsson had been telling the truth about his weak heart. Under the torture it stopped, and he was dead. Ole Ketilsson's ghost must have been happier after that, but Ole's son was not; Olaf died revealing nothing.

"Go and find someone who knows," Haakon said grimly to Knut. "I don't care how you find out." He had just come from counting his own dead, and he was in no good frame of mind. Compared to Olaf's, their losses had been slight, but more good men had died than Olaf Haraldsson's weasel's hide was worth, Black Ayolf among them. He saw them washed and buried with their swords, but not their mail, those who had it. Mail was worth too much, and their widows would need the price of it, even with a full share of the loot. Those of the wounded who had not by now died all looked as if they would survive, or so said one of Olaf's thrall-women who was reputed to have some skill as a healer. She looked at the arrow wound in Haakon's thigh and pronounced it of no matter.

"You will be stiff for a few days, jarl, that is all."

The children were found huddled in a locked storeroom. They were ragged and terrified, but they were all there except for one small girl who had died of a fever and a boy who had raised a hand to one of Olaf's men. The man had been killed in the fighting, so the boy was already avenged, although that would be cold comfort to his kin. For a sacrifice, Haakon killed one of Olaf's cattle over the two pathetic graves and then had the graves properly piled with stones.

And after that there was nothing to keep him in Ireland. With Harud Olafsson still at sea—the gods knew where—Haakon knew he had to return at once to Norway. If she had not already been taken away, he would not let Rosamund out of his sight until Harud's head was stuck on a spear on the shore of the Trondelag.

He paced, waiting for some word of Harud's plans. His men were just beginning to try to shake it out of Harud's captured men, most of whom probably didn't know, when Olaf's thralls began to come back to the steading, grateful for their master's death and eager to tell his secrets.

Thralls in general know much more of the secret ways of a steading than men-at-arms. One ancient

retainer showed Haakon where Olaf's whole treasure
was hidden, enough gold and silver to buy a fair-sized
longship or a herd of cattle. And a woman, who no
one had thought mattered much when they talked in
her presence, had overheard Harud speak of meeting
with traders from the East in Birka.

That sounded likely. Harud would no longer want
Rosamund as his wife now that she was carrying Haakon's
child. He would only want to punish her. What more
degrading punishment could there be than selling her
into slavery? Hedeby, in Denmark, was closer to the
Trondelag, but Birka, in Sweden, was closer to the route
along the rivers of the Slavic lands, which led to
Constantinople and other lands where fair-haired Norse
slaves were valued.

This was not much information to go on, but certainly
the pursuit of Harud—Haakon would not call it the
pursuit of Rosamund, for fear of speaking bad-luck
words—would no longer be quite so much a chase after
a ghost. He would sail home, and if Rosamund wasn't
there, he would go to Birka.

He stayed up all night, restless and wanting something to do to ease the worry in his mind. Olaf's fighting
men were disarmed and turned loose with a few days'
food. No doubt the lucky ones would live to find new
chiefs among the other jarls in Ireland. Haakon didn't
want to be burdened with prisoners.

The thralls were given food, silver, and for the men,
weapons to make their way home. Most left at dawn,
blessing Haakon. And most swore they'd be back to
serve him as free men if he ever took up the steading in
Olaf's place. Even now Ole Ketilsson was remembered
fondly, especially with Olaf Haraldsson for comparison.

Haakon knew it was his right to reclaim the steading,
but that needed more men than he could spare. The
Norse jarls of Ireland were a rough lot, and they would
have no respect for a claim that didn't have a strong

garrison to back it up. Haakon had his own steading in the Trondelag to defend and a fight in Birka possibly, and only after Harud's schemes had been dealt with would there be time to think about matters in Ireland. This wasn't the ending that he had imagined for his quest for vengeance, but a steading in Ireland would be no use to him without Rosamund.

So he stripped his father's steading to its bare walls, and then took down the gates and burned them. They made a pyre for Olaf's dead.

The booty, men, and freed children, he loaded aboard his ships. The pyre was still smoking the next day when they pushed off from the beach, bound downriver for the sea and home.

It was ill luck that let Kare Ingstad choke off the scream of the man Gunnar speared before he could wake the steading. It was also ill luck that Gunnar and Guthrun had been sleeping apart. When they did sleep together, it was not long after one of them left the bed that the other felt the chill and woke up.

As it was, nearly an hour had passed after Kare's attack before Guthrun awoke and went to relieve herself. On the way back, she stopped by Gunnar's room, hoping he might be awake and in a mood to forget his vows and make love. The bed was empty. Pulling a gown over her night shift, she went out to the guards and found that most of them were drunk and none of them had seen Gunnar, either. She boxed the drunkards' ears and took the two sober ones, grumbling, with her to search.

They scouted through the outbuildings of the steading and came to their final stop at Kare's hut. There they found Kare gone and a dead body by the stand of pines, and ceased their grumbling. They ran back to let the jarl's lady know, but found an empty room and a bed that had not been slept in. Guthrun added all these

facts together in her mind; the sum was a crisis. She
screamed and woke up everyone in the house.

When they had come stumbling up out of their furs
and off the sleeping benches, they fanned out, searching the steading from rooftree to cellars, but by then it
was too late. Kare and his captives were well out onto
the fjord, safe from any pursuers who could not stop
and search every *knarr* in the Trondelag. At the steading,
the person with the clearest voice and the coolest head
led, and Guthrun quickly found herself in command.
She now knew Gunnar had been right in his suspicions
of Kare. In between shrieking curses at Harud and
wiping away her tears, she gave orders to the men
around her and saw them obey, although some of them
were old enough to be her father.

Messengers rode to all the nearby steadings, including Erik and Sigrid's. The drunken sentries were locked
up to await Erik's judgment, and someone kept Guthrun
from gelding them on the spot. She put armed men at
every door, bowmen on the roofs, and ringed the
steading yard with torches and fires. No one knew if
they were about to be attacked or not.

Guthrun resisted the temptation to send a band out
to search the forest. She didn't know how many men
Kare had with him or whether he'd left any behind.
She didn't know if he had come only for Rosamund, or
Gunnar, or for the loot in the steading. If a search party
walked into an ambush, half the steading's defenders
might be killed. Then Haakon would come home to
nothing but charred timbers and ashes.

The messengers called out most of Haakon's neighbors before dawn, and they armed every man they
could and sent them out to look behind every tree and
boulder and under every bush. They found nothing.

Sigrid and Erik saw a number of these searching
bands as they rode to Haakon's steading, and Sigrid
thought grimly that if they hadn't found anything, very

likely there was nothing to find. Guthrun met them at
the door to the hall. She was red-eyed, pale, and
tottering from exhaustion. Her voice rasped, but it
remained steady as she told them what she had done so
far. When she said, "I'm glad to see you here," she
could barely get the words out and finally had to sit
down.

"You've done well." Erik looked impressed and gave
her some ale. "Drink this. You've got a clear head about
you, girl."

"Thank you, lord," Guthrun said. "But—it's more
thanks to my lady. I asked myself what she would have
done, and then I did the same." Her voice broke. Now
that Erik was here, she thought she could cry.

"I'll ride out and join the searchers," Erik went on.
"If they've had no luck by dawn tomorrow, I'll call them
in. Then we can think what to do next. If our neighbors
will stand by us, we'll have a proper vengeance."

"No!" Guthrun shook her head and stopped crying.
"No. I won't hear of vengeance now. It would be bad
luck to think it." She pulled herself up to do battle.
"They are not dead."

Erik snorted, but Sigrid looked hard at Guthrun and
thought it over. *Men* thought of vengeance too soon.
"She's not wandering in her wits, Erik. It would have
been easy to kill them both, but Kare seems to have
put himself to the trouble of carrying them off. You
know the kind of man he is. He wouldn't have bothered
without orders from someone to keep them alive."

"Maybe." Erik scratched his neck. "But let's not get
our hopes too high." He patted her shoulder. "We
haven't found their bodies, but that doesn't mean we
won't."

Sigrid glared at him, and Guthrun gave a little moan
and fainted. When she had got Guthrun in bed, Sigrid
went back to discuss with her husband his loose tongue
and the dull knife she would apply to it the next time it

wagged so freely. "It is her lover and her mistress who are missing, you fool!"

"I'll keep the searchers in the woods until nightfall tomorrow," he promised as he mounted his horse. "A man in a hurry won't carry a dead body far. If we've found nothing, then I'll begin to think we can hope for something better than blood-vengeance."

Sigrid hoped even more fervently for Haakon's swift return. They would have to send a ship to Ireland. Haakon might be on his way home before the message reached him, particularly if he had learned anything of this from Olaf—Sigrid was sure Olaf and Harud were behind it. On the other hand, he might be intending to spend time in Ireland putting Ole's former steading in order and thinking all was well at home. He would have to be told.

The homeward voyage was too slow for Haakon's peace of mind, but if he had gone on the wind itself, he would have felt much the same. The three ships certainly made better time in the rough seas than they could have before Snorri Longfoot raised their freeboard. With the extra height, the two smaller ships could carry sail in even the strongest wind.

The children huddled in the ships' holds, too tired to be afraid. The older ones understood what was wrong and forgave Haakon their seasickness. The babies clung to the older ones and whimpered, and Haakon knew that they would have nightmares for some time to come. Not many adults had survived Harud's raid on their village, and the children would have that to face too, when they reached home. That was one more mark on Harud Olafsson's score, Haakon thought when they reached the Trondelag, thinner, wind beaten, and salt stained, and prepared for the worst.

*   *   *

When they told him, hesitantly, that Rosamund was gone, Haakon's silence frightened them. Everyone had expected a berserker's rage, and most were ready to forgive almost anything, including open murder. But instead he went quietly and grimly about preparing for the voyage to Birka. He smiled much less during those days of preparation than usual and hardly raised his voice at all. No one dared to speak to him, except on important matters, and everyone knew that the rage was there, like molten rock rising in a volcano. Eventually it would explode, they thought, the worse for being pent up, and no one cared to risk having it overflow on him.

The few who did not fear Haakon feared Wulf. Somehow he seemed to know what had happened. He padded into Rosamund's empty chamber and let out a howl that would have frightened the dead in Hel. After that he was never far from Haakon's heels.

Preparation for the voyage went on, and a grim sort of comradeship grew out of it. Many of Haakon's men lived to tell their grandchildren of those days on the steading, when no one walked when he could run, stood idle when there was something to do, or slept until he could no longer hold his head up. Through all the stories walked Haakon the Dark—silent, restless, not quite human.

The fifty best men Haakon's neighbors could spare boarded Haakon's ships. He would now be taking nearly two hundred fighting men to Birka, more than enough to deal with Harud, even if he'd found allies in the town.

Another seventy men rode in, unasked, and offered to guard the steading. They included a good many grandfathers and boys, and their pay would take a large bite out of the loot from Ireland, but the steading would be firmly held. Erik would stay and be chief over them.

Meanwhile, all over the Trondelag, men were caulking ships, patching sails, sharpening swords and spears, and scraping the rust off armor. At least a dozen war chiefs seemed ready to make Haakon's feud their own. Rosamund's capture, added to the sack of the village and the enslavement of the children, had made people think of Harud Olafsson as a wild boar to be hunted down before he savaged any more victims. Harud Olafsson might think he had gained a victory—and he might even be right if they couldn't find Rosamund and Gunnar—but it would be his last victory in any Norse land.

Knut One-Eye was less than happy about all the well-wishers he saw taking up arms. "If all those men follow you, they'll expect some reward. And it's late in the year for good raiding. If you pay them from your own silver—"

Haakon only cleared his throat. That silenced Knut as thoroughly as if he'd been knocked on the head. "I have asked most of them to sail south," he said patiently, "and search the Norwegian coast. Afterwards they can meet me off the Frisian Islands, and I won't owe them much for that, unless they find Harud. They can also raid the Frisians as they please. So I have decided I won't be needing to sack Birka."

Knut looked at him dubiously out of his one good eye. It had never occurred to him that Haakon might consider sacking Birka. That would take a fleet as big as Harald Fairhair had brought against the pirates at Hafrsfjord, and the Birkans would never let that many in at once. And if Haakon *could* do it, the Swedes, and probably the Norse, too, would name him outlaw. Still, there was no telling what Haakon was capable of in this mood.

"The men in Birka who have had a hand in this will be few," Haakon said thoughtfully, "and probably are not men of the town. I don't think it would be lawful to sack the town to pay for that."

Knut breathed more easily and decided that he had best make no more arguments about paying extra men. Haakon might be closer to the edge than he had thought. He would doubtless consider it a fair trade to pay out all his silver and become a spearman on someone else's ship if it brought Rosamund back. What Haakon might do with Gunnar when he retrieved him, Knut wasn't sure.

The last work was completed, barrels of salt fish bought and crammed into every corner of Haakon's ships. Extra weapons were brought aboard to arm any man who was willing to follow him and too lean in the purse to have good weapons. They had a full crew, and over. By the time the last bit of weight was aboard, everyone was thanking the gods for Snorri and his extra strakes. Without them, the ships would have been slow, and in bad weather the two smaller ones would have been barely seaworthy.

As it was, all three went thrashing down the fjord in fine style the day Haakon sailed for Birka. No one cheered, either on shore or aboard the ships, but the shout of "Fair wind!" followed them down the fjord. Four more longships were beached at the steading, with their crews patching sails, painting oars, and laying in supplies. They were the first four of his allies, nearly ready for sea—it would not be long before they followed in his wake to Birka.

As Haakon's ships sailed south they hailed every vessel they passed, asking if anyone had seen Harud Olafsson's longship *Lord of the Foam*. It was more to leave no stone unturned than in the hope of learning anything useful. They had a good description of Harud's ship from Olaf's thralls; she was a longship very like every other that sailed in these waters. Certainly there was nothing special for a man to recognize if he saw her briefly or at twilight or passing a long way off in bad weather.

"And if Harud has the intelligence of a louse, he's disguised his ship," Haakon said.

"He has that, unfortunately." Knut scanned the sea gloomily.

"That's not bad fortune," Haakon said. "If he were stupid, he would never have tried to carry them off; he'd have killed them outright where he found them. And left me with nothing but vengeance." He rested his hand on the bow, and it tightened into a fist. "I don't want vengeance, I want Rosamund back. *Then* I will take vengeance." He smiled a dark smile, wolflike. "When I have had leisure to think about it."

From the look on Haakon's face, Knut knew that both Harud and Kare would have long and unpleasant deaths.

"And Gunnar?" he asked uncertainly.

Haakon shook his head. "No. Gunnar will have punished himself by now, if I know him. At first, when I was angry, I thought of it. But this is as much my fault as Gunnar's, for not seeing what Harud could do."

Knut nodded, relieved. Gunnar was Haakon's friend, and if Haakon killed him, he would not forgive himself afterward.

As they sailed into the Kattegat, between Denmark and Sweden, the merchant ships thinned out. Because these were pirate waters, Haakon ordered the lookouts doubled, and everyone slept armed, although there was little chance of trouble. Pirates would only attack if they had overwhelming strength or hope of good loot. Since King Harald Fairhair's victory at Hafrsfjord, the pirates seldom sailed in large fleets, and three shiploads of armed men promised little booty and much hard fighting.

They beat their way out of the Kattegat into the

Baltic against fluky and often contrary winds. Sometimes Haakon ordered the men to the oars simply because he knew he would go mad if he had to sit aboard a motionless ship. Half his mind knew that merely reaching Birka would not save Rosamund, and the other half screamed that every day lost was a day Rosamund spent in despair, or worse. He didn't voice his thoughts to anyone except Knut, but they were plain enough on his face, and no one grudged the sweat at the oars.

It was late afternoon off the southern tip of the island of Gotland when the wind changed in their favor. By nightfall they were plowing along at a good seven knots, with everyone promising the most lavish sacrifices to the gods if they would keep the wind blowing. For the first time since the day Olaf Haraldsson had grinned up at him from the ground in Ireland, Haakon did not have to force himself to fall asleep. . . .

. . . He was in his armor, with a sword at his side, shield on his back, and the golden ax in his hand. There was fresh blood on the golden blade, and the ax's light came redly through it.

Haakon looked down at himself. His armor was also red with blood, and it was the finest armor he had ever had. There were no holes in it, and no holes in him, but he felt short of breath, and his chest hurt, as if he'd finished too long a run or lifted too heavy a weight.

Around him was fog, and underfoot a fine, silver sand that seemed to reflect the light of the ax. He walked forward, experimentally, and the gray fog kept its distance. Through it a golden light began to grow, and then the sweet tone of a horn sounded. A tall figure stepped forward out of the light. She wore full armor, scaled all over like a snake; her shield and spearhead and the armor were all in silver. Her helmet was golden and

had two horns, like the ancient ritual helmets used at
sacrifices, and it hid all her face except the eyes—deep
purple-blue eyes that looked straight at him.

He'd seen eyes like these before, in the bed beside
him most nights for more than a year—but also once
before that, when Thor had showed him a vision of
Valhalla, where the gods went to feast with men who
died bravely in battle. This was a Valkyrie, one of
Odin's handmaids, and Haakon knew with a sudden
tightening in his chest that he was watching his own
death.

No man who is not a fool is fearless. A lifetime of
battles had taught him that. But since Thor had given
him the golden ax, Haakon had found no reason to fear
the gods of Asgard. The Valkyrie beckoned, and he
followed.

They came to Bifrost, rainbow bridge to Valhalla. At
one moment it seemed to be made of clear stone in all
the colors men had given names to and more besides.
And at the next, it seemed to be nothing but the light
itself, shimmering and transparent under the weightless
feet of the gods or the valiant dead.

As they crossed the bridge, Haakon expected a hall
the size of a mountain to rise from the golden light
ahead. Instead there was only a door of red wood,
carved with runes unrecognizable to man. The doors
swung open, the Valkyrie vanished, and Haakon walked
forward into Valhalla.

It was just as he'd seen it before, in the god's vision,
the ceiling lost in golden mist and music. Plates of gold
and silver heaped high with food, and drinking horns
that would not run dry. There were men eating, drinking,
dicing, telling of old battles. Haakon thought that some
of them had faces that he knew, but somehow he could
not be sure. Through the hall moved the Valkyries, as
beautiful as any man's dreams could wish, but with a
serenity that said more clearly than words that they

were not to be touched. And through the mist above the feasters Haakon saw a face he did know—red bearded and blue eyed, young of face, but infinitely old and fearsome. Thor Hammerer, Odinsson. Haakon gaped, and then that great and terrible beauty faded away, and a black-haired stranger beckoned to him from across the hall.

He was lean and tanned, shorter than Haakon and with the unmistakable look of the Gael about him. His black hair and mustache were shot with gray, and in the side of his neck was a fresh scar that must have been a death wound. He grinned at Haakon and waved him to a place beside him, and Haakon saw another scar, this one old and faded, running from the corner of his right eye down his cheek to the line of his jaw. There was a harp bag slung across his back.

"Welcome, then, and I've been waiting for you," he said cheerfully. "I see no holes in that fine hide. Was it your heart, then?"

Haakon nodded silently and looked down at a high-backed chair with a tunic and cloak draped across it, richer than anything he had ever owned. Pearls and gold encrusted the tunic, and it was fit for a king and as heavy as a coat of mail.

He moved the clothes and sat down carefully, the golden ax across his knees. He felt odd, floating, and he watched curiously as the dark-haired man who seemed to know him filled a plate with meat, but somehow Haakon didn't ask his name. He knew without asking that he knew him, had known him, down long years and through many battles, and that the only human who had been closer to him was Rosamund. "You'll be hungry," the man said. He raised his left hand, and Haakon saw it lacked two fingers and a thumb. A Valkyrie came and poured a horn full of ale, and the dark-haired man pushed the plate in front of him.

He was hungry. But when he bit into the food, there

was nothing. And the ale horn faded away in his hand.
He opened his mouth to speak, but the black-haired
man had frozen in midmotion, and the golden light
above was turning blue. The music faded, and Haakon
heard the shrill voice of a seabird. . . .

It was cold and wet, and he jerked himself out of his
leather bag for sleeping with Valhalla's golden mist
fading in his head. It was gray morning, and the three
ships were still moving briskly across a whitecapped
sea, with Gotland barely visible on the southern horizon.

Haakon crawled back in the bag again and closed his
eyes, feigning sleep. He didn't think that that was a
dream he wanted to speak about.

It had been a dream of his own death, of that he was
sure. Every man died sooner or later, and Thor had not
promised him anything else. If he had, Haakon would
have known the god was lying or perhaps was no god at
all.

But a man could die well or badly, and Thor *had*
promised a good death with Valhalla afterward if Haakon
served him well. That much Haakon was willing to
believe, since there was as yet no good reason not to.
And his dream had certainly shown a good death, not of
a wound, but the kind that could take a man to Valhalla
if the gods wished it.

But was this dream prophecy of what *would* be?
Haakon chased that question around in his mind and
found no easy answer. If it *was* true, then his death was
linked to that of a Gaelic harper with a scarred face, and
when he died, Haakon would follow soon after. He
mulled it over until Knut came to wake him, and by
that time Haakon had decided only that he would worry
about it when he actually met the man. He had more
important things to do in Birka than trying to disentan-
gle dreams, which, as every man knew, told lies as
often as not.

XIV

The lead boat towing Kare Ingstad's *knarr* into the creek mouth suddenly swerved to port. Kare shouted to his helmsman to do the same and to his rowers to back water. It was too late for either. The *knarr* slid gently onto the gravel bottom of the creek with a grinding sound.

A quick inspection below showed no leaks. He could surely borrow a few of Harud's men to help get the *knarr* afloat again. Looking farther up the creek, Kare could make out Harud's longship *Lord of the Foam* moored snugly against the bank. She was hard to see because her sides and mast were covered with cut branches. She looked like part of the forest. There was no sign of anyone aboard.

Two of Kare's men brought the prisoners up onto the *knarr*'s foredeck. Kare wanted no mistakes made about his having the prisoners ready to hand over.

Someone ashore must have seen them. A small boat skimmed across the creek from behind the longship, with Harud in the stern and two men paddling. Harud was unarmored, although he had a sword at his waist. Between Harud's feet, Kare saw a bulging leather bag. He grinned.

"Not much longer, men. Then you'll be getting your reward for work well done." They would also be dismissed from his service. With Harud's money, Kare could find better spearmen than these. They'd been good enough for guarding Gunnar and Rosamund, but he didn't want to have them protecting his back again.

Harud scrambled aboard the *knarr*, looked quickly at Rosamund and Gunnar, then lifted the woman down into his small boat. She didn't struggle, but she looked as if she would like to spit in his eye. Harud pointed at Gunnar. "Who's this?"

"Haakon's skald. He was sticking his nose in where it didn't belong," Kare said, "so I figured he'd bring you a good price, too."

"It's not your job to do any figuring." Harud glared at him. "All right, help me get him into the boat."

Gunnar nearly thanked Harud for taking him along. For an awful moment, he had thought Rosamund would be taken and he would be left for Kare to dispose of. Harud handed him down into the small boat, then waved to one of his men to hand up the leather bag.

The man was just raising the bag when Harud suddenly turned and gripped Kare fiercely by both shoulders. Then he hurled himself sideways, dragging Kare over the side with him. Kare's mouth was open with surprise when they landed in the creek. Although it was not very deep, he swallowed so much water that he was coughing and choking when they rose to the surface. He barely saw the arrows raining down on the deck of the *knarr*, but he heard the death screams of his men.

Kare spat out water and saw the lead boat, which had towed him and tricked him onto the gravel, shoot out from the bank again, now full of men who'd been hiding in the woods with the archers. They swarmed aboard the *knarr*; there were a few more desperate screams, then only silence except for the sounds of one man who had leaped over the side and swum for the bank. He was just standing up in the waist-deep water, about to lunge for the shore and the protective cover of the foliage, when the archers let fly again. One of the dozen arrows that struck him drove into his back, and he pitched forward and died in a little wave of bloodied water.

Then there was silence, except for the laughter that made Kare shiver as the hopeless screams of his men had not. Harud's laughter was as maniacal and unpleasant a sound as the stories about him had said it was. But even worse was the laughter from the boat, where Rosamund and Gunnar had thrown back their heads and openly guffawed. They couldn't have looked more amused if Harud had just sworn to set them free.

Kare looked away to hide his anger and shame, but still he heard the laughter and felt their eyes on him. He would have preferred to sink like the last of his men, but Harud had a firm grip on his upper arm with one hand and was holding a knife to his back with the other.

Just before dawn Haakon's ships reached the mouth of the channel that led inland to Lake Mälar and Birka. They drifted, their peace shields hung on all three masts and the figureheads stowed below to avoid frightening the land spirits. After what seemed like half the day, someone ashore noticed them. A boat came out, carrying a pilot to guide them up the channel.

Haakon barraged the man with questions about Harud Olafsson, Kare Ingstad, Gunnar, and Rosamund. He got only vague answers or none at all. After Haakon's ships started up the channel, the pilot remained completely silent, except to give orders to the helmsman of *Red Hawk*, while the other two ships steered by following her.

Haakon kept a grip on his temper, remembering what a closemouthed lot the pilots of Birka had to be. The town's flourishing trade depended on their flawless knowledge of the winding channels from the Baltic to Lake Mälar. Birka's safety depended on their ability to keep the secrets of those channels. Its Thing and merchants kept few warriors, relying instead on the mysteries of the channels to strand any raiders' ships trying to reach the town without the guidance of the pilots.

So the Birka pilots were a close-knit brotherhood, no matter where they'd begun life. Their ranks included not only Norsemen, but Germans, Franks, English, Finns, and even Arabs from the Moslem countries. All swore mighty and secret oaths by whatever gods they followed, and it was said they also swore more potent oaths by the guardian spirits of the marshlands and lakes, older than any of the other powers and long forgotten everywhere except Birka.

So under the pilot's orders, *Red Hawk* led the way to Birka. Once out of the channel and into the deeper waters of the lake, the pilot had no more orders to give or secrets to keep. He became more talkative.

"If the people you're after are in the slave houses, you'll have to go to the south end of the island," he said. "The merchants didn't like having five hundred slaves a bowshot from their houses and shops, and they weren't of a mind to pay more fighters for a guard, either."

"Afraid the warriors might get the idea of ruling Birka themselves?"

The pilot ignored Haakon's question. "So we have a new slave camp, in the south of the island."

He wasn't going to answer any more questions than he pleased or in a way the merchants wouldn't like, but Haakon understood. Several thousand slaves of every race and land changed masters every year at Birka. Some would be desperate men, and willing to kill or be killed to escape or take vengeance.

After the pilot had gone ashore, Haakon called Knut and Orm Persson over. "I'll take *Red Hawk* to the slave camp. You take *Wave Walker* and *Dragon Queen* around to the town itself. Anchor and make camp where they tell you, then let half the men at a time go into town. Give each of them some silver for a drink and a woman—"

"And news?" asked Orm.

"Yes. It ought to buy what we're after. I doubt everyone in Birka is as closemouthed as the pilots."

The ships separated, and Haakon brought *Red Hawk* around to where the pilot had shown him. He left half his men for a shipguard and took Wulf and the rest up the path to the slave camp. It wound across rough ground, overgrown with bushes and young trees and studded with boulders to slow a running man. In places there were deep ditches cut across the path, with light plank bridges guarded by spearmen. The merchants of Birka were taking no chances with escaping slaves.

Haakon and his men could smell the slave camp from halfway up the path. They crossed another bridge and Haakon began to look grim. Beyond the bridge, was a circle where the boulders and brush had been cleared away for some forty paces across. It was studded with gallows and heavy wooden frames, some of them black with old blood.

A man was spread-eagled on one of the frames, tied by his wrists and ankles, and two guards took turns flogging him, while several more stood by. He was naked except for a breechclout, slender, well muscled, and black haired, and he was swearing. His back was a mass of old scars and fresh wounds, but instead of yelling as the whips came down, he cursed steadily in Gaelic—his tormentors, their ancestors, mothers, wives, and children. —

Haakon was about to pass by when the guards stepped back to throw a bucket of water down the man's back. The water turned pink with blood as it trickled down his legs to make a pool on the ground. The man wriggled all over, looked back over his shoulder, and spat at the guards. Haakon stopped so abruptly, the man behind bumped into him.

The black-haired man was young, nineteen at the most. And he was also the man in Haakon's dream. The lines of age weren't there, or the gray in the hair and mustache, or the scars, but he was the same Valhalla warrior.

Haakon hefted the golden ax and found himself stepping forward almost before he realized he was doing it. The guards tried to bar his path, looked at the ax, and stepped back again.

"Who are you?" Haakon said in a voice barely recognizable as his own. His men were staring at him blankly.

"Donal." He must have been in considerable pain, but his voice was steady. He looked at Haakon with curiosity, apparently weighing what he might want.

"Donal, *master!*" snarled the guard. He swung his whip. Haakon raised the golden ax, and the whip coiled itself around the shaft. He jerked the ax back with both hands, and the guard went sprawling. Haakon unwound the whip from the ax, cut the lash free of its handle with the blade, and tossed the pieces at the fallen guard.

The other guards stepped forward, spears raised. "I don't care who *you* are," one growled. "You'll pay for this. That man's never obeyed orders yet, and he's a flogging coming. You've—"

Wulf growled and bared all his teeth, Haakon's men jerked themselves into motion and leveled their spears, and the guard thought better of what he'd been about to say.

In the silence that followed, Haakon did some hasty thinking. He'd no mind to begin explaining dreams.

"Before I left home, I went to a wise woman. She read the signs and told me that it would help me find my wife and skald if I freed a slave at Birka." Donal stared, and his men stared. "This one seems to have too much spirit to make a decent slave," he went on before anyone could ask questions, "so you have two choices. You can kill him with another flogging, which is a silly waste, or you can sell him to me." He looked around at the guards. "Are any of you his owner? And if not, who is?"

Haakon stepped back, while the guards argued among themselves. This man might be a jarl and have the silver, but he also seemed mad. Donal stared at him with only slightly less suspicion than the guards.

Haakon wondered if he *was* mad. Certainly he had decided to free Donal for no better reason than his looking like a man in a dream. A dream that might have been a true vision of the future, or might have been nothing of the kind. Even after his meeting with Thor, Haakon knew that some dreams came from the gods and some from bad ale. And dreams from the gods might still come from Odin, who spoke to men with a double tongue, or from Loki, who seldom spoke at all, except in malice.

But he wasn't prepared to believe that it all meant *nothing*. If his life and Donal's were intertwined, then this was fate, and there was no point in arguing with it. If they weren't, it was still true that Donal would make a most unsatisfactory slave, but likely a good fighting man.

When he had reached this conclusion, Haakon saw that he had rested the golden ax on the ground. He hadn't been aware of doing that. Had he once again decided to make his own decision and listen for the gods' judgment afterward? That might not be overly wise. On the other hand, his bargain with Thor was not for a thrall collar, but free service. Haakon picked up the golden ax and waited a decent interval for it to give some sign. When nothing happened, he shouldered it and walked back to the guards. They seemed to have decided that the madman was not to be argued with.

Thorfinn Solvisson and Hagar the Simple cut Donal loose, and as the last of the thongs fell clear, he staggered away from the frame. He nearly fell, looked once at the faces of the guards, and righted himself. He walked carefully to Haakon and dropped to both knees.

"Get up," Haakon said. "Get up. You are a free man, and free men don't kneel to Haakon Olesson."

"For what I owe you, it seems a small trouble," Donal said, but he got gingerly to his feet. "What oath may I swear to you?"

"For the moment, only an oath to tell me who you are and where you came from. Truthfully." There was another water bucket by the frame, and Haakon signaled to one of his men to bring it. Donal drank half of it in a few gulps and poured the rest of it over his back. He swore again, twitched his back, and told Haakon his story.

He was a man of Clan MacRae, from the Tay Valley in the Lowlands of Scotland, and he'd been caught by Danish raiders, together with his betrothed, Fann, her father, and the few men who were guarding them. "We weren't going far, d'you see," he said thoughtfully. "Not a mistake I'd make again, mind." They had been crossing the Tay in a boat when the Danes appeared. Donal and Fann looked valuable enough to sell, and they'd been singled out for the dubious honor of being knocked on the head instead of killed. When they awoke, they found themselves bound hand and foot, in the hold of a Danish ship.

"We were sold more times than we could count after that, starting with Hedeby. I haven't seen Fann in Birka, but I know she was supposed to be sent here." Donal's face was solemn. "Jarl Haakon, I will swear any oath you like, any service, if you will try to find her. She's too young to—" His voice broke off—Haakon wasn't listening to him. Instead, he stared over Donal's head at a line of slaves coming down the path from the camp.

There were about twenty of them, shuffling along with stout cords on their ankles and their wrists tied in front of them. A dark, bearded man with the look of an

Arab led them, a long, curved sword in his belt. Four more Arabs marched on either side, swords drawn. The ninth man in the line was Kare Ingstad.

Afterward Haakon could not clearly remember what had happened. He had to take the word of other men, and since all of them said more or less the same thing, he had to admit that they were probably telling the truth. He thought he had been calm the whole time, but twenty men swore they saw him walk over to the line of slaves and strangle Kare Ingstad with his bare hands.

He would have killed him if he hadn't had to fight off the Arab trader and his guards. Two of the guards came at Haakon bare-handed, remembering that shedding Norse blood in Birka could be dangerous. He saw them coming and kicked the first one so hard in the stomach that he flew backward into the second, and both went down. A third guard held on to his sword, but Haakon grabbed his sword arm and twisted it until the man's elbow shattered and he dropped his sword with a scream.

Behind him, the Arab trader drew his sword. Before he could bring it down, Donal leaped at him, and the trader turned in time to slash Donal across the face, from the corner of his right eye down across his cheek to the line of his jaw. Then Donal crashed into the trader, both men went down, and Haakon's men swarmed over him.

Wulf had been keeping the last guard at bay, and the man was smart enough to count the odds against him. Donal's former guards decided that fighting a madman for someone else's slaves was not their business. Haakon went back to strangling Kare. Kare's face was turning blue, and his breath was a faint rasp when Haakon became aware of a face looming over him. It was Magnus Styrkasson, shaking his arm. Donal, with his cheek dripping blood, stood behind Magnus.

"Haakon! Stop it! For the love of the gods, if you kill him he can't tell you what he's done with Rosamund!" Haakon slowly loosened his hands, but it wasn't Magnus he was looking at, it was Donal.

"You are wounded," he said slowly. "That—that will leave a scar."

"Nay, I was not such a beauty to begin with," Donal said, not understanding.

Haakon shook himself, let go of Kare, and stood up. Kare collapsed, trying to suck in as much breath as terror and a half-crushed windpipe would permit.

"This one saved your life, Haakon," Thorfinn Solvisson said, pointing at Donal.

Haakon looked sharply at Donal's wound again, then at Kare still writhing on the ground. "I'm—I will find your Fann for you," he said. "I have lost someone also."

"Thank you, jarl." Donal tried to bow, tipped over, and fainted. Thorfinn Solvisson picked him up, while Haakon cut Kare Ingstad out of the slave line with his knife. Kare's eyes were wide with fear. He was almost as afraid of Haakon as he had been of Harud Olafsson. More guards were coming from the slave camp, drawn by the noise. Haakon's men had their weapons out, but they wouldn't fight unless Haakon gave the nod. Haakon didn't *want* to fight; it would do him no good to be unfriends with the merchants of Birka. But he made it clear to the guards that they would all be dog's meat if any of them tried to come between him and Kare Ingstad. They took the warning.

Kare's story took a while, but he'd been half choked to death, and he knew he was talking his life away in the presence of fifty witnesses. It took considerable prodding from Haakon, but Kare talked eventually.

Harud Olafsson hadn't kept any of his promises, except to receive Rosamund. He had sailed for Birka with Kare in the hold with Rosamund and Gunnar, but found no Eastern slave buyers in port when he got there. Harud had no mind to sell his captives to masters in Norse lands, where they might be recognized or found by Haakon. Harud wanted vengeance—slavery without hope.

But Harud also did not wish to spend too long in Birka. He couldn't be sure that tales from the Trondelag or the Rogaland hadn't reached Birka ahead of him. Any day, someone might denounce him. If he fled, he would be outlawed at once and every man's hand would be against him. If he stayed to be heard before the Thing, he would certainly lose his prisoners. Men from Norway might also come and kill him outright.

"So Harud found an Arab pirate named Red Ali, from Cadiz in Spain. He was sailing the next day. Harud sold *them* to Ali," Kare said. "It didn't matter so much about me. The Thing wouldn't be interested in me."

"The Thing is going to have you," Haakon said. He would rather have plunged his hands into a pot of burning coals than have touched Kare again.

The ships needed food, water, and repairs, and the men needed a chance to stretch their legs ashore before they sailed for Spain. There was the matter of Donal's Fann, which turned out to be refreshingly simple. She'd been sold to a combmaker in Birka itself, who wanted a young, healthy thrall-girl to cook his meals, clean his house, and occasionally warm his bed. The amount of silver offered by Haakon, who was in a hurry, left the combmaker more than willing to part with her. So did Haakon's threat to hang him up from the roof beams if he didn't sell.

Fann was no more than fifteen, small, red haired, and plain as a boot. To Donal, however, she was obviously the most beautiful woman in the world, and Haakon found himself turning away from their reunion with a twist of pain in his stomach.

That night he talked with Knut and Orm. They had

spent generous amounts of time and silver in the town
and learned a good deal worth knowing.

"Red Ali sells his best takings to the wali of Cadiz,
who rules there in the name of the emir of Cordova,"
Orm said. "They might not go farther than Cadiz."

"That wouldn't be what he agreed to with Harud,"
Haakon said thoughtfully. "But out of sight of Harud—I
doubt that Red Ali is overly honest, and he might get
the best price from the wali." For the first time he felt
real hope growing. They had been in good health when
Harud took them—and now it seemed they might be in
a city on the sea, and he might not have to face the
nearly impossible problem of snatching them from some
inland town in a country swarming with good fighting
men.

It was less pleasant to learn in the morning that the
Thing of Birka wanted to hear him on the matter of
Harud and his crimes, and also on the matter of brawling
in the slave camp, but court would not be convening for
five days. "If we sail without giving those Arabs weregild,
I doubt the Birkans will give us any satisfaction over
Harud," Knut said. "They need the goodwill of the
foreign merchants."

"They also need to keep the goodwill of the Norse,"
Haakon growled, "and if they argue, I will find time to
show them why."

Orm and Knut looked at each other and decided that
it would do no harm to keep Jarl Haakon distracted
over the next five days. It would do no good to his case
if he punched a lawspeaker in the nose before the case
even came up.

They came to him with questions over every repair to
the ships until he yelled at them that they were
helmsmen, they ought to know the stern of a ship from
their own ass and to leave him alone, and went off to
an ale house to brood.

The five days before the Thing met were the longest

in his life, and his patience might have snapped entirely
if Ragnar the Noseless hadn't come to Birka, with his
three longships and a heavily loaded *knarr*. Ragnar was
a friend, and when he heard about Harud, he immediately promised to bear witness for Haakon before the
Thing and to go to Cadiz with him, with his three
longships. So many of the *knarr*'s crew also asked to
join the raiders that its captain lost his temper, and
Orm lost his and threw the man overboard. That took a
while to settle, and Ragnar filled in the rest of the time
by teaching Haakon enough Arabic for him to be rude
to the wali. Ragnar had traded down the rivers of the
Slavic lands as far as Constantinople and had met
enough Arabs there, and in Hedeby and Birka, to be
fluent. He would be a welcome interpreter if matters
came to talking and not fighting.

Haakon also kept an ear out for the talk among the
chiefs and fighting men in Birka. "Most of them think
you have a case against the Thing for not keeping better
control over who's brought into the slave camp," Orm
said. "Some of these merchants had heard stories about
Harud, but they didn't bother to check *his* story."

"Which is a bad habit," Knut said, "and likely to get
them killed one day, and if the Thing sits on its ass long
enough, it will hear that in plain words, from the jarls
and maybe also from the king of the Swedes. He and
the Birkans will be unfriends in a hurry if he thinks
they'll shelter men he has outlawed."

The king would have to outlaw Harud if Harud
stayed in Sweden long enough, Haakon thought. Ac-
cording to Birkan merchants' gossip, Harud was bound
north, apparently intending to winter on the north
shore of the Baltic, and Harud was not a man who could
stay in any one place for long without making trouble.

"It is not that these jarls are all so clean handed
themselves," Knut said. "No man who bears weapons
and has blood instead of milk in his body can live thirty

years without paying weregild once or twice. If Harud's feud with you were over some common murder, that would be one thing. But stealing your wife, and this after stealing the children—they are beginning to think of Harud as something to be hunted down. Some of them have a mind to sail with you."

"Also, I am sailing on a raid that promises good booty," Haakon said, darkly amused. Most chiefs were honorable men, but honor filled no bellies, and their men would remind them of this if they forgot. It was said that the Moslems of Spain were fighting what was almost a civil war, and so their coasts were guarded by fewer men and ships than usual. And Spain was very rich.

The knowledge of how many armed men favored Haakon's cause certainly helped speed the Birkans in their decision. When the Thing met, it heard no more than the fewest possible number of witnesses in each case, deliberated for only a couple of hours, then gave its judgments:

Harud Olafsson was banned from Birka until he had stood trial before the Thing of his own land. If he came to the town anyway, he would be tried before the Thing of Birka for harm done to men and property. If he fled, he would be declared outlaw.

Kare Ingstad, guilty of oath-breaking and the abduction of two free Norse, would be hanged. Some Birkans, not wishing to lie down too tamely, argued that Rosamund was not, strictly speaking, either free or Norse. Others said that all of Haakon's witnesses spoke of her as if she were, therefore she should be counted as such. With a little help from the number of Haakon's men who drew their weapons, the second party won the day.

The Arab slave trader would receive compensation from Haakon in gold coin for the injuries to himself and his men as though they were Norse, and also for the price of

Kare Ingstad. The Thing of Birka would pay this latter penalty itself.

Haakon Olesson would receive all the supplies his ships and men needed at half payment. He would also be allowed to take aboard his ships any fighting men sworn to the service of the Thing of Birka who wished to go, and the Thing would continue their pay in their absence.

Haakon found these judgments less than generous, but Ragnar the Noseless informed him otherwise. "I'm surprised those tight-purses parted with as much as they did. Believe me, you'll get nothing more without raising swords or waiting half a year."

Haakon grumbled, but he was pleased enough with the number of chiefs and men who asked to join in the voyage to Spain. Each had his own reasons, of course, and few of them went strictly to regain Haakon's Rosamund for him, but Haakon had come to Birka with three ships and slightly more than two hundred men, and he sailed out again with twelve ships and rather more than seven hundred men.

Only one ship was not going to Spain. Her chief had discovered after swearing his oath that his ship was not fit for a raiding voyage that would mean staying at sea later in the year than usual. Haakon found that rather better luck than not, and it solved a problem for him. He released the chief from his oath, on condition that he sail to the Trondelag and take Haakon's messages, and Donal and Fann.

Donal was indignant; Haakon was adamant. "You needn't fear for your soul," he said reassuringly. "Most of the people on my steading have been prime-signed, and Christians can lawfully deal with them." It didn't seem wise to add that he'd seen Donal in his dream, comfortably seated in Norse Valhalla and looking very un-Christian indeed.

"I'm not overworried about my soul," Donal said stubbornly. "I want to fight."

"You won't be fit to fight again this year," Haakon said bluntly. "Go to my house and let my mother feed you. Then we'll talk about fighting. And I have to send Fann home anyway—I can't take her to Spain with a fleet full of men whose manners will grow less the longer they're away from their women. If you don't go, I'll have to send men of my own to guard her, and I don't want to."

Donal gave up grudgingly, and his face was still rebellious when he set foot on the ship, but Fann looked relieved. If Donal's Christianity did not hang overly heavy on him, Fann's wrapped her like a cloak, and she looked at Norsemen, Haakon included, as if they might suddenly sprout fangs. The day of sailing dawned bright and fine, but Haakon hadn't slept. Restless and exasperated, he finally went down to the ships at first light, with Wulf.

Red Hawk lay drawn up bow-first on the shore, ready to spread her wings, empty of men except for one shipguard at her stern. Another spearman stood on the shore and waved to Haakon cheerfully. "Fair day, jarl."

In no mood for talking, Haakon grunted something he hoped would sound polite. He waded out into the water to examine *Red Hawk*'s hull. Wulf, apparently in no mood for a morning swim, stayed on shore, and the spearman eyed him warily. Wulf had never bitten one of Haakon's men yet, but there was always a first time.

Amidships, the water reached Haakon's waist. He was standing with his ear against the planks, a trick that Snorri had taught him to check for leaks, when Wulf suddenly started barking furiously. Haakon spun around to see the dog hurling himself over *Red Hawk*'s oar ports. The shipguard looked frantically around him, trying to point his spear in all directions at once and seeing nothing.

Then a shadow fell across Haakon. He looked up as a

man with a knife came down at him from the deck. The water slowed Haakon, but it also rocked *Red Hawk*, and the man overbalanced. Haakon turned and instinctively caught the man's right wrist and slammed it hard against the ship's hull.

Then he saw that the knife was in his left hand. The man raised it for another stab, and Wulf came hurtling into the water. He closed on the man's throat with a snarl, and the man thrashed about frantically.

The spearman on shore finally realized what was happening and hurled his weapon. The shaft slammed across Wulf's ribs and broke the hound's hold. By then Haakon had one hand on the man's knife hand and the other on his tunic. He heaved the man into deeper water and started to hold his head under when he saw that it wasn't necessary. Wulf had torn the side of his throat out, and blood was flowing into the water around him.

Haakon threw the man back aboard *Red Hawk* and squatted beside him to make him talk before he bled to death. Wulf paddled back to the shore and then jumped into *Red Hawk*'s bow.

"You can tell me who you are," Haakon said, "and I'll let you bleed to death. If you don't, I'll feed you to the dog a bit at a time first." Wulf stood beside him, blood dripping from his jaws.

The man gasped in terror. He began to talk, hoarsely, feeling the life drain out of him. Just as Haakon had thought, he was Harud's man. He'd killed one of his shipmates in a quarrel over loot, and Harud had promised his protection only if the man stayed behind in Birka and killed Haakon. Otherwise, the dead man's friends could have him.

"I was outlaw before I joined Harud," the man gasped. "What else could I do? Where else could I go?"

"Nowhere," Haakon said. "Down Hel-Road, which is where you're going anyway."

By this time both the shipguard in *Red Hawk*'s stern and the spearman on shore had joined Haakon, and both were sweating in fear of his temper, for letting the would-be murderer get aboard in the first place. Haakon let that pass with a few pointed remarks about dark nights and strong ale being a bad combination for a man with work to do. He sent the first man off with a message to Knut to report back to the ships and then took the spearman by the collar and shook him. "If you ever throw a spear so near Wulf again, I'll ram it down your throat sideways—or I'll let Wulf make you look like that."

The guard looked at the dying man on the deck and swore extravagant oaths of repentance. Wulf sat down to lick his bruised flank.

When Knut got Haakon's message, he roused most of Haakon's men out of their beds and back to their ships within an hour, to search all of them. Harud might have left other men behind, and there was also an Arab trader to maybe count among his enemies.

Most of the searchers were not quite sober or even awake, but there were so many of them that an unwanted mouse could hardly have stayed hidden aboard any of the ships. All they found were a couple of men who'd slipped a woman aboard in the night and then fallen asleep. By midmorning the search was finished, and by noon they were ready for sea.

Most of Haakon's men seemed to find the failure of the attempted murder an omen of good luck, but in spite of this fortune, they stayed farther away from Wulf than usual. The tales from the men who'd seen the dead man's throat had lost nothing in the telling.

As they entered the channel to the sea, they passed Kare Ingstad's head on a spear by the shore. By evening they'd reached the open Baltic, and by nightfall Haakon's fleet was well offshore, spreading its sails to a rising wind.

XV

They came out of the blazing sunlight and dust of the hillside into the shadowed courtyard so suddenly that for a moment Gunnar was half-blind and stumbled on the gravel walk.

"Best not to be frightened," one of the guards said. "If Abdullah the Wise buys you, you will have a good master. But he will buy no cowards."

Gunnar looked blankly at the guard, trying to pretend he'd only understood one word in four. He'd been doing that ever since he and Rosamund went aboard Red Ali's ship at Birka. Masters talked more freely in the presence of slaves who could not understand what they heard, and what Gunnar wanted desperately was knowledge. He had already learned with some satisfaction that the Spanish coast around Cadiz was nearly bare of warships because the wali Abdullah had sent them all away to help an ally. The Arabs of Spain did not speak with quite the same accent as the Arabs Gunnar had known in the North, but he had always had an easy command of foreign tongues, and it hadn't taken him long to puzzle out the differences.

He and Rosamund had never been left alone together after leaving Birka, so there had been no way to tell her what he knew. He had wondered if he shouldn't abandon pretense to give her some reassurance that their situation was not as dire as it could be, but to admit to speaking Arabic after the fact might be dangerous, and Rosamund had seemed in reasonably good spirits,

considering. He thought she might be planning what
she would do to Harud if she ever had the chance.

She was often sick in the morning as they sailed
south, but that was the way of breeding women. She
ate hungrily of the coarse food aboard the ship and kept
herself and her clothes as clean as possible. Now, as her
guards led Rosamund into the courtyard behind Gunnar,
he stole a glimpse of her. She stood straight, and she
had somehow managed to brush her long hair until its
fairness glowed like a candle in the shadows.

Red Ali led the whole party into the courtyard. The
whitewashed walls of the house rose two floors high all
around, with shutters made of metal bars arranged like
a fisherman's net at each window. The courtyard itself
was covered with gravel, except for paths of blue polished stone and a pool of water, lined with white tile.
Most of it was shaded by squat trees bearing shiny
round fruits, about the size of apples and colored like a
sunset—*naranjas*—which sometimes found their way to
a jarl's table from the northern markets.

Red Ali stopped by the pool, and two immense
bearded men with swords stepped from an archway on
the far side. Gunnar did not need their shouts to "Do
honor to Abdullah 'ibn Numan, wali of Cadiz under the
lord emir and Allah, the Merciful and Compassionate"
to know that he should kneel to the man who followed
the two swordsmen.

The wali Abdullah was the same shape as Haakon,
thick limbed and barrel chested, although a good head
shorter. His skin was dark brown, and where his beard
wasn't gray, it was so black, it almost looked blue. He
wore an embroidered green coat, open in front to
reveal white trousers and a sash holding a dagger with a
pearl-studded handle.

It wouldn't have mattered if he had worn rags. This
was a man who had been born to command. He stood
thoughtfully, shifting the gaze of his large brown eyes

from one man to another, and Gunnar thought that with
a glance he drew from each face whatever he wanted to
know. But there was a sharp hiss of indrawn breath
when his eyes came to Rosamund.

"Well, flea-ridden dog of the sea, what do you bring
me?" The wali looked down at Ali.

"In Birka I found these two fine Franks, noble Wali,"
Red Ali said. He salaamed again. "You are the worthiest
man in all of Spain to have them in your house. The
man Gunnar is well known as a poet, and this lovely
Rosamund, fair as a maiden—"

"Rosamund is with child, Ali. Were you planning to
hide this from me?"

Red Ali turned slightly pale. "Noble Wali, it was not
my intention to hide any—"

"Save your breath to tell lies to those who will
believe them," said Abdullah. "Your mother, the she-
ass, may not have known when she was bearing you,
but I can tell a breeding woman when I see one."

The wali let Red Ali tremble and try to think of a
good story while he spoke to one of the guards, who
bowed and disappeared. Then the wali turned back
with a slightly amused look. "Since you thought you
were doing me a favor by bringing these poor wretches
here, I suppose I should be merciful and buy them.
What do your wandering wits tell you they are worth?"

Ali was not quite so afraid of Abdullah 'ibn Numan as
he was greedy, and he had seen the look on Abdullah's
face.

The bargaining for Rosamund went on so long and
became so interesting that Gunnar almost forgot he
wasn't supposed to understand most of what he was
hearing. Red Ali pointed out that Rosamund was worth
more, as a woman of proven fertility. Abdullah pointed
out just as firmly that she was worth less, since she
would be useless for nearly a year and her child might
be stillborn, sickly, or a girl. Finally they seemed to

agree on a price, and Gunnar stiffened as the wali
turned to him.

"You are a poet, Ali says. Is he telling more of the
truth than usual?"

The wali spoke a strangely accented French. Gunnar
decided that to understand it might make him appear
wiser and perhaps useful as an interpreter. He nodded
slowly. "I was poet in a great house, lord. They found
my verses pleasing there."

"Well, you may find yourself a poet in a greater
house if you please *me*. Compose a praise to me in my
own tongue before"—here he named a day Gunnar
didn't recognize—"and I will consider keeping you."

"I shall do my best, noble lord. The language—"

"That you will have to learn," the wali said firmly.
"And while you are learning you will work in the
pottery shop, so that I will have some good for my
money, which I am paying this thief." By now the guard
had come back, with four more armed men. One
carried a polished wooden box. From their hairlessness,
Gunnar recognized the two behind the first guard as
eunuchs from the harem. They led Rosamund away, and
she went with her head high and hands clasped in front
of her. The wali's eyes followed her, and the eunuchs
kept their distance on either side of her, as if a magical
barrier prevented them from coming closer.

The wali handed Red Ali the wooden box and motioned
the other two guards to take Gunnar away. He went
with them peaceably, feeling somewhat cheered. Rosamund at least seemed to have a chance of good treatment,
and he might win the same for himself if he could learn
to write poetry in Arabic.

He blessed his further fortune that one of his tasks in
Earl Edmund's castle had been to help keep the kitch-
enware in repair. At least he would not be turning a
potter's wheel or mixing clay with the drudges for long.

As he passed through the gate from the courtyard, he looked back once. The wali Abdullah stood by the pool, with an odd, unsure look on his face as if he were waiting for news that could be good or ill. Gunnar looked away quickly. A wise slave never showed too much curiosity about his master's affairs.

Abdullah 'ibn Numan was indeed waiting. He tapped his foot pensively and appeared to study the fish in the pool until the astrologer Yusuf 'ibn Khalid appeared. The astrologer was immensely tall and long limbed and wore tight trousers and a tunic that made him look half-starved. His narrow face was completely framed in white hair and a white beard. Men who came upon him by surprise in the dark had been known to make the sign against the evil eye.

With him, as always, was his bodyguard and archer, a Slav known only as Pyotr. Pyotr was even taller than his master, with muscles like an ox. He carried a bow as tall as a well-grown boy, and Abdullah had seen him use it to put five arrows in quick succession into a space the size of a man's palm.

"You have bought them both, my lord?" Yusuf 'ibn Khalid salaamed respectfully.

"Yes. That is why I have called you here."

"It is the woman, is it not?"

"Have you seen her?"

"Only here." Yusuf tapped his wrinkled forehead.

"Well, you will have your chance to see her with the eyes of your body before tomorrow's sunset. When you have done this, read the stars for me. Tell me if they encourage my taking her as I wish."

"May I ask what *is* your wish in the matter of this Frankish woman?"

Abdullah nearly told him. Had he lost all caution from one viewing? he thought. That would have answered

more questions than he wished to, even for Yusuf.
Instead he gave a long description of Rosamund and his
immediate intentions regarding her.

Yusuf listened silently, then allowed himself a thin
smile. "Assuming that your manhood has not deserted
you—"

"That is a remark that would earn anyone but you a
flogging, my friend."

"That would not give your shaft new life if the old life
had fled," Yusuf said piously.

"No doubt. But you were going to say?—"

"I was going to say that I see clearly what you want
from her, after she has the child, even if you do not
speak it. But I cannot answer your questions soon. We
are entering the sign of the Virgin, and this woman is
clearly no such thing. The effect of the dominance of
this sign makes it hard to judge the fitness of this
woman—"

"May camels piss in your well! Can you read the
signs for Rosamund or not? And if so, when?"

"I can give you no brief answer that would permit
you to judge properly," Yusuf said coldly. "If you wish
such an answer, you must find another man to read the
stars for you."

The wali sighed. That he could not allow. Yusuf read
not only the stars, but also something of equal or
greater importance—the minds of his fellow Kaasites.
Like most of Moslem Spain, Cadiz was divided between the Yemenites, descendants of men from South
Arabia, and Kaasites, descendants of men from the
north. Thanks to battles and blood-feuds dating back
almost to the time of the prophet Muhammad himself,
the Yemenites and Kaasites found it hard to live together in peace.

Like most of the men who ruled in Spain, Abdullah
'ibn Numan was a Yemenite. He owed his success in

ruling Cadiz to his wisdom and sense of justice, and also to the aid given for the past ten years by Yusuf 'ibn Khalid. The astrologer told the wali of the Kaasites' grievances, and he also spread word of the wali's good-will among them. If Yusuf left the wali's service, he would no longer be inclined to do so. The normal distrust the Kaasites felt for any Yemenite ruler would boil up again, dividing Cadiz at the worst possible time.

With civil war raging in Spain, the wali could keep his power and independence as long as his own people were united behind him and neither side elsewhere declared him an enemy. If Cadiz fell into disunity, one side or the other would surely appeal for outside aid. And then the wali would lose his hold on the city, and most likely his life. It was a chancy time.

The next few months would be the worst time of all. To stay at peace with both sides in the war, Abdullah had left Cadiz almost defenseless. Most of his soldiers were riding inland toward Cordova to support the emir, while the wali's ships had sailed into the Mediterranean to give the appearance of aid to the rebel 'ibn Hafsunn. That was risky in itself, and if war broke out in Cadiz now, the wali would be like a newborn lamb thrown among the wolves.

Besides, the astrologer might be right about Rosamund. He'd been right about Hakim—and at the thought of his dead son the wali went hot with grief as he always did, even in the cool shade of the courtyard.

So he listened while the astrologer explained at great length why it might be dangerous and would surely be useless to seek knowledge about Rosamund in the stars for some time, perhaps until she had borne her child. After Yusuf and Pyotr left, it occurred to the wali, not for the first time, that it always seemed to take longer to explain why something could not be done than to just go ahead and do it.

*   *   *

Rosamund stepped out of the bath, trying not to blush as the attending women studied her body. They gently pushed her down on a couch covered with linen cushions, which exhaled a pleasant scent, and began to rub perfumed oil into her skin.

They had nearly finished her back and buttocks when she became aware of someone else looking her over. A woman's firm voice said, "Turn over, little Frank," in French. Rosamund was now past blushing, but she refused to lie on her back like a dead fish. She sat up, to see a tall, gray-haired woman, now running to fat, but obviously once exquisite.

"I am Aurora, chief wife in the harem of Abdullah the Wise. You are the Frank named Rosamund?"

Rosamund was tired of being called a Frank and almost said so, but then she remembered Gunnar's advice after Harud had massacred Kare's men: "If we are sold, tell them *nothing* they don't ask for, except to save your life." So she nodded and didn't say anything.

Aurora walked around the couch, staring intently. Rosamund wondered briefly if she had an unnatural passion for her own sex, and looked around her for something to use as a weapon.

Finally Aurora nodded to the women to go on oiling Rosamund's skin and smiled. "They did not lie to me. You look enough like Diana to be her daughter." Rosamund looked puzzled, and Aurora shook her head sadly. "Diana was the first wife of our lord Abdullah and mother of his favorite son, Hakim. She died bearing him, and then the boy also died before he was twenty, from an assassin's knife. With each of them, a little of the wali died, also. But in you—ah, Diana might live again. Did not the wali look at you as though you were more than a common woman?"

"I do not know how the wali commonly looks at women," Rosamund said sourly. It was bad enough to be bought for herself. She didn't care for being a dead woman's ghost.

Aurora laughed. "Come, Rosamund. If you know enough of men to be bearing a child, surely you know how a man looks when his desire for you is strong. Or were you raped?"

Rosamund choked and blinked back tears. She would *not* cry in front of this woman. But she could see Haakon's face so clearly. . . . "No," she said finally. "It was not rape."

"So. I thought not." Aurora looked at her kindly.

Rosamund remembered the wali's gaze, roaming swiftly over the people in front of him until it . . . reached her. He had been surprised, she thought. And unsettled. "Yes," she said slowly. "He—he stared, and he looked— sad. And then, as you have said, with desire."

"I'm not surprised. Well, take heart. If he goes on looking at you that way, your life here will be very luxurious. If you give him a son as well, you will think you are in Paradise without going to the trouble of dying."

They dressed Rosamund in loose trousers, a tunic, and a long robe, then led her to a clean chamber furnished with a bed, chests, and a rug. The walls of the room were covered with complex patterns of curved and straight blue lines, but no people or animals. Rosamund remembered that Gunnar had said Arabs were forbidden to drink wine, eat pork, or make pictures of men and animals.

The eunuchs brought her a meal in her chamber, the best food she'd eaten since Haakon sailed for Ireland. There were mutton, eggs, cakes of coarse-ground wheat, fruit in a sweet syrup, and, to her surprise, a cup of wine. Were the Arabs here a different kind from the ones Gunnar knew?

When she finally lay down on the bed, she found herself falling almost asleep. Was it poppy syrup in the

wine, or was it just that this was the best bed she'd had
in far too long? It was a slave's bed, of course, but no
bed was entirely bad just now. And the wali was far
better luck than Harud Olafsson had intended for her.

XVI

From Birka it took ten days before Haakon's ships
were out of the Baltic and into the North Sea again. Off
the Frisian coast they met the ships from the Trondelag,
eight of them, where Haakon had expected only four,
with more than four hundred men. There wasn't enough
beer aboard to see them to Spain and back, so all the
nineteen ships sailed down the channel and put into the
bay of the Seine on the coast of France.

They found all the beer they needed in the Norse
settlements there, and four more shiploads of fighting
men eager to join what was taking on the size of a war.
Two were bands under ordinary chiefs, such as Haakon
had been a year ago. And two others were ships of
Hrolf Gänger, who was jarl in everything but name over
the Norsemen of the Seine steadings.

Hrolf himself was leading a war-band against the
English, but he'd left behind three trusted men to
speak for him in his absence, and they talked together
and decided to send two ships to Spain with Haakon.
The prospects of loot looked good, and it would do no
harm to win Haakon Olesson's friendship for Hrolf or to
sail with Haakon long enough to measure his strength.

At least that was what Ragnar the Noseless told
Haakon after a night of drinking with Hrolf's men, and
Haakon was willing to believe it.

"I *think* I'm flattered," he said. "I've heard that Hrolf collects information on men he thinks may be rivals. I must look stronger to him than I do to myself."

"The gods will never punish you for boasting," Ragnar said. "This is the largest fleet I have ever heard of following a man who was neither a king nor a jarl with sworn friendship with a king."

Haakon looked dubious, but Ragnar generally knew what he was talking about. Suddenly Haakon grinned. He had grown important, it seemed.

In the far north of Sweden, Harud Olafsson brought his ships to the mouth of a little river, beached them, and started cutting trees for a winter camp. They would not go south before spring. And by that time he hoped enough men would have forgotten him so that he could reach the rivers south to Mikligard without a fight every other day. No one except Haakon would pursue him farther than that.

In Ireland the story of Olaf Haraldsson's defeat was told and retold around the fire at Norse and Irish hearths. The Irish thanked their god, and the Norse wondered if Haakon Olesson would now put his nose into Irish affairs, and if so, how soon. No one mourned Olaf Haraldsson.

And in the Trondelag, Sigrid and Erik spent half their time at Haakon's steading and half at home, trying to run them both. Sigrid frequently lay sleepless at night, wondering how many more losses she could endure and whether word would come before winter that Haakon was dead in Spain. Erik did his best to console her, but there was little consolation to give, since he was not a god who knew the future.

Red Ali repaired his ships, paid off the men he didn't want to keep through the winter, and listened to the

rumors in the marketplace of Cadiz. It was said that the
new woman in the wali's harem, the Frank named
Rosamund, was finding much favor in his eyes.

That made Ali think soberly. If Rosamund became
Abdullah's favorite, her fate might also become known
outside Cadiz, and possibly as far as the Frankish lands.
And if Rosamund had powerful kin, they might come
looking for her, maybe with gold, but more likely with
steel in hand.

Ali wished now he had tried to learn more about
Rosamund and Gunnar before he had bought them
from Harud. To be sure, Harud might not have told
him even if he had asked, but there was always someone to be found who knew things. Ali had been too
tempted by Harud's bribe, paid to sell the woman for a
whore or a kitchen drudge. Harud was plainly in a
hurry, and Ali knew he could sell—and indeed did
sell—Rosamund and Gunnar for a small fortune to the
wali, double-crossing Harud in the process. Still, the
thought that the wali might have to pay or fight because
of Ali's mistake prompted the slave agent to keep his
wealth in the form of bags of coins, easily loaded on
horses for a quick departure.

Rosamund lived in comfort, if not luxury, in Abdullah's
harem. The midwives assured her that her pregnancy
was a healthy one, and she felt well enough. The
sickness in the morning had abated, and she seemed to
do nothing but sleep and eat. Perhaps her mother's gift
of easy birthing had been passed on to her.

But the repeated promises of a wonderful future in
the harem if she bore a son, even by another man,
chafed at her. Sometimes she felt like screaming, "This
is *my* child, mine and Haakon's! The wali has no part of
him! And I am not a cow to prove I can breed!"

But that would have made an enemy of Aurora,

and Aurora might decide to pry and discover Rosamund
had a Norse jarl for a husband. If they knew that, they
might move her inland if any Norse ships showed off
the coast. Better that they think her French and content
with her lot.

She was still left alone with the worst question of all.
If there was no rescue or ransom, what could she do
then? Live out her life in the wali's harem and raise
Haakon's child to be a slave-warrior or a concubine? Or
damn herself in the next world to save the child from
that fate in this one? She might be forgiven the sins of
going to Norse worship and lying with Haakon unwed.
But laying violent hands on herself—that was another
matter entirely. *Holy Mother Mary, give me the wisdom
to know what I should do and the courage to do
it*—even if that meant living in the wali's harem and
trying to learn to be at home there for the child's sake.

Gunnar scraped the last of the tin-enamel paste from
the bowl with a wooden knife and carefully spread it
over a small patch of bare clay on the big pot in front of
him. He worked at the enamel until it was smooth,
then set the knife down, stood up, and walked around
the pot three times. Slaves were not beaten for very
many things in the pottery shop—the master potter
knew that the best work did not come from frightened
men. But leaving a gap in the enamel that could ruin a
pot meant a flogging.

The pot looked flawless to Gunnar. He pulled off his
leather gloves and signaled to the two mute boys who
carried pots from the enamel shop to the painters. They
slipped into the harnesses at both ends of the wooden
platform under the pot, lifted it carefully, and walked
out. Gunnar tossed his gloves onto the bench in the
corner, lifted the water jug, and drank until the water
trickled down his chin and soaked his beard. It was hot

in the underground pottery shops, with the poor ventilation and the heat of the kilns, so the master never left his slaves short of drinking water.

Gunnar's work for the day was done. He walked down the hall to the bench where the slaves waited until a guard was free to lead them back to their quarters. As always, his eyes slid to the right, and he was tempted to slip through the narrow archway into the dark tunnel beyond that led—somewhere.

Something unlawful was going on down the tunnel from the pottery shop, something the wali didn't know about, but something protected by someone who was very powerful indeed. That much was an open secret in the pottery shop, and Gunnar, who was still pretending to know only a smattering of Arabic, was well aware of it. Whatever it was was so important and so deadly that the other slaves might whisper among themselves, but they would never, ever, whisper to the wali.

Gunnar was sure that the answer lay beyond the archway. Men went in there carrying pots and came out empty-handed. If he ever had the chance, he was going to sneak in there himself. If he took what he learned to the wali, he might be rewarded with freedom, or perhaps he could ask instead for Rosamund's? . . .

Gunnar sighed. Once again his imagination had leaped ahead to what he might win for doing something he had no idea how to do! There was never a chance to slip through the archway while he was at work. And for all he knew, beyond was a maze of tunnels where he might be lost forever, or a trap with armed men, waiting for fools like him. Then he might lose everything he had now. Even if they only thought he was trying to escape, he would get a brutal flogging and lose his chance to be a poet in the wali's house. If they thought he was spying out their secret, he would be killed, and it would be a surprise to everyone if his body was ever found.

This obsessive hope of winning freedom by exposing these mysterious crimes was disordering his wits, he decided. He seemed unable to compose the verses he would need to present to the wali only twelve days from now.

You are forgetting how to be a slave: Always choose a small but certain good over a large but only possible one. The wali's favor in return for good poetry was a certain good. Discovering the secret crime was only a possible one. And earning the wali's contempt if his verses were poor was a certain evil.

Gunnar put the idea of uncovering the crime firmly in the back of his mind. Now he needed only to think of something flattering to say about the wali, when he knew practically nothing about him, he thought gloomily. All he knew was that the man was honored as a brave and wise leader and had lost a beloved wife for whom he still mourned.

A brave and wise leader, who mourned for a lost wife? . . . Gunnar let out a whoop, and the other slaves started and stared at him. They already thought him a little mad, and now Gunnar gave them a grin that did nothing to revise that opinion.

He could tell Haakon's story, thinly veiled as the wali's, and the ending would give the wali a surprise he might not like, but it would give Gunnar great satisfaction. And if he were careful, and the poem good, there would be little that the wali could do to him for it without looking a smaller man than he would like.

Gunnar chuckled again. He could do it. It wouldn't put Rosamund in any danger, so he *would* do it. He could win a place in the wali's house and hold on to more of his honor than he'd thought likely. With a lifetime of slavery facing him, that seemed important.

XVII

The crests of the Spanish mountains loomed above the horizon when Haakon's fleet heaved to at dawn. The sea was so smooth that he was able to bring all twenty-three ships within hailing distance to give his orders. The calm would mean a good deal of work at the oars, but it would also mean easy pickings outside Cadiz harbor. Most of her ships would be merchantmen, heavy laden and with few oars.

"You've all heard that it's true!" Haakon bellowed. "The wali has sent his own longships and their men away. Cadiz has no fleet!"

The Norse warriors beat on their shields, hooted, and laughed in response to this remarkable good fortune. Haakon held the golden ax over his head and waved it in a wide arc until the flickering, flashing reflection of the dawn's light caught their wandering attention.

"Branch out in the Cadiz harbor. Take every ship you meet, and any loot on it!"

They cheered again: Haakon the Lucky. The men who had cast their lot with Haakon had known there was loot in Spain. It was beyond their conjecturing that the booty would be theirs for the plucking, without resistance.

"*Quiet!* The safety of my wife and Gunnar Thorsten is foremost in my mind. I don't want them used as hostages by the wali, and for that reason, you will take no slaves. And harm no one, unless you're attacked!"

They grumbled at that, but it was already beginning to be said that Haakon the Dark didn't think like other men, and still he kept his war-luck. Maybe he was smarter. After all, there was going to be more loot than they had dreamed of.

"After the ships are yours, let them and their people go free, with this message for the wali of Cadiz: Haakon Olesson has come for his wife, Rosamund, and his poet, Gunnar." He shouted it again in Arabic—just as Ragnar had taught him—and made all the chiefs repeat it over until he was sure they knew it as well as they were going to. They agreed on a meeting place for that night, and he raised the golden ax. It caught the light of the rising sun and flamed so brightly that some wouldn't look directly at it.

"For our vengeance and our victory!" Weapons thundered against shields, and men shouted until it seemed that the noise must have rolled across the water to the sleeping city. Then they sat down and lifted their oars, and the ships spread out like a wolf pack on the hunt.

Ragnar stood beside Haakon and watched them go. "I think we will be lucky if any Arabs even recognize their own tongue, let alone understand the message. Still, something should get through."

"Oh, enough to shake up the wali," Haakon said. "There will be men who speak some Arabic on some of our ships, and Arabs who speak some Norse on theirs. And traders out of both lands are bound to speak French. I think our message will get to the wali Abdullah in a hurry if we take enough of his merchantmen."

Haakon sat down and began smearing a light coating of fish oil across the blade of the golden ax.

Yeshua Ben David spat the taste of sleep out of his mouth, stretched, and looked around him. The ship seemed to be pasted to a calm blue ocean, with the grayish white sails as limp as a beggar's purse. It was still early in the day, though. The wind might still

come. In any case, Yeshua knew that the captain disliked
Jews just enough not to welcome suggestions from one,
even if he was the owner's son.

It didn't matter greatly. The olive oil in the hold
below was fresh, all except a few jugs. It would still
bring a good price in wool from the Berbers in Africa,
unless the ship was becalmed for whole weeks on their
way south. Even if the oil didn't bring a good price,
Yeshua had an ample supply of silver coins in the
strongbox below. His father's looms would not be short
of wool this winter, no matter what, and—

"Hoaaaaa!" shouted the helmsman aft. Yeshua saw
him pointing frantically, and he ran aft to where he
could see what the man was pointing at.

On the horizon, two unmistakably Norse square sails
were rising into view, dangerous as hawks. Even as
Yeshua watched, he saw the flicker of white, telling of
fast-moving oars. The captain came on deck, took one
look, and ordered the crew to the sweeps. The ship's
prow turned slowly toward the distant land. With luck
and sweat, they might be able to run the ship aground and
escape inland. They would lose the ship and cargo
and perhaps would go hungry for a year. But they
would be far hungrier as Norse slaves, providing they
lived through the fight.

There was plenty of sweat. Even Yeshua and the
captain took their turns at the sweeps: No one with any
sense was unafraid of Norsemen. But there was no luck.
By the time the captain was ordering the cargo thrown
overboard, the two Norse ships were overtaking them
rapidly. One of the sailors had a bow, and he ran below
to get it. Yeshua followed him to get the strongbox and
throw it overboard. His father would not like the fishes
getting his silver, but forfeiting it to the Norse would be
even worse.

The archer nocked an arrow and shot. A man in the
longship to port caught it on his shield. From the same

ship three arrows whistled in reply. The archer clawed
at two shafts in his chest, coughed blood, and fell to the
deck. Two other men leaped overboard, preferring
drowning or sharks to the Norsemen. Yeshua followed
them to the railings, ready to heave the strongbox in his
hands. Then one of the longships came crashing alongside.

The impact of the collision threw Yeshua to the deck.
The strongbox fell, and the lid flew off, scattering silver
in a bright river on the pitching deck. The Norsemen
swarmed aboard. Yeshua choked off a scream as a boot
came down hard on his hand and knocked his head into
an oar bench. Dimly he could see Norsemen picking up
the silver.

When his head cleared, he blinked in surprise and
struggled to sit up. Half a dozen Norsemen had the
ship's crew bunched into a herd in the stern. The crew
looked fearfully down the points of their spears, but
no one was bleeding, and they weren't bound. A blond
man prodded Yeshua into line with the rest. The
Norsemen were systematically stripping the ship of
everything that wasn't nailed down—and a few things
that had to be pried or cut loose. A one-eyed man with
a bristly beard stood in front of the captive crew,
repeating something over and over. The second time he
heard it, Yeshua recognized the words as Arabic. The
fourth time, he recognized what they said, in spite of
the Norseman's terrible accent: "Haakon Olesson has
come for his wife, Rosamund, and his poet, Gunnar."

That made very little sense, but the Norseman seemed
determined. He might speak French better than he
spoke Arabic. Yeshua cleared his throat and looked
embarrassed as the words came out in a croak.

"Who is—the Haakon?"

The one-eyed man fumbled for words. "He—our
jarl."

That didn't get them much further, and the one-eyed
man, who seemed to be the chief, apparently decided

there was no reason to try using a language he couldn't speak very well. "Thorfinn!" he bellowed.

Thorfinn Solvisson had spent some time in France before he came into Haakon's service, so understanding grew quickly after he came aboard. "But why does Jarl Haakon think his wife and poet are in Cadiz?" Yeshua asked.

The Norsemen had finished looting the hold, and the ship now rode a good foot higher in the water. They stood listening to Thorfinn and Yeshua, and at that question they let out a general growl like a pack of hunting dogs and crashed their spear butts on the deck. Yeshua almost succeeded in not flinching.

"It is known that Red Ali bought them in Birka," Thorfinn said sharply. "It is known that Red Ali deals from Cadiz. If you say otherwise, you lie."

Yeshua would not have lied in the face of so many angry Norsemen, particularly about a thief like Red Ali.

There had been rumors in the marketplace that the wali had bought a man and a woman from Red Ali for a great price. They were said to be Franks, but Franks and Norse were not so different, and Red Ali had never had a compulsion toward truth telling.

If the Norsemen were telling the truth, whoever brought their message to the wali Abdullah would be bringing him bad news, and he loved bad-news bringers no more than any other ruler. On the other hand, the Norsemen also seemed to be offering Yeshua and his people their lives and freedom in return for bearing that message. It seemed better to be in fear of the wali's anger than to be a slave or a corpse. There were other cities for trading in Spain besides Cadiz, whereas few men came back from Norse chains and none came back from the dead.

"I shall tell the wali or a man of his what you wish," Yeshua said.

"That is enough," Thorfinn said, and the one-eyed

man nodded. Within minutes after that, the Norsemen were back aboard their ships and at the oars. The captain and Yeshua stood side by side until the long-ships were out of bowshot, not daring to speak for fear of destroying the miracle that had spared their lives and freedom. Then they looked at each other.

"Were you telling them the truth?" the captain asked.

Yeshua shrugged. "We have to return to Cadiz anyway. Where are we going, with no cargo?"

They reached port by late afternoon and discovered that some eight or nine ships had gone through the same ordeal. By nightfall there were fifteen, and by midnight, twenty. Aboard some ships there'd been more resistance to the Norsemen and, as a result, more bloodshed. But everywhere the Norse had seemed more interested in loot and getting their message carried to the wali than in victims or slaves.

Rumors ran through the streets of Cadiz like mad dogs on hot days. It was said that the Norsemen would stop all ships going in and coming out of Cadiz until "Rosamund and Gunnar are returned"; it was also said that the Norsemen threatened to enter the city and sack it if the two were not returned within three days; it was said that the Haakon who led them possessed a great magic and could turn himself into a firedrake and burn the city with his breath.

The merchants went to the house of the wali's captain of the port, Abu Zayd 'ibn Badr, but were informed by servants that the master was sleeping. Then the house gates were unceremoniously shut and the city watch called. Yeshua Ben David persuaded the men of the watch not to attack the merchants and start a civil war in the streets of their own city. After that he went to the synagogue and prayed earnestly for God's mercy, as he had been faithful in observing both the Laws of Moses and the laws of Abdullah the Wise.

Some of the merchants went considerably farther

than the nearest synagogue, church, or mosque. They packed their portable valuables, gathered their families, and left Cadiz, certain they were leaving a city doomed to destruction by the Norse.

Well ahead of even the fleetest merchant went Red Ali. He rode a good horse whose saddlebags held only money and a change of clothes. What Ali had most feared had already happened, whether or not the Norse sacked Cadiz. He would be years regaining what he would lose by fleeing the city, but then it would be years before he was safe anywhere within reach of Abdullah the Wise.

The captain of the port, Abu Zayd 'ibn Badr, locked himself in his house and hoped that the Norsemen would go away. If he took the news to the wali, the wali would think that this was his fault, and Abu Zayd did not even wish to contemplate the results of that.

The chaos in the harbor and the panic in the port spread throughout the city. In the wali's pottery factory, no one knew exactly what was happening in the city outside, although there were many rumors and much confusion. In the pandemonium, anyone who'd bothered keeping watch on a certain archway might have seen a tall, fair-haired man slip through and vanish into the darkness beyond.

Gunnar had no pressing need to learn the secret of the tunnel. His poem was finished—it even had two endings, one rather bold, the other not, for use depending on the wali's mood. But when opportunity so obligingly presented itself, he couldn't resist that dark, inviting doorway, although he very shortly wished that he had let well enough alone.

He'd brought flint, steel, and a lamp, so once he was far enough down the tunnel to use them safely, there was light to hurry by and therefore not much danger of being gone long enough to be missed. In fact, in the confusion that seemed to be spreading through Cadiz, he would have a fair chance of escaping. But then what would happen to Rosamund? She was in the harem in the wali's country house two hours away.

The sight that greeted him in the secret workroom drove everything else out of his mind. The evidence displayed all steps in the process: the clay molds for false linings, the jewels and spices, the opium—all were there littering the tabletops. Gunnar stared at them in sheer terror. This was a secret to lose a man his head.

Each clay pot had an inner lining carefully formed to match the outer shape of the pot, and to each piece of the inner lining was pasted a jewel, a pearl, a quantity of gold or silver coins, or a flat leather packet. Gunnar found pepper or opium in the packets he dared to open. The pottery shop was being used for smuggling stolen goods out of Cadiz, under the wali's nose.

Who was behind such a careful operation? There had to be a good many hands at work here, and a good many eyes turned away, but they would only be underlings. Somewhere in Cadiz lurked a very powerful thief.

Gunnar could be sure of at least one thing. The man in all Cadiz who would find it easiest to be such a thief was the astrologer, Yusuf 'ibn Khalid. As the friend, counselor, and seer of the wali, Yusuf could give more orders with fewer questions asked and afford more bribes than any six men in the city.

Gunnar had heard a dozen versions of how Yusuf had come to have so much power over a man normally too sensible to let such a thing happen. Yusuf had predicted the death of the wali's favorite child, Hakim, son of the beloved Diana. With his father's encouragement, Hakim had ignored the prophecy and one night fell victim to a band of assassins. Stricken with grief and shame, his father had ever since been more willing to listen to Yusuf than to any other man and less willing to believe him capable of wrongdoing.

From what Gunnar had heard, he wouldn't have been surprised if Hakim's murderers were in the astrologer's pay. If Yusuf was the master thief, Gunnar was going to have to carry his new knowledge as carefully as a basket of fresh eggs. Yusuf could end his life with as little trouble as a dog snapping a rat's neck. He might even think himself free to strike at Rosamund. For that he would pay, but perhaps too late to save her.

Gunnar found himself sweating from more than the damp heat of the shop. He blew out his lamp and stealthily made his way back to the archway. He didn't stop expecting a strong, sudden hand on his shoulder or a dagger in his back until he was stretched out on his pallet in the slave quarters again.

It was dark, so from his balcony Yusuf 'ibn Khalid could barely see the rooftops of Cadiz and could only imagine the Norse ships lurking out at sea. In fact, it was so dark that he was not aware of the presence of his archer, Pyotr, until the man came directly up to him and spoke.

"My lord?"

Yusuf started, but recovered himself quickly. Not even Pyotr could be allowed to see that the coming of the Norse had made him uneasy. "Pyotr, I want you to find a village where there are Christians and followers of the True Faith. Then I want you to make trouble between them."

"Poison a well?"

"Yes, or steal cattle or break family treasures . . . or kidnap a child. Anything that can be blamed on the Christians and will rouse the Moslems against them. You may use as many of your men as you feel you need."

"My lord Yusuf, I have no such men. I have always—"

"You have never thought I was a fool, so do not start now. Of course you have men in your pay. How else could you have given me such good service for so long?" Pyotr smiled but said nothing. Yusuf continued. "Will you need more money than you have now for this work?"

"I do not think so."

"Good." Yusuf was prepared to be generous, but he was also glad to hear that. It meant that Pyotr was taking no more money for himself than might be expected of a good servant who knew that he might outlive his master and wanted a comfortable old age.

"Then go and do it, Pyotr," Yusuf finished. "And do not be tenderhearted or allow your men to be. The followers of the false prophet Jesus seek to die for their belief in him. I am always happy to oblige them."

"I understand, my lord," Pyotr said. He vanished into the darkness, and Yusuf relaxed somewhat. The work would be done well—Pyotr had money, a good head for choosing men with as few scruples as he himself had, and no love for Christians. Of course he had little love for Moslems, either, or indeed worshipers of any god. It was doubtful that Pyotr worshiped anything, except perhaps his bow and arrows, and some dim Slavic nature force.

The wali Abdullah had always been careful of the interests of the Christians of his land, and there was much less hostility between them and the local Moslems than was true elsewhere. That meant one less quarrel for Yusuf to exploit, and now seemed a good time to change things, with everyone already uneasy over the Norsemen. Trouble between Christians and Moslems could be easily started, and it would give the wali something to think about besides the Norsemen—when he finally did learn of their presence. The wali was enjoying himself at his country house, and Yusuf had every intention that he should stay that way as long as possible. Then Yusuf could make his own approaches to the Norsemen if they turned out to be interested.

Certainly something would have to be done to conceal his own long-standing plots and thefts, which might easily be exposed in this confusion. With the Norsemen blocking the harbor, his stolen goods were stacking up in the wali's shop and hence growing more dangerous by the minute.

If trouble between Christians and Moslems was not enough diversion, Yusuf would go further, but only if he faced exposure and arrest before he could gather his wealth and leave Cadiz. In that case he would make use of people he had placed in Abdullah's harem. Even if he used them only once, some of them would surely be discovered and implicate him as their leader. However, he was equally certain that Rosamund's death would leave Abdullah the Wise in no fit state to take revenge before Yusuf 'ibn Khalid could put several days' travel between himself and Cadiz.

XVIII

Yeshua Ben David found that he could not sleep at all, so he rose early, told his wife to gather the children and valuables, and sent messages to his father and their master weaver. Then he prayed again, dressed, and was one of the first of the city's merchants to appear again at the gate of the captain of the port.

This time Abu Zayd's servants weren't even willing to tell the merchants if their master was within. Some of the merchants wanted to arm themselves and break into the house, but Yeshua and other cooler heads argued otherwise.

"If we kill him, is that going to make him go to the

wali for us? If Abu Zayd will not do his duty, we will take the message to the wali ourselves." Yeshua sighed. "He may not reward bad-news bringers, but he can hardly punish forty of the city's merchants at once. Abdullah the Wise does not kill the cow and then expect it to give more milk."

So the merchants withdrew and prepared to ride to the wali's palace. From the safety of the harbor's watchtower, Abu Zayd saw them go. Earlier that morning, he'd seen Norse sails on the horizon and knew that the longships were still offshore. Today would bring more looted ships into Cadiz and more outraged captains and merchants to his door. And now the wali was going to hear about the Norse anyway, but from these men first; that was going to spell no good for Abu Zayd.

He waited until the streets were clear of merchants, and then ordered his fastest horse. He also ordered his guards to find Red Ali, or at least to learn where the man had gone. If Red Ali had brought this disaster on Cadiz, he had a very large debt to pay, and the sooner the better, so that the wali had someone to behead besides Abu Zayd.

The wali did Gunnar Thorsten the honor of sending guards and a horse to bring him out to the country palace for his poetry recital. That it was an honor was not immediately evident to Gunnar. It seemed that rough hands and rougher voices dragged him out of a sound sleep only minutes after he closed his eyes. Before the dawn shadows began to shorten, he and his guards were mounted and riding south out of Cadiz.

Gunnar found the wali awaiting him in the courtyard, surrounded by bodyguards. This time Abdullah was seated in a chair of carved wood, inlaid with ivory and mother-of-pearl and padded with silk cushions. Outside the ring that the guards made around the wali stood nearly a dozen men, all richly dressed and unarmed, most of them with gray in their beards. The astrologer and his pet archer, Pyotr, were not among them.

Gunnar smiled. If the wali had brought all the poets of Cadiz to hear the barbaric Norseman fumble his way through praise verses, that simply meant more listeners who, in a short time, were going to get a surprise. It also meant more witnesses to the wali's embarrassment if Gunnar used the bolder of the two endings for his poem. That might be dangerous, but Gunnar didn't mind. He was inclined to risk-taking because the wali had evidently invited a crowd of poets to witness Gunnar's expected failure. The wali might move Rosamund inland, though, if he were offended.

Since his audience was talking to itself and taking very little notice of him, Gunnar examined all the doorways and windows he could see from where he stood. There was movement behind a large, ornate screen on a balcony facing him. Was Abdullah's harem being allowed to listen without being seen? Was Rosamund there?

Gunnar took several deep breaths and waited for the wali to grant him his attention. The wali smiled, and Gunnar thought he might be amusing himself, letting Gunnar stand about on one foot. Finally the wali made a shushing motion at the other poets and lifted a brown hand.

"You may begin."

Gunnar fixed his eyes on a point somewhere over the wali's head.

> "Land the brave chief's father held,
> By love of friend and fear of foe.
> Wealth he got, and wife, and sons,
> And honor—God would have it so. . . ."

The Arabs all opened their eyes wide, and the poets ceased to look superior. Gunnar's Arabic was accented but fluent, and the poem was properly composed in an Arabic verse form.

Abdullah 'ibn Numan leaned forward, his dark eyes interested and his expression surprised but watchful. As a young soldier he'd learned that if he reacted to surprises by standing with his mouth gaping open, someone was likely to run a spear between his teeth and up into his brain. He would then die with a stupid look on his face and no reputation worth mentioning afterward.

Abdullah thoughtfully put his chin in his hand and got ready for further surprises. He realized that Gunnar was telling a story, in the manner of the Frankish and the Norse poets. Arab poetry simply gave a picture in words of the blossom, the beloved, the moonlit night, or whatever other inspiration the poet found. Gunnar would add variety to his guests' entertainment, the wali decided, and thus to his reputation as a host. Most unusual and useful.

The fact that he told a tale didn't prevent Gunnar from creating fine imagery. The wali listened with appreciation as the sea warrior forgave the men who attacked by treachery because they had followed a bad leader. One could almost see the flickering light of the driftwood fire driving the shadows back across the stony beach and hear the whine of the cold wind of the northern seas.

Certainly Gunnar's sea warrior was wise as well as brave. He seemed to know the same thing that Abdullah had learned: You can either destroy your enemies completely or win them over until they become friends. He'd found no middle ground between those two courses in forty years.

> "A castle strong they boldly stormed,
> And fair the maiden found within.
> Her father's men she would defend,
> With woman's arms, not fearing sin."

A very romantic tale, it seemed—the nobleman's daughter gave herself to the raider and saved the lives of her father's servants and slaves. It also cut rather sharply for the wali. His beloved Diana had sworn to enter his harem if he would pay off the debts her father owed and keep him from being sold into slavery. She'd kept her bargain and done even more. There'd been nothing said about making Abdullah 'ibn Numan love her as much as his own life and afterward give the same love to the son she bore him. Abdullah asked himself sometimes if his life might not have been easier if Diana hadn't done so much more than she promised.

Easier, perhaps, not happier. Allah has never promised that there shall be only honey or only vinegar in a man's life, but always that the two shall be mixed.

The wali pulled his mind away from Diana. He had not been attending, and that would never do. The other poets would resent such discourtesy to their art. Gunnar might be a slave, but he was their equal as a poet, and they were a touchy lot.

Now it seemed that the maiden had also become the beloved of her captor. She was carrying his child, then:

"Harud tore Rosamund from Haakon
By treachery, merciless as death.
Yet their love shall endure and grow
While either one of them draws breath."

Gunnar bowed his head to signal the end of the poem, then raised it and stared hard at the wali. Abdullah met the stare and thought that he had had friendlier looks from men into whose bodies he had just thrust his lance.

The other poets were nodding and tugging at their beards. They were favorably impressed, in spite of themselves. So was Abdullah. Gunnar was indeed a fine poet, and he had earned himself a place in the wali's house.

He'd also earned himself fifty strokes of the bastinado on the soles of his bare feet. Using the name "Rosamund" for the hero's beloved was sharper wit than the wali was going to allow. The sooner Gunnar learned this, the better. Fifty strokes should do nothing worse than keep him from walking comfortably for a few days while it taught him better manners.

Abdullah raised a hand for his guards, when a babble of voices broke the silence of the courtyard, followed by the sound of fast-moving feet. Abu Zayd 'ibn Badr, captain of the port, dashed in, with two guards, their swords drawn, behind him. More guards followed with their backs to the wali, holding off a mob of angry men in merchants' clothing. Abu Zayd threw himself on the gravel at the wali's feet, while the poets gathered up their robes and scurried out through every open door and archway. They didn't want to be anywhere near what looked like an attempt to murder the wali.

By the time the last poet had vanished from sight, the guards had the merchants enough under control that the wali was at least in no danger of being trampled to death in his courtyard. He looked down at the groveling Abu Zayd.

"I presume you have some excellent reason for coming here?"

"Lord Wali, I—there is—the merchants—"

"If you cannot find your tongue, Abu Zayd, I shall have it cut out and placed in your hand." The wali looked at the merchants and pointed at the first one who was able to meet his gaze. "You! Who are you, and what brings you here?"

"I am Yeshua Ben David, noble one. I am a tailor and a merchant in cloth. There are more than twenty ships of the Norsemen off our shore. They are intercepting all the ships they can, looting them, and then sending them back to port. They do not kill often, but always they send a message."

"And what might that be?" The wali found that his mouth was suddenly dry.

Yeshua Ben David seemed to commend himself to the mercy of his god, then said slowly, "'Haakon Olesson has come for his wife, Rosamund, and his poet, Gunnar.' They say it over and over again."

A long, uncomfortable silence enveloped the courtyard. The wali continued to stare at Yeshua Ben David but saw no more of him than if he'd been a piece of the wall. Then he looked at Gunnar. He had to admire the poet—he must have understood the message, but not a flicker of an eyelid showed it.

At this point Abu Zayd staggered to his feet. The sight of him gave the wali back his voice. "Get out of my sight, and leave your office and the city. If I see you again before I find your successor, you will lose your head as well as your post." The captain of the port left without even taking the time to bow again. The wali turned back to Yeshua Ben David.

"I am glad to see that at least one man in Cadiz has more courage than a rabbit. Is there more to this tale?"

"Yes, my lord."

"Then tell me. You will not be poorer for it."

"Thank you, Lord Wali. I—I would ask instead that you be generous with the kin of the three men of my ship who died at Norse hands. All left wives, and two had children."

The wali nodded. "They shall not want, as long as you tell me the truth about what is happening in my city."

By the time Yeshua Ben David finished his story, the wali knew all that he could without questioning Gunnar and Rosamund, and he had no mind to do that in the open courtyard—his pride would not stand for it. Tonight, discreetly, with no one else present, he would question them.

Meanwhile, he would send this Haakon a message to come ashore and discuss matters. The northern barbarians were even slower of wit than the Franks, and the wali doubted he would find it hard to get the better of this one, either with words or weapons. He had enough hidden archers to solve the problem that way, if necessary. He was determined not to surrender Rosamund for any cause, and he had no mind to hand over Gunnar, like a thief giving up a stolen donkey!

He gave orders to return Gunnar to the slave quarters and watch him, appointed Yeshua Ben David captain of the port for the time being, sent a message to the Norseman, and ordered that Red Ali be found. Abdullah did not greatly care whether they brought Ali to him alive or even in one piece, but he did intend to have the man accounted for by the time the sun set on this shameful day.

XIX

Rosamund and Gunnar spent that night sleepless, Rosamund in the harem with what seemed like forty eunuchs outside her door, Gunnar in his own quarters, which were more luxurious than the pottery workers' but were also ringed with guards. They had both been brought to the wali that night, separately and then together, and they had been very well behaved indeed. They had done as they were told, spoken truth, and prayed fervently—to any god they could think of—that the wali wouldn't take it into his head to send them farther inland. He didn't seem to find Haakon very threatening, which meant he would be surprised. Haakon would undoubtedly lay Cadiz in ruins if he couldn't get to them, but that would be small comfort to Rosamund and Gunnar. And probably to Haakon, once he was through.

"It still makes me uneasy, sticking your head so far down the wolf's throat." Knut looked at the lights beyond the harbor that were the city of Cadiz.

Haakon frowned and grunted, a plain indication that he wished no more arguments, but Knut ignored him stubbornly. When he wished, Knut could appear not only one-eyed but blind and sometimes completely deaf as well.

"Foolhardy," Knut added.

"The wolf will need a wide gullet not to choke on five hundred Norsemen," Haakon said.

Ragnar the Noseless raised his eyebrows. "He will let you in with so many?"

"He said I should bring the men I trust most," Haakon said. "He did not say how many."

"That being the case, I expect he has enough of his own not to worry," Knut said, gloomily unconvinced.

"Thor's hammer, that is enough!" Haakon said. "We have seven hundred more men on our ships in his harbor. They will burn his city for him if we don't come back, and he knows it."

"As to that, I've served some men who wouldn't quibble at losing a city, to keep something they'd a mind to have," Knut growled.

"I doubt that Abdullah 'ibn Numan is that sort," Ragnar said. "He has been wali here for more than twenty years, and the merchants speak well of him. He doesn't sound to me like a man to throw away his city over a woman. It may grate his pride a bit, but he won't do it."

Knut opened his mouth to make further protests, met Haakon's look, and threw up his hands.

Haakon polished his ax. "You still lack one of Bjorn's skills, Knut—you don't know when to stop arguing with me. You insist on telling me three times what I'm only willing to hear twice."

Five hundred Norse, flanked by the wali's escorts, marched north from where the ships had set them ashore. The wali's men were mounted, and they reined in their flighty mounts to the Norsemen's pace. There were not many of them—enough to look important and give honor, but not enough to try anything, Haakon decided.

It was a two hours' march to the wali's country palace, itself two hours south of the city. The longships pushed off again behind them and, with the aid of the morning land breezes, cruised just offshore, within sight of the city itself. There they would wait—for Haakon's return, and if he didn't return, the Norse would destroy Cadiz. The roofs of Cadiz were white with the robes of the people who had turned out to keep a jumpy eye on the Norse in the harbor. And below, the streets were jammed with others, carrying their goods on their backs or leading pack animals, heading inland for safety. No one knew what either the wali or the Norse might do.

Haakon's men wore mail or leather shirts, and they went sword in hand, bows strung, and spears ready. As the Spanish sun rose higher, hotter, they began to perspire and grumble, but Haakon glared them into silence. They were in alien land, and although they had not been attacked so far, that could change from one grove of trees to the next. They settled in to march and marveled at the bright sky overhead, the *naranjas* and olives on the farms, and the village houses of whitened stone, with roofs of colored tile.

The villagers mostly scattered when they saw the Norse coming, but as they passed a third cluster of

white houses, there was a sudden spurt of shouts and
screams. The village dogs barked furiously, and Wulf
echoed them as smoke began to rise over the rooftops.

"Battle lines!" Haakon shouted.

They made a shield wall, and the wali's escort milled
around them uncertainly. If this was an ambush, they
didn't seem to know about it. Haakon relaxed a fraction
and looked curiously at the village as a score or so of
people in dusty, ragged clothes burst from between the
houses. More villagers were pursuing them, throwing
stones.

Ragnar cocked an ear to the shouting. "Those are
Christians. The others say that they have poisoned a
well and stolen from the wali's treasures by magic."

The Christians didn't look capable of stealing a sack of
oats. There were women and children with them, stumbling along as the men tried to shield their backs.

"Open the lines!" Haakon shouted. It was no quarrel
of theirs, but he remembered that Thor had implied
that mercy often counts for more than pride when the
god gave Haakon the ax as a reward for the jarl's mercy
to the *Wave Walker* crew. He thought the golden ax
head had begun to glow. It was hard to tell in the dusty
sunlight, but in any case he was not willing to stand by
and watch a slaughter.

If the Norsemen questioned his actions, they didn't
disobey; the Christians were too grateful for any refuge
to care who offered it. They ran through the gaps in the
shield wall and collapsed, panting, while the Norse
slammed their shields closed behind them.

"Now, then." Haakon stepped forward, ax in hand,
and the Moslem villagers halted a prudent distance
away. The wali's escorts still weren't doing anything.
They had no orders for such a contingency, and considering the temper the wali had been in lately, no one
wished to take a chance on trying to guess his wishes.

One of the Moslem villagers with more courage than

most raised his fist and shouted. Haakon didn't need an interpreter to translate *that*. He whistled. "Wulf—him!"

Wulf leaped from his position at Haakon's heel, and before the man knew what was coming, massive jaws full of sharp white teeth had fastened on his ankle. He screamed, then screamed again as Wulf pulled hard and tumbled him in the dusty road. Wulf stood over him growling, his eyes fixed hopefully on the man's throat and one ear cocked for Haakon's order. The man choked off his screams and hiccuped in fear. The mob backed off; spears and arrows they understood, but the dog was something out of hell.

Haakon chuckled. "Fetch."

The man began shrieking again as Wulf dragged him by his ankle across the rocky ground and deposited him proudly at Haakon's feet.

"A fine dog, that," Ragnar the Noseless said with some amusement.

Haakon looked at the man on the ground. "You are going with us to the wali Abdullah, and you may tell *him* why you were rousing a mob against defenseless folk."

The man screamed as if he had been impaled and started to get up. As he rose, Haakon drew his fist back and hit him carefully in the jaw. It seemed that the wali put a healthy fear in his subjects.

The man dropped down again with a moan, and they tied a cloak to two spears and dumped him on it. They moved on, with the unconscious man on his sling and the wali's escorts still carefully pretending that nothing had occurred. The Christians went with them, although some of them looked as if they weren't sure they hadn't fled from the devil they knew to a devil they didn't.

Abdullah 'ibn Numan had a premonition of a difficult situation the moment he heard that Haakon was bringing five hundred armed men with him to the meeting.

He would not call it a premonition of defeat—he was
still certain he could match wits with any Norseman
and come out ahead—but he found himself wishing he
had another thousand fighting men in and around Cadiz.
Wishing being no more useful now than usual, he also
did something more practical. He had Rosamund and
Gunnar brought out into the courtyard, both heavily
guarded, but both clearly visible. There'd never been
much chance to deny that Rosamund and Gunnar were
in Cadiz, not when Haakon knew about Red Ali. Now
at least the shoe would be on the other foot—Haakon
wouldn't be able to claim that they were sick or hurt.
And the Norse would be able to see that Rosamund and
Gunnar would probably live better in this land than
they did at home.

The wali's determination to meet with Haakon faltered
when they brought Rosamund out. He had ordered her
finely dressed, and she was beautiful enough to take his
breath away. Her pregnancy made her look even more
like Diana than ever. Diana had died in childbirth, and
the wali always remembered her pregnant. He swallowed
and turned his face away. He would not disgrace himself in the presence of a woman who had endured so
much and remained dry eyed through it all, but it was
no easy thing to face a beloved ghost, to see Diana back
again.

The captain of his guards coughed politely from the
main gate. "My lord Wali, the Norse have come. There
are a great many of them." He salaamed respectfully.
"Enough to surround the palace."

"So be it. Let this Haakon come in with whom he
chooses, and I will talk to him."

Including Ragnar the Noseless, Haakon took thirty
men with him, enough to make his point. Wulf paced
sedately at his side, ears pricked. Haakon examined the
wali with interest—a squarely built man, with the look

of a war chief, who sat in a carved wooden chair. A white-bearded man in a robe and an archer with a huge bow and arms like an ape stood beside the wali's chair. And behind him, in the shadow of a doorway, was Rosamund, with Gunnar beside her.

Rosamund gasped as she saw Haakon. Wulf let out a wild yelp, but Haakon's hand shot out for his collar. Pyotr, shielding the wali, unslung his bow.

"I will take weregild for the dog as I would for a man," Haakon said quietly, and Ragnar translated.

"I am the wali of Cadiz, and I did not think we were here to talk about dogs."

"That is a matter as much worth talking about as a man who steals another man's wife. An honest dog is worth more than a human thief." That was not polite, nor was it intended to be, and Ragnar gave Haakon a pointed look before he translated it. Seeing the wali's wrathful expression, Haakon thought that Ragnar might be right. It would be a mistake to make the wali so angry that he would do something foolish to prove he had more courage than a Norse chieftain.

"I do not mean yourself, of course, when I speak of thieves." Haakon smiled—friendly and reasonable. "I mean the man who stole Rosamund and Gunnar in the North. I will have my reckoning with him in time, but you have done nothing against me out of hatred, so I am prepared to be generous, knowing that when you bought these people, you did not know that they were mine."

The wali choked. "I did not. But I did buy them, lawfully in the sight of Allah and the ways of my people. And my laws. Do you think to set aside Allah's will, or the law of the wali of Cadiz?"

"Hmm! You will set yourself against *our* gods and *our* laws if you do not give them up, and that is not a safe thing to do. The man is my sworn friend, and the

woman is my lawful wife." That was only a small lie
about Rosamund, and Haakon certainly intended to
make it truth.

The wali looked at him coldly. "I have already taken
the woman as my wife." Haakon thought that the wali,
too, was lying. He risked a look at Rosamund and saw a
faint shake of her head.

"No woman may be taken to wife while she is already
married to another. At least not by our laws, and I do
not think yours are so different in this matter."

Silence. Haakon could accuse the wali of lying outright,
but it would probably start bloodshed. Haakon would
probably have fought if the wali had accused *him* of
lying. The fact that both of them were lying had nothing to do with it.

"Do you set yourself against your *own* laws?" Haakon
prodded.

More silence.

Haakon looked back at Rosamund. She was as pale as
a snowdrift, and there were beads of sweat on her
upper lip, but otherwise she looked ready to wait until
the end of the world if it took that long for Abdullah the
Stubborn to make up his mind.

Haakon decided that Rosamund had more patience
than he did. If the wali didn't yield in the time it took
to count to a hundred, blood was going to flow. Barely
moving his lips, Haakon started counting.

The wali Abdullah looked at the Norsemen carefully.
He could see the little twistings of muscle as Norse
hands tightened on bows, on spear shafts, and on sword
hilts. He looked back at Pyotr, whose free hand was
twitching as if it were ready of its own will to pull an
arrow from his quiver. Beside him was Yusuf, blank
faced and portentous, as usual. Whatever Yusuf might
be thinking, no man ever saw it in his face.

There were no more than thirty Norsemen behind
this stubborn chieftain. A single gesture would put an

end to all of them. But they were only a handful of the men who had followed this Haakon. Nearly five hundred more were at the gates of the wali's own palace, and as many again were doubtless still aboard those ships offshore, ready to strike at a city that he himself had left defenseless.

The wali could keep Rosamund and his pride only by sacrificing his land and people to these northern sea wolves. And when it was over, the people who were left would surely turn on him—he had enemies they could call on for aid. His rule would be short, his life would not last much longer, and maybe even his two daughters and their children would die for his pride. It would go that way, even if he survived the battle and every Norseman died.

And Rosamund, whom he and this Haakon stood bargaining for—what did she think of them? The wali found that he had to know.

He looked at her and broke the silence with a soft word, which might have been either a prayer or a curse.

She stood silent and straight, but her eyes were riveted on Haakon, and her face seemed to be lit from within. Abdullah knew that look. He had seen it on Diana's face when she looked at him—the look that only a most lucky man got, a man fortunate enough to find the one woman meant for him and for no other man in the world, a woman who would never give that look to any other man, even if she had to give her body.

Allah forgive me. I am blind. He could never keep Rosamund now. Other men might think he owned her, praise him for it, and feed his pride, but he would know otherwise and feel no pride where it mattered. *So it is written, and only a fool goes on fighting when he sees that.*

The wali cleared his throat. He was still not going to fall down and bow to this Norseman. "I have paid a

large sum for these people. In justice, I should receive
something in return."

Haakon looked thoughtful. Swallowing pride was always a hard thing for any man, and the wali of Cadiz
was reasonably proud. "I will give you half of what you
paid for them," he said. "Not because they are not
mine, but because we have caused some—inconvenience
in your city."

"That is an understatement, Haakon Norseman.
However, I will accept that." The wali swallowed and
turned to Rosamund and spoke French.

"Lady Rosamund, you are free, but I wish that you
should know in what way I think of you. Always you
would have been honored in my house."

Rosamund smiled, and his heart turned over. She had
never smiled at him before, and he saw the sun come
out in her face. "I know, lord," she said gently. "I am
sorry that you could not find your Diana again in me."

Abdullah 'ibn Numan was not known as the Wise for
no reason. He lifted his hand in farewell to her, and
Rosamund smiled again. Then she dashed across the
courtyard to throw herself into Haakon's arms. Gunnar
Thorsten followed at a more dignified pace, although
the wali wanted to laugh at how obviously the poet also
wished to run.

Rosamund's guards spoke no French and were caught
by surprise. Three tried to follow her. They had taken
no more than four steps when Wulf hurled himself into
their path, mouth open and fur bristling. His teeth
gleamed, his growls were like boulders grinding together in the surf, and his eyes seemed to be glowing red as
fire. Altogether he looked like something guarding the
damned in hell.

Pyotr nocked an arrow to his bow. The guards stopped
in their tracks, and one retreated so suddenly that he
backed into the drawn sword of a comrade. He yelled
and clapped both hands to his backside, and the wali

laughed, but he reached up a hand and snapped Pyotr's bow out of his hands. "You are too quick with that." He looked around him at his guards and the Norsemen, the two groups eyeing each other suspiciously. "The woman and the poet are freed," he said in Arabic, and waited for Ragnar to translate for the Norsemen. "By my will, there will be no blood between this man and me, and no man of mine will break that peace. This is clear? Good." The wali kept Pyotr's bow. He thought it would be no bad thing for Pyotr to stay unarmed. Turning to Haakon, he said, "Since we now have no more reason to be enemies, shall we seek ways to be friends?"

"I have nothing against that," Haakon said. "It depends on what the wali suggests."

"You can return what you stole from the ships of Cadiz, to begin with," the wali said firmly.

Haakon shook his head. "My men will not go home with no gain to show for the voyage. Likely they would sack your city when I left if I made them give it back. Also I swore fair payment to them. I will not make peace by breaking oaths."

"Hmm. It is not my wish that you break an oath." It occurred to the wali that if he confiscated the wealth of Red Ali and Abu Zayd, there should be enough to aid the merchants and the kin of the dead. After all, none of the merchants had actually *lost* his ships. But still ...

"Instead I will pay full price for what you were cheated of when you bought my wife," Haakon said.

"Done." The wali considered that he could up the sum by a reasonable amount.

Haakon grinned. Gunnar had been there, and he was willing to bet that Gunnar knew to a penny what had been paid.

"You will be my guests," the wali said, "you and your men—for enough time for a feast and sporting contests." And time to size up this troublesome Norseman and decide how far to go with their treaty. "And we shall pledge ourselves, you and I, to friendship, honesty, and peace."

"Done, and a fair bargain," Haakon said, "but there is one thing more. I have with my men some Christians from one of your nearby villages and a man who claims they have worked an evil magic, which I very much doubt. The rest of the village was throwing rocks, and that does not seem to me to be justice."

The guards who had escorted the Norsemen looked blank, as if they had noticed no Christians, and the wali glared at them. This was embarrassing. He thought that even Yusuf was looking annoyed, a most unusual display of emotion. "Our Christians have always lived in peace," he said carefully, "by my will. There must have been a reason for this. When I was a young man, there were Christians in Cordova who blasphemed Allah and said that Muhammad was a false prophet. They were useless creatures who sought martyrdom. I would not care to protect such fools."

"No. Men who ask for death cannot complain if someone obliges them," Haakon said. "But these do not strike me as fools, and they say they have lived at peace until today, and that someone is spreading evil tales about them. . . ." His voice trailed off, but he looked the wali in the eye. He had stopped, just short of telling the wali of Cadiz how to govern his city, in front of his own household.

The wali appreciated the tact but still took the message. Peace with the Norsemen would depend partly on whether he was seen to give justice to the Christians. Well, there was no harm in that. But how had it come about that this Norseman was standing here in his own courtyard and passing judgment on *him*?

He did not know and doubted he ever would. The will of Allah is not easily understood by mortal man. However, he did know one thing, which he did not expect to forget. He had made a great mistake in thinking this Jarl Haakon a barbarian and had paid a very light price for it.

XX

The feast hosted by Abdullah the Wise continued for most of the next two days. The harvest had been good, and it sometimes seemed that the wali was determined to feed all the Norse until they were so full they could not move a muscle or lift a weapon. One man from Birka made a witty verse of it, of how the men of Haakon the Dark would become the first band of Norse to be feasted to death; they were all in great charity with the wali and the wali's men as long as the food kept coming.

Nothing could have kept the men from stuffing themselves. It would be a long, cold voyage home, with little hope of getting hot food until they made landfall. They did grumble at the lack of pork, and even more at the lack of mead, ale, or wine. Another verse said that Arab men must be so weak in their manhood that they had to avoid rich meat and good drink in order to be able to satisfy their women, and Haakon shouted at the singer not to sing it again, or he would be able to count his teeth on one thumb.

The absence of wine was Haakon's idea. He knew that the Arabs of Spain did not observe Muhammad's prohibition of it, but he asked the wali to do so anyway while the Norse were at his table. For now Haakon's men felt kindly toward the world; some of them would change once the wine got into them. The Arabs would

be better off having their manhood insulted by sober
Norsemen than their shops wrecked and their wives
and daughters insulted by drunken ones.

Gunnar composed none of the verses. He walked
around silently, his thoughts obviously elsewhere, looking
long faced and gloomy for a man just snatched from
slavery. Haakon thought Gunnar might be waiting for
Haakon to challenge him for letting Rosamund be
abducted in the first place. To set his mind at ease,
Haakon made a point of saying he would not, but
Gunnar's mood didn't lighten, and Haakon had other
things on his mind just now besides a gloomy poet. One
was getting to know Rosamund all over again. A dozen
times during each night he would reach out and touch
her, to be sure she was really there, alive, breathing,
and warm. After he'd done that two nights running, he
began to believe that he really *had* found her, and that
her presence was not a trick played on him by some
malevolent god.

He spent most of each day bargaining with the wali
Abdullah. There would never be a better chance to win
trading rights in Cadiz. If the wali was willing to give
Haakon and Haakon's chosen traders freedom of his
harbor, it meant a great deal of wealth over the years. If
he could talk the wali into trade rights for *all* Norse, he
wouldn't get as wealthy from it, but he *would* get a
name to be remembered in all the Norse lands. The
kind of word-fame a man got from victories in trade was
not the same as war-fame, but it was still worth having.

The wali was willing to give Haakon a good part of
what he wanted, for a suitable price, but he firmly
declined to open his harbors to all Norse. He would
give Haakon and any Norseman who had sworn friendship with Haakon such rights as any foreign traders had
in Cadiz. These were substantial, and in exchange
Haakon would give his protection in Norse lands to

traders from Cadiz or any others to whom the wali wished to extend his friendship.

Haakon thought it over from all sides. The wali clearly wanted to become the protector of Spanish Arabs trading with the Norse. For this protection he would doubtless charge a suitable price, of which Haakon would not get one brass piece. At the same time he would be asking Haakon to assume a heavy burden, including some danger of blood-feud with anyone who slew an Arab.

On the other hand, Haakon would then become the protector of Norsemen trading with Cadiz, and he could ask his own price for the necessary oaths of friendship. In particular, he could ask it of King Harald Fairhair, and that might be useful, although the king wouldn't like it. King Harald of Vestfold wished to push his influence and his rule into the Trondelag, and the Trondelag did not wish to have him. An agreement with Cadiz would give Haakon a sharp spear to wave under Harald's nose.

The more Haakon thought about it, the more he came to believe that what Abdullah the Wise was offering him was worth having. So Haakon agreed, they thrashed out the last of the details, and the bargain was made under the disapproving gaze of Yusuf 'ibn Khalid, who seemed to Haakon to be everywhere. Yusuf's disapproval did not appear to bother the wali, but it made Haakon suspicious. Was the astrologer in a position to force his master to break the agreement afterward, or would he act on his own to make the life of Norse traders in Cadiz unbearable? Haakon wondered. He didn't like Yusuf's weasel face. Haakon decided to ask Rosamund and Gunnar what they thought.

Rosamund honestly didn't know. She had heard how Yusuf had gained his influence, but in the harem they did not talk much about what he'd done with it since.

Gunnar said that Yusuf would be no friend to the
Norse, or to anyone else who might detract from his
own power with the wali. He also added gloomily that
he didn't know what they could do about it. Haakon
threw up his hands in exasperation and went off to see
that his men hadn't got into any wine, which was a
more immediate problem.

Gunnar sat down to see if some brilliant idea about
Yusuf had come to him in the last few moments and
found that none had. Yusuf would certainly do his best
to smash the agreement and sow trouble between Arab
and Norseman as soon as he saw his chance. Anything
that made the wali stronger and gave him new friends,
Yusuf saw as something that made his own position
weaker, and he might even be right. Abdullah 'ibn
Numan was not the sort of man to be ridden with a
tight rein forever, and Yusuf was a jealous man.

Gunnar could kick Yusuf's feet out from under him if
he could reveal his treacherous thefts, but Yusuf could
conceal the stolen goods faster than Gunnar could
convince the wali to investigate, no doubt. Then Gunnar
would look like a treacherous troublemaker, and the
wali would certainly wish to put his head up on a spike.
And that would most certainly ruin Haakon's treaty. No
one would gain anything but Yusuf.

He thought it through again, and it came out the
same. On the morning of the wali's games, he was still
wondering if this was a risk he wanted to take.

The wali and Haakon had been careful to choose
contests that would give neither Norse nor Arab a clear
advantage. They wanted only sweat spilled today, not
blood, and Haakon had a clear memory of the games
between his own men and Ivar Egbertsson's.

The day began with spear-throwing, each side using
the spears they were accustomed to. The lighter Arab
spears weren't as well designed for throwing, and there

was enough wind to make the heavier Norse spears fly straighter. After the Norse completely won that round, Abdullah's captain of guards, sullen, gave his men a look with teeth in it.

Prompted maybe by that, the Arabs decided to give the Norse spears a try. The Arabs proved quick to learn to handle the other side's weapons and won back every point they'd lost in the first round. Both sides swarmed cheerfully down to the beach for the swimming contest.

Haakon limited that to ten men on a side because far more Norse than Arabs could swim. But the Arabs who were at home in the water swam like fish. The first four swimmers were two Arabs and two Norse, and they were so close together when they passed the floating barrel at the finish that the judges gratefully declared a tie.

After that, tempers stayed even, and the wali and Haakon congratulated themselves on an afternoon to cement friendship. The Arabs won the wrestling contest. All but one of them were smaller than their Norse opponents, but they were faster and trickier, and they won seven falls out of ten.

The Norse were the victors in the running contest. The Arabs were not slow footed—and they were more used to the heat—but the longer legs of the Norse gave them an advantage that could not be taken away as long as they were determined to use it. After the defeat in the wrestling, each Norse runner covered the course as if his own life and the lives of all his kin depended on being first.

"Now they will all be too tired to make trouble," Haakon said, and the wali laughed.

By now a fair-sized crowd had gathered to watch the contests from beyond a line of Norse and Arab guards. Parents held children up to watch, loud-voiced men sold bread and fruit from carts, and a herd of goats being driven to market bleated angrily as they were caught in the crowd. Relieved of their terror of the Norsemen, the people of Cadiz turned out curious to see the blond barbarians up close.

Who won the stone-throwing depended on what one considered important, accuracy or distance. The Arabs hit the marks more often, and the Norse threw farther. But the precarious friendship was growing more solid: Good throws by either side were cheered in Norse and Arabic.

Haakon also saw that his own men were cheering each other on without regard to who had followed him last year and who had followed Ivar Egbertsson. They were all his men now and seemed to have forgotten that they'd ever been anything else. Clearly this was a good-luck day.

The luck nearly didn't survive the horse race, but the wali Abdullah the Wise proved his name, and Haakon threatened darkly to knock heads together, and matters subsided. The trouble arose because even those Norse who were normally at home on horseback were unprepared for the fine-bred, nervy Arab mounts, and the horses took an equal exception to them. All but two of the Arab riders crossed the finish line before the first of the Norsemen, and only five of the Norsemen finished the race at all. Luckily there were no major injuries to either men or horses—if the Norse couldn't stay on them, they could at least fall off without too much damage. Only Kalki Estridsson seemed really hurt, and the wali's own physician came to examine him. Kalki had struck his head, and the physician said he should lie still for some days, but he could go aboard ship and would probably be a well man before he got home.

The physician salaamed and departed in haste before the Norse could decide to demand some surety for that, and the wali raised his hand. "We of Spain are clearly masters of the land," he intoned, "but the Norse are equally masters of the horses of the sea." He made a wide gesture, taking in the longships, which, he knew, rested off the shore of Cadiz. "There, on the sea, there is much that we can learn from you."

Knut looked at Kalki's slumped form being carried off by Hjalmar and Thorfinn Solvisson. "Ah, well," he said. "It was his own fool fault, for getting up on the silly beast in the first place."

No pleasant speeches could improve Gunnar Thorsten's mood. If the seven loveliest houris of the Moslem paradise had appeared before him, each carrying a bag of gold for him and wearing nothing else, he would have asked them only, "Do *you* know what we can do about Yusuf 'ibn Khalid?" Certainly he still didn't have even a faint idea.

The crowd was now so huge that Norse and Arab guards had to join forces to push them back far enough for the men setting up the archery targets to do their work. Gunnar walked aimlessly along the milling edge of the crowd until he saw something that finally, miraculously, gave him an idea. It was a cart, drawn by two mules, and filled with pots packed in straw. The pots were all of a pattern that Gunnar had seen in the tunnel, and one of the carters was a man he'd seen carrying them.

Gunnar grinned. Yusuf was using the confusion of the games to get his ill-gotten goods out of the way. Certainly they must have been stacking up dangerously while the Norse blocked the harbor. So now the evidence was under the wali's nose, and if Gunnar could expose it, Yusuf wouldn't be able to cover it up quickly enough. The pots surely had contraband in them—if the pots had only air in them, Gunnar didn't want to think about the wali's reaction. He squinted his eyes—he was almost sure, but if he got any closer the carter would recognize him, and if he got suspicious and started a row, there could well be a riot. Gunnar looked wildly around for inspiration, and his eye lit on the archery targets—Hagar the Simple, who was first up and who could hit anything! Gunnar dived back through the crowd to Hagar.

It was a mark of how Hagar's mind worked that he never said a word of protest about being called the Simple, even though Gunnar suspected he wasn't lacking in his wits. Hagar merely felt that as long as the world contained bows, arrows, and something to shoot at, there was very little else to talk about. He listened patiently as Gunnar explained what he wanted done, then nodded and said: "You play for high stakes."

Gunnar couldn't have produced a better summary of the matter if he'd thought about it for days. The stakes might include his own life if he was wrong—at least the wali would probably ask for it. Haakon would undoubtedly not grant it, but Gunnar knew that peace between Norse and Arab might depend on his going quietly to his death, no matter what Haakon said. If he started a riot and jeopardized the treaty, he might have it coming.

Gunnar sweated through the opening formalities, praying that the cart wouldn't get out of range and trying not to look at Hagar, who was trying not to look at the cart. He would probably have the chance for no more than one shot, certainly no more than two. Both had to look like accidents, and neither could be allowed to hit an Arab or there *would* be trouble, whether Gunnar was right or wrong.

The judges nodded; Hagar nocked his arrow, raised the bow, and pretended to stumble. The shaft went wide, clipped one of the mules in the ear, and broke a pot. The mule reared, tipped the carters off their perch, and overturned the cart in a shower of Arabic curses and broken pots. Gunnar ran for the wreckage.

The carters were frantically snatching up armfuls of pots, and the mules were jigging hysterically and braying. The crowd gathered around interestedly, trying to help and getting in the way.

Gunnar knelt and scooped up jagged pieces. A jewel gleamed in one, and Gunnar gave a shout of triumph. One of the potters dropped what he was carrying and came for Gunnar with a knife. Gunnar threw a piece of pot at the man and flung his left arm up in time to keep the knife's point out of his ribs. The blade slid down his arm and cut it nearly to the bone. Gunnar yelped, and the arm hung uselessly, pouring blood. He couldn't get his own knife out without dropping his precious piece of pot, so he backed away from the carter and shouted for the guards.

Haakon and the wali shouted at their men with nearly one voice, and guards converged on the carter in such numbers that he completely disappeared under their bodies in a cloud of dust. Gunnar stood swaying, his left arm bloody from shoulder to wrist. Then for good measure four more guards ran up to grab him. He looked at them blankly and collapsed, still clutching his piece of pot.

By this time it was obvious that more than a private fight was involved. The wali began pushing his way through the crowd, intent on the cause of this chaos. He nearly died for it.

Like the wali, everyone was watching the row. No one was watching Yusuf or Pyotr except Hagar the Simple. Gunnar had said not to trust them, and Hagar didn't. He saw Yusuf blink twice at the big archer. Pyotr pivoted with grace surprising for his size. Then his eyes locked on Hagar: Pyotr didn't trust Hagar either, and rightly so. One hand scooped up his bow, and the other drew an arrow. Hagar didn't move until Pyotr was nocking the arrow and looking at it.

Pyotr's elbow was drawing back and the arrow was pointing ominously at the wali when Hagar seemed to become a blur of arms and legs, with an arrow suddenly flying from the middle of it. It sank into Pyotr's back as he released his own shaft, and Pyotr's arrow sang wide of the wali's head and buried itself in a mule's backside. The mule reared and began kicking the cart to pieces. Pyotr staggered, went down on his knees, and looked very surprised as he died. Leaning on his bow, Hagar, "the Simple," looked around to see what would happen now.

Yusuf 'ibn Khalid saw the wali spin around as the arrow went by, and the astrologer saw his own death written clearly on the air. He hiked up his robes and ran. Hagar swore. He couldn't shoot without a good chance of hitting someone in the crowd.

"Jarl Haakon!" Hagar pointed toward the crowd.

Haakon had reached the cart, and his men and the wali's were beginning to push the crowd back when he heard Hagar's shout. Then he saw Yusuf explode out of the press of spectators, running for his horse, a hundred paces away. Haakon snatched the golden ax from its sling, swung it around his head to get up speed, and threw. It smashed broadside into Yusuf's back between the shoulder blades and sent the astrologer sprawling. Before he could get up, Haakon was on him, both hands around his neck. Yusuf struggled like a madman, but Haakon was half again his weight, considerably younger, and just as determined. Finally Yusuf went limp. Haakon stood up, scratched and dusty, just in time to face Abdullah the Wise. "What pig-spawned idiocy is this?" the wali said in an awful voice.

Haakon knew enough Arabic to translate that. "None," he said. Ragnar appeared, looking appalled, and Haakon went on. "Gunnar generally knows what he's doing." He hoped he did.

"Then let him say what that was," the wali requested acidly. He looked at his guards. "Get that arrow out of that beast and find out where it came from."

Gunnar was in no condition to say anything. But the wali's men dumped Yusuf, both carters, and an arrow that was unmistakably Pyotr's at their master's feet.

They pried Gunnar's piece of pot out of his fingers, and the wali looked at it most thoughtfully.

The carters looked at the wali's wrathful expression and became eager to implicate their former patron. They were "but poor men, O Defender of the Unfortunate," and helpless in the hands of Yusuf the Astrologer, who had the evil eye and would have cursed them had they disobeyed.

"Where you are going, the evil eye will not trouble you," Abdullah said. The guards dragged the wailing carters away, someone picked up Yusuf's limp form to lock up until such time as he could talk, and the wali's physician arrived to stitch up Gunnar's arm.

The wali looked from Haakon to Yusuf. "Most instructive," he said briefly and turned on his heel.

XXI

By sunset Gunnar was conscious enough to hear the pleasant news that Yusuf 'ibn Khalid had realized he had nothing to lose by confessing except long and painful sessions with the wali's torturers. A messenger came to Haakon to inform him of that and added that Yusuf would be publicly executed, with those who had helped him. To be included were Abu Zayd, former captain of the port, the cart drivers, and a network that proved to stretch throughout the wali's palace. Pyotr was already dead. The messenger sounded regretful.

"It is my lord's belief that if the Kaasites hear their champion was a common thief, they will not say too much against his death."

Not knowing who the Kaasites were, Haakon said solemnly that he hoped that was true. When Gunnar had explained it, he hoped so indeed. A treaty allowing for trading privileges in a city torn apart by civil war would not be worth much to anyone.

In the evening another messenger appeared, summoning Haakon, Gunnar, and Rosamund to the wali's presence for a final audience and an exchange of gifts. They went with Ragnar, their interpreter, in the best clothes they had, Rosamund in the harem clothes the wali had given her, since that was all she had. They found the wali alone except for his guards, in a small chamber with a blue tile floor that softly reflected the light of half a dozen torches in bronze holders. He sat on a couch with guards at either end and looked considerably older and more tired than when Haakon had seen him last.

"I regret that we have been the cause of your losing a friend," Haakon said. It seemed tactful to express some regret over Yusuf's fate.

The wali shrugged. "It must be as it is written. I cannot mourn for a friend who has turned thief. His honor was dead long before his body, so what could his life have been like?"

That seemed unanswerable.

The wali handed Haakon two scrolls. "The agreement we have reached. One copy is in Arabic, one in French. I understand that the way of writing among the Norse is slow, so I do not ask for copies from you now. But send them to me with the first of your sworn friends. In the meantime, my chief men and yours will be witnesses to what we swear."

"Your trust honors us, and yourself," Haakon said politely.

"I thank you," Abdullah said. He looked at Haakon tiredly. "I think that you will go a long way, my friend. You are a very strong wind, and difficult to stand against. It would not surprise me to hear one day that there is a crown on your head."

Haakon felt a little cold breath on his back at that. Never a crown, Thor had said. Never a crown, or die. He smiled. "That also will be as it is written. Crowns have brought bad luck to many men, I can endure well enough without one."

"Perhaps you are wise. Certainly I would not wish a friend a crown. But there are other gifts in my power." He clapped his hands, and a bustle of servants appeared in the doorway.

The wali's gifts were rich, befitting a man of pride—lengths of embroidered silk and entire bolts of fine wool, silver cups, and a curved sword with a jeweled scabbard. A slave bowed low and presented Haakon with a chain of gold links, each as large as a man's thumb, hung with enameled golden disks.

For Rosamund there were three rich gowns in the Arab style—which Haakon suspected might prove sadly lacking in warmth in a Norse winter—and a small chest. The chest was nearly filled with silver coins. Nestled among the coins was a necklace of fine amber, worth a longship all by itself.

For Gunnar there were also new clothes and a dark-haired girl, who salaamed and kissed his foot. Gunnar turned red.

"Her name is Riziya," the wali said. "She knows all the suitable skills."

Rosamund wondered what those might be.

Gunnar looked at the girl dubiously. "Lord Wali, I am hardly worthy—"

"We are grateful," Haakon said hastily. To refuse would be an insult, and he did not think that insulting the wali, even now, was a particularly safe thing to do. He wondered what Guthrun was going to think of Riziya. Ragnar the Noseless was laughing.

"We are grateful," Haakon said again. He wished he knew what to give the wali in return. He couldn't take away from his men's share of the loot. That would get

him an ugly and ill-omened name. Besides, it had been
stolen from Cadiz, and that might not be tactful.

The wali smiled. "I understand that you may find
some difficulty in offering a suitable gift. You came to
Cadiz prepared to fight a war rather than make peace.
However, I am a collector of fine weapons. Your ax with
its golden head is like no other I have seen. If that can
be your gift to me, I could ask no other."

Haakon unslung the golden ax and held it out in front
of him because he didn't know what else to do. He said
carefully, "Lord Abdullah, this is an ax sacred to the
gods of the Norse. I have sworn many oaths on it. Will
it be fit for your house, in which you worship Allah?"

"There is no god but Allah," replied the wali. "So if
this ax is sacred at all, it has Allah's blessing. It will find
a place of honor in my house, I assure you." He looked
pleasant and determined.

Haakon felt himself sweating. Even if this peace were
Thor's will, would the god let his ax go to the Arab?
And if he wouldn't, what was going to happen? Haakon
was greatly reluctant to wake Thor's temper, especially
if it burned Abdullah the Wise. He motioned to a guard
and held out the ax to him, deciding that the guard was
more expendable than the wali. Gunnar, he noticed,
was watching him nervously.

The guard came forward, reached for the ax—and it
jerked itself away just before his fingers touched it. The
guard decided this hadn't really occurred and reached
out again.

The ax flipped away.

The guard looked all around, not meeting anyone's
eyes. He seemed to hope the answer might be written
on the walls of the room. Then he took a deep breath
and reached for the ax with both hands, while Haakon
locked his muscles to hold the weapon in place.

The ax pulled itself up out of the guard's reach until

it was nearly vertical. Haakon almost lost his grip completely.

Rosamund's eyes opened wide, and he thought she crossed herself.

The guard backed away, staring at the ax as if it were a snake as Haakon lowered it to the floor. He was tempted to push it out in front of him with his toe and invite the guard to pick it up, if only to see what would happen. He decided against it. Things were strange enough already. And Thor was keeping his temper admirably, but his wish was quite clear, and you never knew. The guards were staring wide eyed and were making signs against the evil eye.

The wali Abdullah looked as if he knew what he'd seen but wasn't positive that it had really happened. He looked from the ax to Haakon's face and back again.

Haakon decided he had best break the silence before the ax did something else. "Lord Abdullah, it seems that it is—someone's—will that the ax remain in my hands. I would gladly honor you with it, but it seems to me that it would be an ill-omened gift." His poet was giving it a look of great respect, Haakon saw, and his wife was now firmly pretending that it didn't exist.

"I have heard you praise our longships," Haakon said. "Our horses of the sea." From somewhere inspiration had come. "I will give you one, with everything aboard her that does not belong to the men themselves. May she carry your banner proudly, and may none but brave men ever walk her decks." Ragnar translated, and his look said firmly, not *my* ship.

The wali smiled. A most acceptable gift. He said so, with polite formality, and Haakon breathed a sigh of relief. Paying the ship's owner would probably take most of his own gains from the voyage. But he had come for Rosamund and not for silver. Haakon thought he had the best end of the bargain: *He* had Rosamund.

From the wistful look on the wali's face when he looked
at Rosamund, it was evident that Abdullah the Wise
thought so too.

The wali pressed an invitation to stay another night
in the palace, and Haakon accepted because Ragnar
whispered that it would be tactful. He sent Rosamund
back to the ship with Gunnar and the wali's gifts, and
orders to select the smallest longship and arrange for
her people to be divided up among the other ships.

When they had left, the wali and Haakon and Ragnar
settled in to linger over their wine and talk trade,
comfortable now that all bargains were struck. It was
late when Haakon and Ragnar went away to their
rooms.

The wali sipped a little more wine, alone, when they
had gone, and then called for his chief wife, Aurora, to
share his bed. She was no longer beautiful, but she had
been his wife for a long time, and had given him his
eldest daughter and a son who'd died as a baby. And
now she gave him good advice, wit, and massages that
soothed him. Tonight he needed that, not to lie awake
and think about Rosamund—who had not been Diana,
after all.

Haakon parted from Ragnar outside his door and
looked at the bed. It was a fine affair of silks and
hangings, and it made him feel boxed in, as if he were
choking. Rosamund had thought it a wonderful bed,
but Rosamund was on *Red Hawk* tonight, and the more
Haakon looked at it, the more he didn't like it. Finally
he took half the bedding, dumped it on the floor on the
other side of the room, and curled up in it.

He was just falling asleep when a faint scraping at the
window jolted him awake. Reaching out for the golden
ax, he rolled clear of the bedclothes. There was a
shadow, dark against this side of the window, and he

heard the hiss of a sword cutting air. It thumped into the rest of the coverlets on the bed, and Haakon heard the swordsman curse as he realized there was no body beneath them.

Haakon got to his feet cautiously, the golden ax ready. He swung it upward silently to strike. Moonlight came through the window, golden light blazed from the axhead. The swordsman stopped, blade raised, and peered through the semidarkness.

Haakon began to get his night sight. His attacker was a young man, half a head taller than Haakon. He wore dark rough clothes that might have suggested poverty, but the sword in his hands said otherwise. It was a magnificent weapon, less curved than most Arab swords, and in the moonlight Haakon saw the fine silver wire wound around the hilt.

He had seen Haakon now, and with hands on his sword, he began to speak in a low, anger-filled voice. Haakon's Arabic didn't go much beyond the words "Abu Zayd" and "Norsemen."

"Dead," the man said, and spat at him.

Haakon understood that, but there didn't seem much answer to make to it. He pointed at the window.

"Go."

The man laughed. The laughter had a harsh, hysterical note. He leaped over the bedding, swinging at Haakon. He'd come to fight, and there was nothing for Haakon to do but fight back.

The man was virtually chasing him around the room. The swordsman had a longer reach and the strength and determination of a berserker. The tip of the sword slashed Haakon's clothing, and he swore and dodged. When the sword struck the head of the ax, sparks flew, and the room echoed with the clang. The blade bit into the handle of the ax, and chips sprayed into Haakon's face. Somehow the man kept him from the door.

Haakon wondered where the guards the wali had

posted were. Had they been surprised in their sleep by
accomplices and killed? Or drugged? Or only bribed to
be deaf? And if so, by whose order? The swordsman
came after him again, and Haakon realized that he was
alone in this. That meant getting in close with the
ax—not easy against a supple, fast-moving sword. Even
a minor wound could put him at a fatal disadvantage, he
thought as he lifted the ax, ready to move in. It was
better to take the offensive than try to talk sense and
risk being cut to pieces in this little room.

He charged, grappled with the man, and leaped back
panting as the swordsman too jumped back out of the
ax's murderous arc and swung his sword. Haakon could
feel the sweat running down into his eyes, and he shook
his head. His hands and shirt were wet with it, and he
knew that if he weren't careful he would slip on the
slick tile floor. The little room was stifling, even with
the faint sea breeze that came through the open window.
The fight seemed to be taking hours, and he knew that
he would tire soon. And when the swordsman saw it,
that would be the end. He tried to force himself to
maintain an impossible level of endurance, and as if to
mock that, the tip of the sword took skin from his ribs
so that he felt blood ooze.

He began to lose track of the course of the fight,
blocking the sword strokes automatically in that stifling
box of a room, always with the swordsman between him
and the door. But he gradually found that his weary
muscles were still responding, as if something gave new
strength to his legs and arms, even though to him they
felt like lead. The haft of the golden ax was warm and
alive in his hand.

The swordsman now was tiring, and he began to look
at Haakon and the ax with puzzlement. He was younger
than Haakon, and bigger, and Haakon should have
flagged first. But still the ax blocked his sword blows,

and it seemed somehow that the blade itself glowed with more than the moonlight.

The swordsman's breath came in ragged gasps now, and his feet were unsteady. Haakon backed up just a little, to let him run if he wanted to, but the swordsman came on. Haakon realized he was facing the most dangerous of opponents—the man who is willing to die if he can also kill. He shifted his grip on the ax and then moved in to finish the matter.

The swordsman dropped across the bed, with a mortal wound in his thigh and another in his stomach, and his face twisted into a ghastly mask. He had only the strength to curse Haakon as he died.

Ragnar appeared in the doorway, with the wali's guards, somewhat belatedly. "That is the son of Abu Zayd, the port captain," he said, as the man spouted out his final sentence.

"The port captain?" Haakon leaned wearily against the wall and gave the wali's guards an awful look that made them quail.

"Yes. His father was executed, and this one blames it on us." Ragnar looked down at the body. "'Stinking pig-eating Norsemen,' was what he said just now. He wanted vengeance."

He nearly got it, Haakon thought. He looked at the wali's guards again. "I think we have had enough of the hospitality of Abdullah the Wise, who plainly still has Yusuf's spies in his palace. I expect he will find them." The guards flinched. "You may explain all this to him in the morning, if you have the courage."

By dawn the gift ship lay abandoned on the shore, and the other twenty-two longships were well out to sea.

XXII

Haakon's fleet had weather-luck all the way north across the Bay of Biscay, no small gift at that time of year. The bay was a vicious body of water at the best of times, with all its winds blowing onto lee shores. The early autumn was *not* the best of times, although it was somewhat better than the late autumn, and as for winter, only a man who was desperate or mad sailed the bay in the teeth of its harsh gales.

But having had their luck there, they lost it off the capes of Brittany, where France jutted far out into the open ocean. Like a woman with a long skirt, Brittany trailed a mass of reefs, shoals, and jagged rocks, which would gut unwary ships well out at sea. They were still off the Breton coast when the wind died and fog wrapped the fleet like a blanket. These were dangerous waters for groping blindly, and Haakon knew there were only two choices. They could make their way into shallow water, drop the anchor stones, and wait for the fog to lift. Or they could break out the oars and row out to sea. There was no way to steer through the reefs in the fog, but they could set a course away from them with a sunstone, a translucent piece of Iceland spar that clouded when it was turned to the sun.

Haakon decided on that. It meant more work but also more sea room when the wind rose again. If the ships were anchored when the wind came up, they might find themselves too close to a rock-fanged lee shore.

The oars slid through the leather flaps over the oar

ports, and the ships crept westward across the glassy surface. By peering down to see how long a chip of wood thrown overboard from the bow would take to pass the stern, Haakon had a fair judgment of *Red Hawk*'s speed. She was moving fast enough that by nightfall they should be in deep water.

The blanket around the ships faded from pale gray to dark gray, and from dark gray to black. Haakon munched a piece of fish pickled in olive oil from Cadiz, crawled into his sleeping bag beside Rosamund, and let *Red Hawk*'s rocking lull them both to sleep.

He awoke suddenly with darkness all around except for a faint grayness ahead and an even fainter light, closer at hand, that he knew all too well. The head of the golden ax was glowing softly. When he touched the handle, he felt the power in it. The god was using his messenger, but what was the message?

Shielding the glowing head with his cloak, Haakon crawled out of the bag and went forward. It never hurt to have a clear view ahead. When he reached the bow, he pulled the ax out, looked around for any curious eyes, and held the ax out over the side.

The golden light blazed up suddenly, like a fire doused with pitch. Haakon blinked and drew the ax back to feel the head. It was cold and damp like any other metal at sea on such a night. He held it out again, this time over the other side. The glow fluttered and died. He repeated the test until he had turned in a full circle. It was enough to tell him that when the ax was held over the starboard bow, it glowed more strongly than in any other direction. Whatever it was that the god wished to show him, it lay to starboard.

So, very probably, did enough reefs and shoals to wreck the whole fleet and drown every man. If Thor did not know that, he was not the patron of sailors that he claimed to be. Haakon leaned on the shields slung along *Red Hawk*'s side and thought it over. Then he saw that the grayness ahead was growing lighter. It wasn't just dawn coming; the fog was actually thinning out. That made a difference. But Haakon wasn't going through those reefs unless the fog burned off enough for safety, not with Rosamund in the ship and other ships following him.

If the gods wish it otherwise, let them take the golden ax back and give it to a thrall.

By dawn the fog was nearly gone, the sky was clearing, and the fleet was sailing close-hauled in a freshening breeze. Haakon grinned. He didn't care to argue with a god if he didn't have to. With a little help from the rowers, he steered *Red Hawk* through the fleet until she was on the far starboard side. That should put him closest to whatever there was to see.

The morning passed. Nothing. By noon Haakon was beginning to wonder if there was going to *be* anything to see. His stomach was reminding him that he'd eaten nothing since last night's fish, when a shout came from the lookout forward.

"*Hoaaaa*, Haakon! A flag off the starboard bow! Can't see a ship, though."

Haakon hurried forward, and Rosamund came up to join him in the bow. Looking off to starboard, Haakon couldn't see a ship either, only something that did look very much like a flag on a pole. It seemed to come and go as the spray of breaking waves veiled it. Straining his eyes, Haakon saw what looked like wet, black rock, and when the waves receded, he thought there were broken ship timbers.

A shipwreck and survivors on the reef?

The shipwreck seemed certain, the survivors likely. Or at least likely enough that Haakon knew what the ax's message had been.

It wasn't going to be easy. Beyond the flag lay more reefs and rocks. Rescuers would have to get upwind of the shipwreck and drift down to it. Not too close, either—the spray shot up higher than a ship's mast from the force of the waves on the reef. Too close, and there would be two shipwrecks instead of one.

They had a good deal of time to think about the problem as *Red Hawk* beat her way past the flag. By the time they were ready to douse the sail and break out the oars, Haakon had had an empty meal barrel dragged out and leather stretched and nailed over the end to make it watertight. They threaded a hundred paces' worth of walrus-hide rope through two holes cut in the barrel and sealed them with more leather. With the barrel to hold it up, the rope should float through the breakers to the wreck. Anyone alive on the reef could grab it and be hauled back to *Red Hawk*, with the barrel to keep him afloat.

It was as good an answer as the time allowed. The wind was rising, and not only *Red Hawk* but the whole fleet would soon be too close to a lee shore for comfort. Haakon hailed *Wave Walker* and *Dragon Queen* and ordered them to stay close to *Red Hawk* but farther from the reef. If *Red Hawk* drifted too close to the reef, they were to throw lines on her and start towing. With three sets of rowers at work, Haakon was confident he could snatch at least *Red Hawk* from the rocky jaws, if not the shipwrecked survivors.

With Haakon himself at the steering oar, *Red Hawk* drifted toward the reef, and the oarsmen worked to keep her heading into the waves. Haakon didn't want a rolling deck underfoot as he tried to haul half-drowned men aboard.

They were close enough to be drenched in the spray from the breakers when Haakon finally shouted, "Now— hold her here!" The barrel dropped overboard, dragging the rope after it. By now they could see three bodies, or what looked like bodies, on the reef, and one man sitting up. Haakon hoped the man wasn't too far gone to grip the rope and hold on. If the barrel wasn't

smashed to pieces on the reef, he thought, watching it
bob wildly in the breakers.

The barrel survived its dangerous passage. One wave
larger than the rest carried it right over the lower rocks
and dropped it on top of the reef. When the wave
receded, two of the bodies had gone with it, but the
sitting man was on hands and knees. He looked half-
drowned and unaware of the barrel.

"Grab it, you!—" Haakon bellowed. The wind snatched
his words away. One more strong wave would smash
the barrel or carry it off the reef again. Haakon began to
think that either he would have to swim in through the
surf with another rope or watch the man die before his
eyes.

Then the man rose to his knees and fumbled at the
barrel. Haakon realized that he was tying a piece of
rope of his own to the barrel's rope. Now he would stay
with it as long as the knots held, even if he lost his grip.
A clear thinker, that one, to raise the flag and keep
rope by him on the chance of rescue, and a strong man,
still to be moving about after his shipmates were dead.

As they watched, he finished tying himself to the
barrel, lifted it in his arms, and stood up. When the
next large wave rolled in, he leaped out as far as he
could. The leap propelled him past most of the sharp
rocks, and the barrel protected him from the rest until
the receding wave carried him into open water. They
pulled the rope in, shouting at him to hang on.

By the time the half-drowned man was hauled aboard,
Red Hawk was dangerously close to the reef. The other
two ships were ready to throw their lines and start
towing, when Haakon saw that the reef made a sharp
angle just to the north. That way lay a good half mile
more of open water before the rocks. The rowers put
their backs in it, and they got the ship around the
angle, with *Wave Walker* and *Dragon Queen* keeping
pace. Beyond it was more time and sea room to throw

their lines, but it seemed to Haakon that he was five years older before they were safely out to sea again.

It was only then that he had time for the rescued man. Haakon found him forward, with Rosamund watching over him. He wore someone's spare shirt and was wrapped in a sleeping bag. An empty bowl lay on the deck beside him. His eyes were open, and they turned toward Haakon with a bright curiosity. Haakon thought that he looked more alive now than he had at first.

"You are the chief who saved me?"

"I am."

"Then I have had a true vision. I saw you, lord, last night when I crawled ashore. So I shall keep my vow." The man's Norse was good, but accented, much like the Arab traders of Birka. He was a slight man, long nosed and dark haired, with dark hawk's eyes.

"What vow?" Haakon said.

"I shall build you a great ship, as Allah wishes it. The greatest ever to sail. A great ship." He tried to repeat the phrase, but the words came out slurred. The third time, his lips only moved, and no sound came out. His eyes drifted shut.

Haakon thought there were too many gods in this matter for comfort, but maybe the man was mad.

"He's sleeping again," Rosamund said. "He woke up once before and ate porridge. He says he is Yazid of Alexandria, a shipbuilder, and he has worked here in the North for many years."

So maybe he was not mad. And maybe he would build Haakon a ship—if he remembered his vow when he awoke and Haakon held him to it. Certainly his coming had not been ordinary. Haakon looked down at the Arab thoughtfully.

XXIII

By the time the fleet rounded the capes of Brittany
and headed up the channel to the North Sea, Yazid was
on his feet again. He did not talk much, which might
have been a sign of mourning for his dead shipmates, or
maybe only weariness. When he did speak, it was plain
that he knew ships and the sea. So maybe it didn't
really matter whether he could build a ship or not. He
appeared to be a useful man, and if Thor had sent him,
it was no doubt with a purpose. Haakon looked at
Rosamund's round figure standing in the bow and decided that he wasn't interested in worrying over that now.
He was interested in going home.

The fleet entered the Bay of the Seine to take on
fresh water, divide the booty, and give the men a
chance for hot food and some time ashore. The allied
ships from the Norse settlements took leave of Haakon
there, as did one ship from the Trondelag and one from
the Baltic. Their chiefs had a mind to try their luck with
Hrolf Gänger, and to winter in France would make an
earlier start in the spring. The rest of the ships from
Birka left Haakon off the Danish coast, to make their
way home by the inshore route along the coast of
Jutland.

There was much goodwill on both sides at the parting.
Haakon had brought them wealth, luck, and easy victories,
been fair in distributing the loot and dividing the work,
and left no man who followed him with less reputation.
There was very little more that a Norseman could ask of
a jarl; Haakon heard this praise so often that he became

gruff to conceal his pride. He muttered into his beard until Rosamund finally burst out laughing and told him that he wouldn't fool a child, that he obviously enjoyed being Haakon the Dark, and indeed why shouldn't he, for it was a great thing to be. He kissed her and was silent after that.

They reached the mouth of the Trondheimsfjord before noon on a gray, blustery day, with the waves growing white crests even as they watched. There still seemed to be a great many ships following them, and Rosamund asked Haakon how he was planning to feed all these men, whom he would undoubtedly invite to stay on the steading for weeks.

As they came about on a course toward the land, the waves suddenly sprouted white clouds of spray, and Haakon laughed. "Rosamund, there's your homecoming feast!" A moment later twenty or more ship-sized black backs rose into view. Foam boiled up as wide black flukes churned the water.

"*Hvalblast!*" shouted a dozen voices, quite unnecessarily. Even if they had been blind they would have heard the whales spouting and thrashing and smelled the rank fish on their breaths.

"Get out the boarding lances!" Haakon shouted.

They had no whaling harpoons aboard *Red Hawk*, but all the ships had twelve-foot boarding lances, made by Hagar for taking the Arab ships. Someone shouted, "They aren't for throwing, Haakon!"

"They were made by Hagar," Haakon yelled. "Do you think he's ever made anything that couldn't be thrown? Tie the ropes to them!"

Rosamund came up to stand beside him. He put an arm gently around her waist to hold her against the motion of the ship. "Can you really kill a whale with that?"

"I don't see why not." The largest of the whales

flipped up its tail and sounded. "That's our homecoming feast, swimming along. We could feed every man who sailed with us off one that size."

Rosamund laughed. Her cheeks had been pale, but now they were flushed like ripe apples from the salt wind. "Haakon, I didn't mean it! This is too dangerous just for the sake of a feast. We can find something to feed them, and I'll gladly eat salt cod if I can eat it at home."

"So will I, but there's not so much danger. We're a strong ship and not far from land, even if a whale does ram us. *You* are going to sit down, though. If you fall . . ."

For once she was willing to take care of herself without arguing. She went and sat down in the hold, braced herself against one of the ship's ribs, and swathed herself in a fur.

"Good hunting, my love." Haakon would run into danger no matter what she said, she decided. Likely she would have to get used to it.

By now other ships had spotted the whales, and the fleet was scattering with shouts and laughter.

They are having fun, Rosamund thought. She saw Hagar the Simple standing in the bow of *Wave Walker,* holding a lance with a deceptively negligent grip.

Haakon picked up his lance and was checking the rope when *Red Hawk* shuddered and seemed to rise slightly out of the water. A moment later the back of the biggest whale Haakon had ever seen broke water dead ahead, so close that his tail must still have been under the ship. Haakon raised the lance and murmured a prayer he'd once heard from a man who came from a village in the far north, where they were closer to worshiping the whale than any of the proper Norse gods.

Great lord of the ocean, you have fathered many calves and lived long. Now I offer you an honorable death while you still swim strong and proud. Will you accept it?

He wasn't sure how long he should wait for the whale's reply, but this jarl among whales seemed to deserve nothing less.

The whale swam on, ignoring *Red Hawk* as if she were only a blob of foam. Haakon decided that must mean acceptance. He raised the lance and then thrust it fiercely down into the whale's back.

A moment later Haakon was cursing. The whale's flukes didn't miss a beat. For all the notice the creature was taking of the lance, it might have done no more than scrape a few barnacles off his back. Haakon doubted that was all, but knew the lance head couldn't be very deep. When the whale *did* notice, it would probably make him very angry indeed. He shouted for another lance.

Someone had cut the shaft of the second lance in two before tying on the rope, to make it a good throwing spear. As Haakon raised it the whale awoke to the fact that something was wrong. Haakon hurled the lance downward as the whale's flukes came up. So did what seemed like half the ocean. For a moment Haakon didn't dare breathe. Then he was standing, drenched and dripping, as the ropes to both lances went taut, stiff as iron bars, and the whale plunged out of sight. One man yelped as a rope slammed him against the ship's side. Haakon jumped as the same rope just missed him. He scanned the water where the whale had disappeared and saw a wide patch of blood spreading across the waves. He'd put the second lance deep into the whale's vitals.

That didn't necessarily mean the fight was won. Mortally wounded whales could live long enough to take their killers with them. Haakon found himself not entirely easy in his mind when he looked around and saw not one ship of his fleet within hailing distance. If the whale did strike *Red Hawk* hard enough to breach her planks, they would have to cut him loose and save themselves. No one else would be close enough to help.

How long the whale would stay under, no one could guess. Haakon posted men with axes ready to cut the ropes if they had to, had the ship sounded for leaks, made sure Rosamund was still sitting down, then sat down himself to wait.

Almost as if that were a signal to the whale, the ropes quivered and started to go slack. "He's coming up!" Haakon shouted. Then the ocean came aboard again as the whale broached. If he'd intended to smash *Red Hawk* on the way up, he missed. He rose just ahead, almost exploding from the water. At the top of his leap the first lance pulled loose, and the crew threw themselves flat as it flew back and buried its head in the stern post. Then more water came aboard, swirling around Haakon's calves as the whale plunged back into the ocean and struck out for the land, towing *Red Hawk* behind him.

The remaining rope was again as rigid as an iron bar, and over the bow, a wave rose so high that green water came over the side. *Red Hawk* might have been thrashing her way through a rising storm. Some of the crew grabbed helmets and buckets and started bailing, and others had a try at the oars, but Haakon shouted at them to stop. At this speed the oars would most likely be torn out of their hands, and the whale seemed willing to run himself aground without any help or encouragement.

The hills of the Trondelag were looming above *Red Hawk* when Haakon saw that the whale was heading straight for a cluster of small fishing boats, their nets spread between them. He ran for the steering oar and leaned on it desperately, trying to make the whale alter his course.

Even with four men on the steering oar, the whale could no more be guided than could a boulder careering downhill. Haakon cupped his hands and shouted, "Get out of the way! We can't steer!"

The fishermen had seen the whale and were scattering, frantically hauling in nets. Then the whale was among them, rising directly under a pair of boats. By some chance one boat remained upright and slid off the whale's back like water off a stone. The other capsized, and her men bobbed about in the water as *Red Hawk* swept past. They seemed to be cursing more in anger than in fear, Haakon thought. Most of these fisherfolk could swim like seals, and in any case there were three or four boats still afloat to pick them up. Haakon turned his attention back to the whale, ready to cut the rope. The whale looked ready to swim right onto the shore and halfway up the hills. They would have to be sure he didn't pull *Red Hawk* over the rocks.

Haakon waited until he could be sure the whale was too close to shore to turn back out to sea. He got another lance ready to throw just in case he was wrong, told everyone to lie flat, and nodded to the axmen. Their axes bit through the rope, and the inboard end lashed back like a giant whip. As the rope went limp, the whale ran aground in a great flurry of water and sand. *Red Hawk* crept in cautiously, while Haakon took soundings with the last lance. When the water was no more than chest deep, he dropped over the bow and waded warily toward the whale. A beached whale was not necessarily a dead whale.

Suddenly a pair of flukes the size of a ship's sail were poised above his head. Haakon flung himself sideways before they came down. Even though he was cushioned by three feet of water, the buffeting of the whale's flukes tumbled him head over heels and made his ears ring like a gong.

He rose, spitting out water, to see that the whale had

made his last effort. The creature lay almost motionless now, rolling slightly from side to side and occasionally twitching one fluke. Blood spurted from his blowhole each time he breathed, and each breath was increasingly shallow. He was past doing any harm; it was time to put him out of all pain.

Haakon walked to the whale, picked a spot just above the right eye, and thrust the lance in. Blood gushed out, the sea around him turned a deeper red, and the labored puffs from the blowhole stopped. A moment later the whole ship-long body shuddered and lay still.

The man who'd taught him the whale's prayer hadn't mentioned another to be said when the whale was dead. So Haakon stood and said a version of what he'd sometimes said over the body of a brave opponent. He wondered if there was a place of honor like Valhalla for the spirits of wise beasts that died valiantly. It seemed likely enough.

However, he had more immediate questions to answer, such as what to say to the fishermen. They were rowing toward him and the whale as hard as they could. He didn't like the looks on their faces. They'd lost gear and a boat, which could mean the difference between life and starvation for some of them.

Looking past them to the sea, Haakon saw the answer: *Wave Walker* was coming in, a rope stretched over the side leading aft. A wave lifted the body of the dead whale she was towing, and Haakon could see Hagar the Simple in the bow, with one lance left. They could give the second whale to the fisherfolk, enough meat and oil to keep a score of families fed through the winter. And by spring he could send them a new boat.

That would be enough for justice and even for generosity, which was always a good idea. No one ever suffered from a reputation for just dealing. And no one with enemies ever lost through friendship with men who might watch the sea for their coming. With Harud Olafsson still alive, that might be important.

XXIV

"You are a dog, and I will have you hanged from the tallest tree on this godforsaken coast!" Harud Olafsson gave his helmsman a furious stare.

"No." The helmsman shook his head stubbornly. "They will not do it." Behind him a dozen men of the crew growled in assent.

"Damn you!" Harud shouted.

"Our homes are gone," the helmsman said. "Likely also our women and thralls. Likely everything. You are jarl now, if there is anything left to be jarl over."

Harud spat. "I've no great wish for a piece of dirt in Ireland. We will go to Mikligard in the spring. There is wealth there. You will see."

"No. We are going home." The helmsman looked at him curiously. "Your father is dead."

"My father was no great loss," Harud said, and the helmsman shuddered in spite of himself. Harud was right, but there was also something black at the center of this one. Truly he was the old jarl's child. The helmsman studied him with a waning respect.

"You may go to Mikligard if you wish, jarl, and hide there from Haakon Olesson, who may not be dead yet, but we are going home to see what is left there." He turned his back on Harud and walked away to the ships.

When they were well out to sea, Harud still stood on the desolate coast of Sweden and shook his fist after them. They had left him the ship's boat and enough salt

fish and water to get him to a nearby Swedish steading—
if there was one. They expected there was, but they
didn't care greatly, and they grimly set their faces for
Ireland—and what was left to find there.

It was raining as Haakon and Rosamund rode up the
trail toward Erik and Sigrid's steading. Half a dozen
armed men rode with them, with Donal and four
more on ahead. Rosamund had taken to Donal on sight—
he was a fellow countryman of sorts, and he sang with
the voice of angels when he played his harp. He was
also still wild at not having gone on "the jarl's fine raid
into Spain," and Rosamund had laughed and told him
there would no doubt be as much fighting as he had a
taste for in the jarl's service. He seemed in no hurry to
take himself back to Scotland, she noticed, and wondered how Fann was going to take to that.

Haakon was so quiet beside her that Rosamund
suspected his stomach and his head were still rebellious
from last night's homecoming feast. He'd certainly eat-
en enough whale meat for three men and consumed
enough ale for six. When he had fallen into bed, she
thought he had been more senseless than sleeping.

They had found the steading running smoothly in
their absence, under Erik and Sigrid's hand. No one
doubted that it had been Kare Ingstad who had killed
Bjorn. It was conjecture as to how the murder had
come about, but Haakon thought that Bjorn's ghost was
likely content with Kare's death in Birka.

Snorri Longfoot and Yazid of Alexandria, once intro-
duced, found common ground almost instantly and
were soon seen in the ship house, heads together over a
drawing on a piece of wood.

Wulf seemed pleased to be home and found his usual
place by the fire in the great hall. He was quickly
labeled the most well-traveled dog in Norway.

Gunnar had ordered his slave girl, Riziya, to make

herself scarce until he found the right opportunity to explain her to Guthrun.

Guthrun cried and clung to him, cried and clung to Rosamund, and spent most of the feast just watching them to make sure they were home.

Rosamund also found herself crying, at night when Haakon had gone to sleep. All the restraint of the months of captivity, when she would not let herself weep, overflowed in the night, and her tears ran freely. *Holy Mother of Christ, I thank you for my safe delivery home.*

She cried and woke exhausted; still another matter was on her mind, and homecoming couldn't mend it.

The only remaining thorn in Haakon's side seemed to be Harud Olafsson, who was still a free man. Traders who had come to the Trondelag from Sweden had told him a tale that had cheered him somewhat, but he wouldn't be content until he had put Harud's head on a spike.

But for Rosamund, nothing had changed since Harud had stolen her away. She still had to face the question of the Angel of Death, and she knew now more than ever that she could not do it. There would be no refusing without causing tongues to wag and maybe making enemies for Haakon. But she could not accept. In Spain she'd prayed too often to the Virgin. God or the gods, or whoever listened, knew she was too much a Christian to offer human life to the Norse gods.

The rain turned into snow before they reached Erik and Sigrid's steading. Donal helped her down while Erik's stablehands led the horses away. A thrall-girl came out to show them into the hall, and Sigrid stood on the steps beaming at them.

Erik was nowhere in sight. "A free tenant's house burned down last night," Sigrid said. "Erik rode out this morning to see about rebuilding before the winter

comes or finding them some place else. Since he's not
back yet, I expect he will sleep out."

Rosamund and Haakon looked at each other. Such
devotion to his duties was unlike the Erik the Bald
they'd known. What was happening to him?

They settled in by the fire with Sigrid and told her all
the news they could think of.

"Guthrun has spotted Gunnar's thrall-girl," Haakon
said, laughing, "and we think there will be war before
spring. And our shipwreck survivor is at work with
Snorri, going over the ships. As far as I can judge from
the work he's done already, he wasn't boasting about his
skill."

The conversation rambled on from there, and Haakon
began to yawn. Finally Sigrid suggested that he go to
bed if he found them so dull, and he grinned and
yawned again and went off to the sleeping chamber.
Sigrid poured out two small cups of German wine for
herself and Rosamund, and then she went over to a
chest in the corner. "This is a homecoming gift, child."

It was a gown of the finest wool, dyed to the same
blue-violet as Rosamund's eyes and embroidered in
gold thread at the neck. It was Norse in style, beautiful
and welcome after the odd, exotic clothes they'd dressed
her in in Spain.

Sigrid smiled. "I'm afraid it will look better on you
after you've had the child. But I don't imagine Haakon
will notice that. Rags would look good to him if you
wore them, you know."

Rosamund ran a hand over the cloth, soft as skin.
"How could you find the time for this? The dyeing
alone—"

Sigird patted her cheek. "The dyeing was certainly
the hardest part. I nearly emptied my dye-box, and I'm
afraid some of the thralls will be wearing oddly colored
clothes for a while. But I found I had more time on my

hands than I wanted, and nothing to do but sit and think evil, ill-luck thoughts. And if I made a gown for your homecoming—why, then you'd have to come home."

"You've never been idle," Rosamund said affectionately. "Where came all this time?"

"Erik," Sigrid said. "He found me hard to comfort, I think, until I knew you were safe home, and so he made himself very busy instead. Now he has the habit of it, it seems." Erik, after a lifetime of kindly laziness, was now doing the work of two men half his age, in running his own lands, Sigrid's, and Haakon's.

"Not that I begrudge it to him," Sigrid laughed. "He will leave a better name in the Trondelag for it. But still—there were too many nights alone, so I turned to the dyepot and the needle. I found—child, is the baby troubling you?"

Rosamund shook her head. *Sigrid*. Sigrid had time. Sigrid was older, highly respected, thoroughly Norse. And she was even closer kin to Haakon than Rosamund. Why not make *her* the Angel of Death if the Trondelag needed one?

Sigrid was looking at her, puzzled. Rosamund kissed her. "Sigrid, I'm sorry. It's something I've been thinking about ever since we landed. I'll have to speak to Haakon about it before I tell you, though."

"Something that touches Haakon's pride, is it?"

"Yes."

"Wise of you. I'd like to know, but not if it will make Haakon fuss. Men's pride is such a delicate thing, I sometimes wonder why they don't wrap it up in silk and keep it in a box. Well, go off to bed, and if he's awake, you can tell him. And if he's not, you and that baby still need some sleep."

"Yes, Mama." Rosamund said it so dutifully that Sigrid laughed, but she pushed her along anyway. That was her grandchild Rosamund was carrying, and Sigrid had every intention of seeing it was done properly.

* * *

Rosamund didn't want to wait. She prodded Haakon awake when she got into bed. He sat up groggily, and when she thought he was paying attention, she looked him in the eye and said, "Haakon, I cannot be an Angel of Death. I'm a Christian, and I'm going to have to stay that way."

He put out a hand to her face. "My dear—"

Rosamund nodded. "I know. That will make a great deal of trouble, and it is my fault for not telling you straight off that I didn't even know what one was. But now that I do, I can't, and I thought I had best say so and get it over with. *But* I have thought of something else too—your mother."

"Mother?" He looked puzzled, and then his face lightened. "You are smarter than I am, my heart, for thinking of that. Mother *will* do it, too." He grinned. "It is a position of great respect. Rosamund, I am sorry you have been troubled with this. I was afraid when they asked you—but then you seemed so calm about it."

"The more fool I," Rosamund said. "And I was drunk."

Haakon fell back on the bed laughing. "We will tell them that with the baby coming, you will have no time."

"That is true enough, I expect," Rosamund said. "He is going to be a lively one. He has already been to Spain and back." She put his hand on the curve of her belly to feel their child kicking. *Home,* she thought, watching Haakon's face light up with surprise as he felt the baby move inside her. *I have come home.*

Glossary

curragh: small boat made of wickerwood and covered with hide.

forswear: to renounce an oath or to swear falsely.

Hel: in Scandinavian mythology, the underworld region where spirits of men who had died in their beds reside, as distinguished from Valhalla, the abode of heroes slain in battle.

jarl: tribal chieftain.

knarr: broad-beamed ship, deep in the water, with a high freeboard.

Norns: deities who tended men's destinies.

skald: Norse reciter or singer of heroic epics, a poet.

spaewife: female fortune-teller or witch.

thane: retainer or free servant of a lord.

Thing: northern assembly of free men for law, debate, and matters of regional importance.

thrall: a member of the lowest social class; a slave to a master or lord as a result of capture or an accident of birth.

wadmal: coarse, woolen material used for protective covering and warm clothing.

weregild: a value set by law upon the life of a man, in accordance with a fixed scale. Paid as compensation to kindred or to the lord of a slain person.

wyrd: fate.

COMING IN FALL 1984 ...

HAAKON: BOOK 3
HAAKON'S IRON HAND

by Eric Neilson

Haakon is plagued by peril when he defies the god Thor to settle a blood-feud. Battling against fierce weather and the machinations of a greedy king, Haakon is caught in a vicious war between two savage peoples before he can attempt to exact ultimate revenge against his archenemy Harud Olafsson.

Read HAAKON'S IRON HAND, on sale in the early fall, 1984, wherever Bantam paperbacks are sold.

Haakon-3

"FROM THE PRODUCER OF WAGONS WEST COMES YET ANOTHER EXPLOSIVE SAGA OF LEGENDARY COURAGE AND UNFORGETTABLE LOVE"

CHILDREN OF THE LION